TOO FAR GONE

A SAM POPE NOVEL

ROBERT ENRIGHT

For Sophie and Olivia,

CHAPTER ONE

Three months was a long time.

As his feet slammed against the concrete, Sam Pope could feel himself once again reaching his physical peak, having spent the past few months recovering from a brutal attack on the streets of Rome. With the Vatican in his eyeline, he'd emerged from a car wreck, run off the road by a murderous man with bad intentions.

The bullet wound he'd suffered in his shoulder still hummed with every step, jogging through the humid, spring breeze.

The bullet that had ripped through his back and out of his stomach, missing his spinal cord by a matter of millimetres, had left an impact.

Every beat of the pavement sent a shudder up his spine, reminding him of how close he'd been to paralysis.

Or worse.

But in the three months since, in his reclusive recovery on the outskirts of Naples in the south-west of Italy, he'd come to realise that his hunter hadn't been shooting to kill.

The man had shot to wound, dropping Sam to his

knees and helpless against a very clear execution. Every night since, Sam had felt an unnerving sense of familiarity.

As if he knew the shooter.

It felt as if his mind had played tricks on him.

As the man had approached, with Sam on his knees, ready for his fight to finally end, the man had spoken.

'I've been waiting a long time for this.'

The voice.

The Mancunian accent.

Sam shook his head, realising he was allowing the ghosts from his past to haunt his present.

A present containing enough horror to last a lifetime.

It had been just over a year since the bombing of the London Marathon, a traumatic event that not only shook the city of London but had sent Sam on a one-track mission against the criminal underworld. Before that, he'd allowed the grief of losing his son to fuel his desire to fight back.

Using his position working for the Metropolitan Police in their archive division, Sam had sought out criminals who had beaten the system, providing his own brand of questionable justice.

Having spent over a decade as one of the UK's most decorated snipers, Sam had returned to his loving family after an off-the-book mission had gone wrong.

The memories were hazy.

All he could remember was a dark room inside a stone building before two bullets were sent through his chest and he was left to die in the dark.

He survived.

Sam Pope was built for survival.

It had taken him from the mountainous waste lands of Afghanistan to the deep trenches of the Amazonian jungle.

Mission after mission.

Target after target.

After his decorated career had come to an end, he was prepared for his new life as a loving husband and doting father. Yet the war was not done with him.

Somehow, the cruel hand of fate pulled him back into the firing line by snatching his son from him.

A drunk driver and a broken justice system.

It had sent Sam on a dark spiral, one which his ex-wife, Lucy, could no longer be a part of.

A spiral that spun around the haunting image of his son lying motionless in the middle of the road.

His Jamie.

Gone.

The pain had brought him to the edge where the only solace he could find was in the mercy of others. Eventually, the path led him to some of London's most notorious criminals and their despicable acts upon the innocent. While Sam knew the fight would never bring his son back, the thought of stopping others suffering the same fate at least brought a moment of peace.

It had made him the UK's most wanted man.

It had made him the underworld's most feared opponent.

And it had brought him to the brink of death.

Now here he was, running through the streets of Naples, trying his hardest to return to a war he knew he would never escape.

Training to fight back.

Rounding a corner, Sam almost collided with two elderly women, one of them barking at him in a thick, Italian accent. He held his hands up in way of apology, before picking up the pace as he headed onto the street of his temporary abode. The wide streets were already crammed with cars, the slowly rising sun cutting through the grey clouds and bouncing off their windscreens. The streets were lined with tall, stone buildings, all of them filled with a myriad of shops and flats.

The city hummed with life, the cacophony of traffic bouncing off the brick framework of the surrounding buildings.

Sam knew he was far from home.

Away from the fight.

But through all the noise, he could hear it calling.

Reducing his sprint to a gentle jog, Sam came to a stop as he approached the alleyway, taking a few moments to calm his heart rate, and stretched his legs. He had run over ten kilometres and felt a slight stiffness in his shoulder. The bullet wound had healed, but from the friction he felt, he knew the damage was likely to be permanent.

Stretching out his back, he walked towards the metal fire escape that clung to the building like a rusty, metallic arm. The steps were coated in a shiny drizzle and Sam navigated them carefully. As he approached the top, he reached into his pocket and pulled out the key, twisting it sharply in the lock before slamming his shoulder into the stiff door.

The apartment was cheap, and the door was a testament to the price.

But it was all they could afford.

Well, all Alex could afford.

Sam knew he owed Alex Stone his life. As part of the team who had blackmailed him into hunting his own mentor, they'd bonded over their shared hatred for the man in charge.

Trevor Sims.

The man had been a high-ranking official in the United States army, but had soon sold out for the lucrative world of private security. His lust for power and lack of ethics had seen him command a brutal task force.

It would also lead to his death in an underground bunker just outside Rome.

The same room had also been the final resting place of Sam's mentor, Carl Marsden.

During his time in the army, Marsden had been his commanding officer, molding Sam into the perfect soldier. It was he who had led Sam to Project Hailstorm, the elite squadron that would almost kill him.

It was also Marsden who brought Sam back from his lowest ebb, telling Sam to fight for something when the burden of his son's death pulled him dangerously close to an early grave.

Marsden had been there for Sam, and Sam felt the pain of failure more than the final remnants of the bullets that had rattled his body three months prior.

Sam couldn't save Marsden.

The deceased Sims had blackmailed Sam into helping him hunt Marsden through Europe, with wild theories of terrorism. It was only when Sam had managed to rendezvous with his superior that he realised how high up it went and just how far they would have to go for the truth.

Marsden had entrusted him with the proof before sacrificing himself for Sam's freedom.

Sam should have left.

But he couldn't leave a man behind. It was something that had haunted him for years and the recent events had brought that to the forefront of his mind.

'*I've been waiting a long time for this.*'

The voice.

The Mancunian accent.

It wasn't possible. Was it?

Shaking his head clear, Sam could smell the alluring aroma of coffee wafting through the apartment. The muscles in his legs were starting to stiffen and he slid his feet out from his cheap, second-hand running shoes. After he'd recovered from the back-alley surgery that had saved his life, Sam had asked Alex to pick some up.

With their limited funds, it was all they could afford.

They were all Sam needed.

His brown hair usually kept short and neat was now overgrown, the fringe flopping down over his brow and he brushed it aside, tucking it behind his ear. His beard was thick, although Alex had helped him maintain its unruliness with a pair of scissors.

The smell of cigarette smoke soon joined the coffee in the air.

A voice followed.

'How was it?'

Sam stepped into the doorway of the open-plan flat, looking beyond the tiny kitchen that was tacked onto the wall. By the open window, which overlooked the cramped streets below, was Alex.

Sat in a long T-shirt and shorts, her brown legs shimmered under the sunlight that was threatening to burst through the rain clouds. Her dark hair was tied back in a tight ponytail and her youthful face regarded him with a smile.

She had a mug of coffee in one hand and a cigarette in the other.

'Not bad,' Sam replied, stretching the ache in his back. 'No stopping this time.'

'Good.' Alex smiled. 'You'll be running the New York marathon in no time.'

Sam grunted, knowing she yearned for a return to her hometown as soon as possible. He hadn't told her about his investigation into the bombing of the London Marathon the year before, nor the dangerous path he'd trodden since.

She knew bits of his story, that he'd been blackmailed into joining the Blackridge Task Force just as she had, but beyond that, he'd tried to keep her as knowledge free as possible.

As safe as possible.

Alex was twenty-six years old and had racked up quite the record for illegal street racing in the States. While Sims had used it as leverage, she'd used it as a means to an end, to keep food on the table for her younger siblings while their mother chased a dragon she would never catch.

Now, like Sam, she was alone in a foreign city, hunted by a rogue security company with a burning desire to get home and put things right. Sam had promised her he would get her family back.

She'd saved his life.

Sam was a man of his word and would make good on his promise.

He stepped forward and followed her gaze out of the window, watching as the narrow back roads of Naples began to fill with impatient drivers furiously honking their horns.

'How do you drive in these streets?' Sam asked, shaking his head at the congestion.

Alex took a final puff on her cigarette and then stubbed the end out on the windowsill, letting the smoke rise from her mouth.

'Pure talent.' She slapped him on the shoulder, causing him to grimace. 'Besides, who else is going to pay for your sneakers?'

Sam nodded, knowing that she'd returned to her past life in order to fund their eventual exit from the city. While he didn't approve of her racing, he was hardly in a position to lecture her about staying on the right side of the law. With the Polizia di Stato still looking for them, their chances of finding work were dwindling. Alex had gotten word of a few races in Naples and they'd made the journey to the city and seamlessly blended in.

Now, as Sam continued his road to recovery, Alex was doing her best to get them out of there.

Sam knew he had to honour his promise to the woman who had done so much for him, but there was a nagging doubt in his mind that things weren't finished.

Not yet.

'I'm gonna take a shower,' Alex said, yawning and stretching out her athletic frame. 'I'd ask you to join me, but you have your reasons.'

Sam turned to her with an apologetic look.

'I just don't think it's a good idea.'

'I get it, one and done,' Alex joked. 'I'm kidding. There's coffee in the pot.'

Alex winked and then made her way towards the run-down bathroom, ready to wrestle with the plumbing for a shred of hot water. They had spent a passionate night together in the midst of the hunt for Marsden, but with their lives now firmly resting on the other, Sam had made it clear they couldn't muddy the waters any further. There had been a few times when he'd been tempted. Alex was a stunning woman after all.

But Sam knew he had to keep her at a distance.

For her own good.

He heard the gushing of water slam against the bathtub and reached out to the phone that sat on the side. The Nokia 3210 was like a fossil in his hands, its clunky buttons sticking in the pad while its green screen looked like an old computer monitor

Sam wasn't one for modern conveniences, but as he clumsily laboured with the keypad, he realised just how far the world had come.

Sam dialled the eleven numbers.

The same eleven numbers he dialled every day.

He lifted it with a resigned sigh.

'*It has not been possible to connect your call. Please try again…*'

He hung up.

'Damnit, Paul. Where are you?'

Every day since Alex had procured the phone, Sam had called Paul Etheridge. The man had been in the army with Sam, but what he lacked in adventure, he more than made up for it with his technical genius. Etheridge had made millions in the cyber security game, before helping Sam track down a missing girl destined for a life of horror in the European sex trade.

Etheridge was one of his few allies left.

He was also the man he'd sent the USB stick to.

The USB stick that Marsden had died for and that Blackridge and more importantly, the powers that be were willing to kill for.

Marsden had said it contained *the truth*.

About Project Hailstorm.

About Sam.

Everything.

Sam had posted it to Etheridge before he'd tried, and failed, to save Marsden's life.

Now, with no contact and no idea where Etheridge was, Sam knew his fight was far from over. Despite his promises to Alex, ones he intended to keep, Sam knew the hunt for that stick would continue and there wasn't a drop of blood that would be spared.

With a deep sigh, he returned the phone to the shelf, stretched out the ache in his spine again and told himself that the fight is never over.

Not by a long shot.

CHAPTER TWO

WHO IS WATCHING OVER US NOW?
  Article written by Helal Miah

No one should ever take the law into their own hands.

I've been writing articles for The Pulse *for over four years now, covering everything from the rise in transport costs to the ongoing circus that is our government. I've always taken everything based on facts and then sprinkled it with my opinion.*

It's won me many friends.

It's made me a ton of enemies. (Seriously, check out my social media!)

There is one subject I want to talk about today. A subject that has split the city of London, as well as the rest of our county and one that the press and the powers that be want to paint in a particular way.

Sam Pope.

Now, as I stated at the beginning of this article, I am of the belief that NO ONE should take the law into their own hands. This isn't the wild west, where someone gets to clean up the streets with a Smith & Wesson and a cool catchphrase.

We have a justice system in place for a reason and I am a firm believer that having said system makes our country one of the safest places to live. But something happened a year ago that shook foundations so hard, the pillars they support almost collapsed.

I am, of course, talking about the horrendous bombing attack on the London Marathon.

A horrific event that claimed the lives of seven innocent people, stricken from the world by a reported cowardly act of terrorism. The world watched on in horror as one of the most famous annual events was rocked by the heinous act, and I respectfully undertook the minute's silence we held for those cruelly taken.

But it was this moment when Sam Pope become a known entity in this country.

The authorities have quite rightly labelled him a dangerous vigilante, a well-trained soldier who has murdered over thirty people in the last year. For this, we cannot praise the man.

But is there more to it?

I've read countless reports about his storied past within our armed forces, fighting bravely for our country. But what has never been made public is the reason he stepped out of the shadows and became the most wanted man in this country.

Until now...

A recent source, who unsurprisingly wants to remain anonymous, has informed me that Sam Pope is not just a crazed ex-soldier with a grudge against the country. With further investigation into the lives Sam's crusade has claimed, I've found several links between those people and organised crime. What is even more appalling, is the very real possibility that those people were given the leeway to do it by those in power, for their own agendas.

This might sound like fear mongering or nonsensical click bait, but there are clear links.

After Sam Pope's much publicised assault on a heavily guarded drug base in Dulwich, South London, two senior police officers soon, sadly, passed away. Inspector Michael Howell was arrested amongst

the corruption and found dead in his cell, having hung himself.
Further investigation placed two of the men associated with the crime
lord, Frank Jackson, at Howell's house, both found deceased.

Why would there be two dead criminals at a police Inspector's
house? Could it be possible that the reported links between our senior
police officials and organised crime are in fact binding?

I don't want to speak ill of the dead, but the notion that Howell,
who was a senior officer with no armed experience, would storm a
crime scene with a known vigilante is farfetched.

Another senior figure, Sgt Colin Mayer was found murdered on a
small boat in Dawlish, Cornwall. His disappearance just before the
storming of the High Rise gives additional credence to the idea that
those links do exist.

My sources dictate that Sam Pope acted because he believed it
was right.

The only innocent people who were killed were those in the
Marathon itself, and the people who died by his hands were either
known criminals or corrupt officers.

Again, I do not condone the act of murder nor do I believe that
vigilantism should be celebrated. But I don't feel we should sweep
these startling connections under the rug.

The same link can be made by the abrupt withdrawal of Mark
Harris from the Mayoral campaign at the end of last year. The man
was almost a shoe in for the job.

Handsome, charming, and with a clear gift for the public role,
Harris had set his stall on 'cleaning up the streets of London.' He
even used Sam Pope as his opposite, as if positioning himself as an
antidote to the Sam Pope issue. Harris was so sure of his success, he
publicly backed a task force to bring Sam Pope to justice, using the
man as an example for the rise in gun crime.

So why did he step down?

After a mass shoot-out in the Port of Tilbury, an avalanche of
information poured forth about a terrifying sex trafficking racket, run
by the Kovalenko family. Teenage girls, abducted for the sole purpose
of sex slavery, were discovered in the aftermath.

12

The father of one of the girls, who wishes to remain anonymous for the safety of his family, said he spoke directly with Sam Pope himself.

While the harrowing experience will no doubt haunt his daughter forever, the father spoke about how Sam went through hell and high water to find her.

To bring her back,

To save her from her fate.

Not only did he achieve this, he put an end to the despicable enterprise, with further reports of the wider Kovalenko family meeting their grisly demise in a Ukrainian night club.

And then Harris stepped down amid reports that he had monetary links to a shell company owned by the Kovalenkos.

So again, I want to state, I do not condone the use of violence to solve anything.

Nor do I believe anyone should take the law into their own hands.

But with the facts pointing towards those in power shirking their responsibilities for their own gain and making a mockery of our justice system, then I ask: Is Sam Pope truly wrong?

If those we put in charge to look after the safety of this country put their own needs first, then who fights for the people?

There have been no reported sightings of Sam Pope in over three months, beyond rumours of an incident in Rome where a US private security operation went wrong. A private security operation with strong links to our very own military. The trail of bodies is being pinned on Pope, with the headline reading that he is one step closer to the edge and that we are no longer safe.

But without Sam Pope, who is watching over us now?

What he does may not be legal, but is it necessary?

The law is the law and we shouldn't allow anyone to be above it. But with the country in turmoil, with our government comparable to a circus, and our trusted authorities trying their hardest to lose our confidence, do the streets really feel safer without Sam Pope?

It's a sad day when we fear the law, not for what it does, but for what it doesn't.

––––––

'This needs to be shut down. Now.'

General Ervin Wallace slammed the tablet onto Deputy Commissioner Ruth Ashton's desk and leant back in the chair. His colossal frame crept over the sides of the comfortable seat; his suit strapped tightly to it. While he carried a few extra pounds due to his time behind the desk and the unstoppable clutches of Father Time, he was still an imposing figure. A career soldier who had climbed up the ranks through his sheer determination and ruthless efficiency, he commanded as much respect as he did fear.

He knew he received both from the Deputy Commissioner in bucket loads, along with a strong attraction.

Ashton was approaching fifty, her brown hair, now frosted with grey, was pulled back into a tight bun. Her sharp facial features looked even more prominent, most likely due to the stress of Sam Pope's disappearance.

While she was heavily expected to take the reins once the Commissioner stepped down, she knew having a man of Wallace's considerable weight behind her would make it a formality. She'd taken personal responsibility for the task force which had failed to catch Pope and now, with the powerful General breathing down her neck, she felt the pressure building in her temples.

She reached across her immaculate desk and lifted the tablet.

'It's a free press, General,' she said helplessly. 'A trashy internet blog.'

'I don't give a damn,' Wallace said firmly, his meaty fingers clasped on his lap. 'This Sam Pope nonsense has gone on long enough and the last thing we need is fear mongering from the uneducated.'

Wallace regarded Ashton with a disappointed glare,

revelling in his clear power over the woman. It was a feeling he'd become addicted to.

Power. Control.

It had seen him not only run an elite, off-the-books task force but also gain a controlling share in Blackridge, the private security company that had tried, and failed spectacularly, to stop Carl Marsden a few months before.

The previous field commander, Trevor Sims, had unsuccessfully tried to recruit Pope as a way to placate Wallace. They had blackmailed him with a threat to his ex-wife, but it wasn't enough. Pope had reached Marsden first and according to Marsden, before Wallace regrettably had to end his life, was now in possession of the information Marsden had given up his life for.

Information which could ruin him completely.

Information he would hunt Sam Pope to the ends of the earth for.

Sims had died for his failure and while a similar fate wouldn't await Ashton, Wallace had made it clear enough that if she failed him again, her career would be over.

Power.

Control.

Wallace smirked as Ashton tried to conjure up a solution.

'I can have someone speak to this Mr Miah if you like?'

'Ruth.' Wallace leant forward, lowering his tone. 'If I wanted someone to slap his wrist, I'd have asked one of the grunts out there.'

Wallace jerked his neck towards the door which lead to the offices of some of Ashton's finest detectives.

'This is the Metropolitan Police, Ervi—' Wallace flashed her an angry glance. '—General.'

Ashton sighed, ashamed that she'd lost her first name privileges. Wallace stood up, straightening his tie.

'Then police it,' he commanded. 'If the public begin to think we are not here for their safety, then we lose even more trust. It's not just me they're looking at, is it. Howell? Mayer? Soon, they'll start looking higher up the chain.'

'Okay. Okay,' Ashton said fitfully. 'I'll get someone to speak to him.'

'Send Pearce,' Wallace said coldly. 'He claims he has no links to Pope, so make him clean up this mess.'

Ashton licked her lips nervously. Detective Inspector Adrian Pearce had been the first person to suspect Sam Pope of walking the wrong side of the thin blue line, way back when Sam worked in their archive department. Respected for his diligence but shunned for his work leading the Department of Professional Standards, rumours swirled that Pearce not only agreed with Pope's mission but was actively helping him.

They had tried everything to get him to crack.

Countless interviews.

Busy work.

Hell, they even moved him to a broom cupboard.

But the man was unflappable, almost to the point that Ashton questioned whether he really did know anything. But the glimmer of delight in Wallace's eye made up her mind.

'Consider it done,' she said firmly, standing herself and buttoning her tunic. She'd made sure to wear her smartest uniform when she'd been informed Wallace was on his way to see her.

Wallace nodded calmly.

'And Singh? Is she still a problem?'

Ashton shook her head. DI Amara Singh had been the bright spark of the Met for a few years. Her rapid rise through the ranks had as much to do with her credentials as it did with her filling a necessary diversity quota. Despite her diminutive size, she packed a punch and excelled as an Armed Response Officer. Putting her in charge of the Sam Pope Task Force had at one time seemed like a master stroke.

Now it could end up being Ashton's undoing.

They had suspended Singh for her perceived aiding and abetting of Pope, which was soon disproven. It may have driven a wedge in the blossoming union between her and Pearce, but Singh was soon back at her desk.

Ashton had reduced her to nothing more than a highly paid, highly skilled administrator, but the woman was as strong as she was.

She would not break.

There was a steeliness to Singh that Ashton admired, but now, with the General wanting blood, it was something Ashton feared may make her even more of a target.

'Singh is no longer a problem.' Ashton smiled. 'Unless she blocks the photocopier again.'

The joke fell on deaf ears and Wallace sighed. He turned and marched towards the door of Ashton's office, pulling it with such force that it shook the frame. He turned his head, locking his eyes on her once more.

'This needs to be controlled, Ruth.' His words were laced with menace. 'Wild accusations may just rile the wrong people. People who may not be as patient as I am.'

With that, Wallace stepped through the door and into the office which fell deathly silent as he entered. The door slammed shut behind him and he stomped purposefully across the walkway towards the door, straight back and broad shoulders.

To the watching world, he was a man in complete control.

A man to be feared.

But in reality, Wallace was feeling the walls closing in

and the inevitability of making a phone call that he'd made personal assurances, would never be made.

For the first time in a long time, the man to be feared was feeling that very same emotion.

CHAPTER THREE

The unrelenting heat from the sun bore down on the metal factory, weighing down the oxygen in the room. Outside, the derelict road that lead into the abandoned building was covered with dust and gravel.

No one ventured out.

No one at all.

Just over a mile away, the historic town of Hasankeyf stood. One of Turkey's most ancient towns, its incredible architecture was surrounded by derelict cliffs, riddled with caverns where the natives once lived. Now, situated near the Tigris River, the city was marked for death, the inevitable flooding due to the construction of the *Ilisu Dam*. Despite the objections of the habitants and the nationalists, the city was not long for the world.

Neither was the man strapped to the chair in the warehouse.

Abdul Qadir could feel the blood pouring from the gaping wound above his eyebrow, the outcome of a vicious strike by the man stood before him.

Despite the exhaustive heat, the large man wore a plastic apron strapped to his bulky body, the muscles slightly laxing into a slight gut due to *Father Time*. His dark eyes were locked onto him like a wolf ready to make the kill. Thinning black hair swept across his head, the sweat trickling down the side of his bearded face.

His meaty forearms bore sinister scars which were evident behind the thick hair.

Qadir had long since given up the idea of survival.

He had been a journalist, investigating the Afghanistan Military's involvement in a recent assassination of a prominent rebellion leader in Syria. The man had been found stripped naked, castrated, and hung from a bridge.

A message had been stapled to his naked torso.

Talin.

Relent.

As he wept for the wife and young child he would be leaving behind, Qadir knew he should have listened.

His torturer slowly lowered the metal chain from the harness he had affixed to the metal beam of the roof, pulling the chain link down hand over fist.

The man's reputation proceeded him.

Ahmad Farukh.

Aljulad bin Baghdad.

The Hangman of Baghdad.

Farukh had been one of the Taliban's greatest generals, leading a series of brutal missions throughout the organisation's reign of terror on the country. His bloodlust had seen even his own superiors question his motives, but the ruthlessness of his work kept them at bay.

If they had a problem, then they would point him in the direction and then look the other way.

Men.

Women.

Children.

Found, mutilated and hanged without a moment's hesitation. The stories were so horrifying, Qadir remembered tales in his playground that spoke of The Hangman as if he were a real life bogeyman. Now, as the chain slowly lowered, and the leather strap that comprised the noose slid gently around his neck, he realised that some legends were indeed true.

And in that truth, his horrifying destiny lay.

Qadir shook with fear, his already drenched trousers filling with urine and the pungent smell wafted through the heat to Farukh.

The Hangman turned and looked at Qadir with a disappointing shake of the head.

'In death, one will be remembered in one of two ways,' Farukh said, his Arabic slow and purposeful. 'Either as a coward or as a conqueror.'

Qadir felt the tears flooding down his cheeks as the noose rested on his collar bone, the cool leather pressing against the blood that had trickled down to his chest. As he finished his prayer, he turned to face his executioner. Qadir's wavy black hair was matted to his head, thick with sweat and blood.

His left eye was swollen.

His right was shut; the blood gushing from the wound dripped from his lashes.

His lips were split, and blood seeped through them from the teeth that Farukh had removed with the rusty pair of pliers that were tossed lazily to the side of the room. The man had no fear of covering his tracks.

To the rest of the world, he was a ghost.

An urban legend.

A bump in the night.

Now, as Farukh lit a cigarette and let a plume of smoke casually lift from his mouth, Qadir saw what he truly was.

Evil.

Weeping as quietly as he could, Qadir shut his eyes and took a deep breath. All this for doing the right thing. For doing his best to tell his people what was truly happening with his government. That they would pay a man such as Farukh to erase people like they were mistakes.

To make them disappear.

Farukh watched with a perverted pleasure as his latest victim shook in his chair, praying to a god that Farukh knew had long since abandoned him.

Abandoned them all.

It was why men like him survived.

Were a necessity.

He rested the cigarette between his lips, careful for the end to not singe his thick, greying moustache. He wrapped both of his war-torn hands around the chain and with his vast might, heaved the chain.

The leather tightened.

A few small bones in Qadir's neck cracked as it pulled tight.

A feeble gasp of air was soon shut off as Farukh heaved once more, crushing the man's larynx as he lifted the man from the ground, the metal chair accompanying him as he ascended towards the heavens.

Not towards the grateful arms of Allah.

But towards an agonising end.

With one final yank, the chair lifted to eight feet, the weight of it pulling Qadir towards the ground. The man shook, the noose claiming his final moments in the world.

Farukh stared at his latest victim, taking a long, satisfying pull on his cigarette.

In an instant it was over.

The chain stopped swinging.

The chair gently swung from side to side.

Qadir was dead.

As casually as a jolly punter lifted a pint, Farukh lifted the small bottle of gasoline which he'd placed on the side, popping the cap and he carelessly sloshed the petrol across the dusty floor, the liquid covering the stone and surrounding fixtures.

The smell wafted through the suffocating heat, trying its best to mask the stench of death.

Farukh slid the apron over his head and tossed it into the puddle.

Taking one final drag of his cigarette, he flicked the butt towards the petrol. Flames shot up like the bowels of hell themselves, quickly spreading across the gasoline trail before consuming the nearby equipment. The heat rose quickly, but with calm steps, Farukh walked towards the exit to the fresh air and beating sun outside.

As he stepped out, he lit another cigarette, before cupping his murderous hand across his brow to shield the sun.

The historic landscape of Hasankeyf was a beauty to behold.

He smiled, taking another drag before heading towards the Jeep parked half a mile down the road.

Behind him, the factory fell to the relentless fire and inside the terrifying blaze consumed the motionless body of Qadir.

Within moments, Farukh would be gone.

Once the authorities had extinguished the fire and realised what had happened, there would be two names they would confirm.

Abdul Qadir. Deceased.

Aljulad bin Baghdad.

The Hangman of Baghdad.

———

'I don't like it.'

Sam crossed his arms across his broad chest, his recently healed bullet wound causing his shoulder to ache.

As a light drizzle sprinkled the Italian evening, he looked out of the window of the small flat to the street below. A few hours before, gridlocked traffic had brought the city to a crawl as everyone returned to their homes. Their normal lives.

A world away from where he was.

Now, a few cars glided up the wide roads, their lights cutting through the rain as it splattered from the skies above.

Behind him, Alex rolled her eyes, slightly limping as she walked to the small rail where they hung the few clothes they owned. When she'd taken Sam to the veterinarian to save his life, she also had the young vet treat the bullet wound in her own leg.

Growing up in the Bronx in New York, Alex had been in her fair share of scrapes, especially as she ventured into the world of street racing. There had been a nasty collision when someone tried to run her off the road as she hurtled towards the finish line, sending her careening into a parked truck. The impact had sent a shockwave through her body and the whiplash was immense.

But the pain of being shot was unlike anything she'd ever felt, and she was grateful it had been a flesh wound.

Sam had applied a makeshift tourniquet at the time, which the young vet had told her had probably saved her life.

An act she'd repaid when she'd collided with the gunman who was ready to execute Sam in the middle of the street.

But now, as she slid her toned arms into her jacket, she was beginning to tire of Sam's worry.

'Well, it doesn't matter whether you like it or not,' she said coldly. 'We need the money.'

Sam turned from the window and sighed. The bond they'd built over the past few months had outweighed the original attraction that had seen them spend the night together on a Berlin-bound train. Now, he cared deeply for the young woman. She was in just as deep as he was, yet she didn't know it.

While she had street smarts in abundance, and the skills behind the wheel of a car that would make an F1 driver blush, she didn't have the same survival skills he did.

She'd never needed them.

Until now.

'So, who is this guy?' Sam asked.

'His name is Matteo.' Alex pulled a cigarette out of her pocket and lit the end. Sam gently pushed the window open and she nodded her thanks. 'He just needs a driver.'

'That's it? That's all you know?'

Alex blew the smoke into the air and shook her head.

'What do you want me to do, Sam? Check his fucking papers?'

'No, I need you to be smart,' Sam said coldly. 'I know I've been out of action and you've been making some money racing, but this guy shows up out of nowhere with a job for you to do? It sounds suspicious.'

'Just to let you know, most guys who are involved in street racing usually are suspicious.' She took another pull. 'He showed up a few nights ago, said I drove well and that he needed a driver for a job.'

'And that's it?'

'That's it.' Alex stubbed the cigarette out on the window ledge and stepped past Sam. 'He's paying good money which we need if we're going to get back to New York.'

'I know you want to get back to your family, Alex, but…'

'But what? What, Sam?' Alex snapped. 'My brother and sister are waiting for me and god knows what the fuck has happened since we've been gone. For all I know, my mum's OD'd and they're in some foster home. Or worse. If I could drive this car across the damn ocean, I would. Matteo is paying enough money for us to get there and you can bet your life I'll do anything to get home.'

Alex was shaking, the anger and pain from being away from her siblings was threatening to detonate like a bomb. Sam stepped forward and protectively wrapped his arms around her. Despite her pride, she fell into his hug and Sam gently rubbed her back.

She knew he cared.

Probably too much.

It was a notion that was lost on her. Her deadbeat dad had never been around, and her mum had long since lost herself to addiction. Alex had had a few boyfriends in her time, none of them amounting to more than a few months of passionate sex before she cut any emotional ties.

It was a comfort she didn't need.

But Sam was different. His past was his own, one he was reluctant to share, but his compassion for her was obvious. She adored the love that had grown between them, one that hadn't led to any further trysts between the sheets but one that had grown to a genuine friendship.

As she stepped away from him, she offered him her striking smile.

'Your hair is getting a bit long,' she finally said, chuckling as the fringe flopped over his brow.

'I need you,' Sam said quietly. 'You've kept me alive all this time and now I'm fighting fit. If this guy is dodgy or worse, a cop, then all this goes away. All the hope you have of getting home is gone.'

'This guy isn't a cop,' Alex said, stepping away from Sam and heading towards the door. Outside, the spring shower had gotten heavier, the rain clattering against the metal stairs and echoing like a maraca. 'Just have a bit of faith in me to know what I'm getting myself into.'

Sam readied to respond and then thought better of it. One thing he admired about the woman was her fearlessness. He was just concerned that her drive to return home would turn that to recklessness.

Deep in thought, Sam finally turned back to the window and looked out at the city, watching the rain fall.

Alex took a step towards the door.

'Everything will be fine, Sam.' She yanked the door open, and a chilled breeze blew through the small apartment. 'I promise.'

With that, she stepped out and pulled the door closed. As her boots clattered the metal of the stairs, Sam could feel an unease in his stomach.

Something didn't feel right.

Without a doubt, some very powerful people would be looking for him, with enough resources to run a small country. Besides, the people hunting Sam didn't like to leave behind a trace.

He knew that. He used to work for them.

Ervin Wallace was a terrifying human being, but he wasn't stupid. After Alex had saved his life, there was no doubt in his mind that Wallace would be turning over every stone possible to reach him. All he needed was a whiff of where he was, and the man would turn his attack dogs on him in a heartbeat.

If Alex was walking into a sting operation, the worst that she saw happening was she might get arrested. But unlike Sam, she had her actual passport.

Alex Stone.

The name would flash up on so many Blackridge databases it would look like a Christmas tree.

They would have her locked away until Wallace got there, and his patience was thin at the best of times. Despite her toughness, Sam knew she would have a pain threshold that Wallace would be all too eager to discover.

27

Once that happened, she would be nothing more than a loose end.

Another death on Sam's conscience.

'Fuck it,' Sam said, hurrying across the room to the small cupboard and pulling the tatty leather jacket Alex had purchased for him from a local charity shop. It wrapped snugly around his muscular frame and he stretched out his back, ignoring the dull pain that faintly resonated from his injury.

He wasn't fully fit.

But he was still enough.

With his chances of keeping Alex in his eyeline dissipating with every second, he rushed out of the door, leaving the frame shaking as he slammed it behind him.

CHAPTER FOUR

The *Pannuci Ripairazano Auto* sign had long since faded, with the letters barely legible. Some time ago, it had been a successful repair shop, run by a local family just making an honest living. Offering expertise and a friendly atmosphere, their business soon hit the skids when the patriarch, Salvatore was taken ill.

When he passed, the business fell upon his two sons who soon sold up, splitting whatever money they could and letting the business fade away, like the sign that once hung proudly above it.

As Alex Stone walked down the narrow side street towards the abandoned garage, she wondered how long since it had seen any business.

Legal business.

Shivering slightly in the spring chill, she marched past a few parked cars, ignoring the men stood on the other side of the road sharing a cigarette and some friendly banter. One of them called out to her, eliciting a giggle from his friend. While not fluent in the native tongue, Alex knew it wasn't complimentary.

She passed a couple more cars and a few parked

motorcycles and then stepped onto the rain soaked asphalt that led to the workshop.

As the wind danced through her hair, she approached the large, rusty shutter that fell below the sign like rotten teeth. Beside it, another metal door stood, the padlock missing.

This was the place.

As she raised her fist, she paused.

What if Sam was right?

Alex wasn't afraid of breaking the law. She'd done it for most of her life. She didn't take pride in being a criminal, but she did from doing what she needed to keep her siblings on a better path. She'd been happy to rip up her own future to ensure theirs.

And while Sam's overly cautious approach to her racing was annoying at times, she understood. They were in danger and the sooner they could get to America, the better. But his concern for this meeting was gnawing at her like an unfathomable toothache.

'Come on, Alex,' she muttered under her breath, before slamming the side of her fist against the metal, rainwater splashing down her wrist.

She shot a glance over her shoulder. The two men had gone and behind her the side street was eerily quiet. In the far distance, she saw someone round the corner, but the street lights and rain shrouded them in darkness.

Just a local resident, heading home after an evening out.

A large clang echoed from the other side of the door, startling Alex, who cursed herself. Sam had gotten in her head and she composed herself as the large metal door groaned open.

A large, bearded man appeared from the shadow, his dark eyes hiding beneath a thick brow and a shaved head. His leather jacket hugged his bulky frame tightly and Alex could see the gun tucked under his arm. He glared at her, looking her up and down before arching his neck and grunting.

Alex snapped into action.

'Ciao to you, too,' she said slyly, stepping over the threshold and into the dark garage.

The metal door slammed shut behind her.

Alex stepped cautiously into the derelict building, her eyes scanning the dusty remnants of a once thriving work-shop. Dimly lit by a few lamps placed strategically around the room, she walked past a few pits, once used to allow the mechanics enough space to stand underneath the vehi-cles they were working on. Cluttered work benches lined the walls, along with a few distasteful calendars. A shell of a car still stood proudly on its bracket, the wheels gone and the interior looted. She slowed, interested in the model of the car, but received a firm nudge from the brute who had decided to chaperone her.

She shot him a dirty look, then carried on forward, feeling a sense of unease as they approached a lone metal chair in the middle of the workshop. From the shadows created by the makeshift light, a well-dressed man stepped out, a smile etched across his handsome face.

'Ciao, bella.'

Matteo.

Decked in a black bomber jacket, jumper, and jeans, he looked like he was heading for a date as opposed to running a job.

A job she knew nothing about.

Matteo approached her, his slick, black hair parted to the side and his stubbled jaw still smiling.

'Matteo.'

'Please. Take a seat.' He offered politely, his English struggling through a thick Italian accent.

'I'm fine,' Alex said nervously, glancing as the large

bouncer who had followed her stood to the side, his arms folded across his wide chest.

'We need to discuss,' Matteo said again, his white teeth glistening in the faint light. 'I insist.'

Behind him, a woman and two men stepped out from the shadows, all of them decked in similar black attire. Alex felt her stomach drop. She recognised the dress code.

She'd adhered to it once herself.

Sensing her fear was becoming palpable, she offered a friendly smile to Matteo, who stood a few feet from her.

'You know what?' she said as confidently as she could muster. 'I think I'm going to go.'

As she turned, the doorman stepped in her path, an ugly smirk contorting his face.

'Okay, let's cut the bullshit,' Matteo said, his Italian accent replaced instantly with one similar to her own. 'Sit your fucking ass down in the chair or I'll have Luca do it for you.'

Alex turned back, facing Matteo whose smile had completely vanished. Alex felt her fists clench, but weighing up her odds, she didn't think she would last long. Resigned to her fate, she calmly walked past him and approached the chair.

'Good accent, by the way,' she said dryly, dropping into the chair. 'You learn that while sucking these guys off?'

'You got a foul mouth,' Matteo replied. 'Keep running it and I'll let the boys here try it out.'

The threat was very real, and Alex did her best to remain calm.

'So, you're Blackridge, huh?' Alex asked.

'No, I'm Matt Brecker.' He motioned to everyone else. 'We're all Blackridge. Believe you were, too?'

'Not my finest moment.'

'It should have been,' Matt said, his arms behind his

back as if standing to attention. 'Better than running these streets like a gutter rat.'

'Girl's gotta make a living.'

'Pretty face like yours, I'm sure you could have excelled at other lines of work.' Matt smiled.

'You're a charmer.'

'It worked didn't it?' he said smugly. 'Didn't take much to get you salivating at a big pay day. Now, why don't you tell me where he is?'

'Who?'

Alex felt a nervous sweat begin to trickle down the back of her neck. Considering her situation, she wondered if antagonising the group was the right way to go. Matt grinned.

'Your loyalty is admirable.' He reached into the pocket of his jacket. 'Where is Sam Pope?'

She glanced around the room, making eye contact with the bloodthirsty crew that were spread out around the workshop. They looked like a pack of starved hyenas waiting for their alpha to give them go ahead.

'I...don't...know,' she stammered unconvincingly.

'Sure you do.' Matt pulled a pair of leather gloves from his pocket and made a show of sliding his hands into them. 'So why don't you save yourself a hell of a lot of pain and me a needless workout.'

'Are you going to stop talking?'

Alex immediately regretted her remark, as the back of Matt's leather clad hand struck her viciously across the jaw. The blow was swift, and she felt the blood trickle from the split in her lip. As she took a breath, Matt squatted down in front of her, his hands relaxed over his knees and he regarded her with pity.

'Let me tell you how this is going to go. I'm going to ask you a few more times and in some ill-placed sense of loyalty, you're going to keep giving me a smart answer. I'm then going to have to hurt you pretty badly. Then, once you've been through more pain than you ever though imaginable, you're going to tell me what I need to know. So why don't you just save yourself the bother?' Matt smiled and nodded. 'So, I'll ask again. Where is Sam Pope?'

Alex drew the blood into her mouth, swashed it around with some saliva and spat it straight at him. The projectile caught him on his cheek and shoulder, and he stepped back in disgust.

Like a cobra striking, his fist caught her on the bridge of her nose, breaking it instantly and sending her and the chair crashing to the ground. With her arms shaking, Alex pushed herself onto her elbow, the blood dripping from her nose and tears streaming from her eyes.

The pain was excruciating.

Her fear was almost uncontrollable.

Her mind raced back to the underground bunker on the outskirts of Rome, where she'd lay in agony, a bullet wound in her leg. But then, she had Sam Pope fighting for her life.

A fight he would win.

Now she was alone.

'Get her up,' Matt spat, dabbing at his cheek with his gloved hand, wiping away the phlegm with a sneer of disgust on his face. The two henchmen stepped forward, roughly grabbing Alex by the arms and hauling her upwards. The female member of the group reset the chair and they dumped her onto it. All of them watched without a hint of remorse as Matt stepped forward again.

'That was disgusting,' he said calmly. 'If you do that again, I will cut out your tongue and you will have to write out the address with your own blood. *Capisce?*'

Luca chuckled and Alex eventually nodded her cooperation. Matt, surprisingly, looked relieved.

'You're making a big mistake,' Alex eventually said.

'Alex, please.'

'What do you actually think will happen if you find him?'

'We will do what we do.' Matt shrugged.

'Yeah, but the thing is, what you guys do doesn't even equate to half of what he does.'

'Shut this bitch up.' One of the guys snarled. Alex looked at him and gave him a blood smeared smirk.

'Scared?'

'Enough!' Matt shouted. 'Jimmy, hand me a hammer.'

Alex's eyes widened with fear, as the black clad man known as Jimmy stormed across to one of the work benches and began shifting through the clutter. Moments later, he stepped towards his boss like an obedient dog returning a stick.

He placed the hammer in Matt's hand.

Matt turned to Alex with a look of disappointment on his face.

'This is really going to fucking hurt.'

Alex closed her eyes and took a deep breath, her resistance goading him into making good on his threat. Shaking his head, he lifted the hammer.

A loud banging thundered through the workshop.

Matt stopped, his arm raised high and he turned his head. Someone was banging on the door, the impact echoing through the abandoned workshop. The rest of the group stood to attention, hands ready at their waists, fingers itching to release their sidearms.

Alex opened her eyes, thankful for her stay of execution. Luca turned back to look at Matt, who impatiently nodded for him to investigate.

As the large man lumbered towards the door, his hand tucked to the inside of his jacket and clasping the grip of his handgun, Matt slowly lowered the hammer to his side.

Everyone waited quietly as Luca pulled back the bolt on the door and with a hard tug, yanked it open.

———

Despite the lack of visibility, Sam had been able to keep Alex in his line of sight. Annoyingly, she walked briskly through the streets of Naples, her speed enhanced by the spring shower that had washed over the town. It was near midnight and the weekday drinking scene was coming to a joyful close, with a few groups of inebriated locals stumbling through the streets. It made Sam's job easier. The more people on the street, the less likely Alex would notice him.

Keeping his distance, he watched her round a corner, walking down one of the many narrow sideroads that sliced through the city. Eager not to lose her, Sam skipped across the road, stepping between two parked taxis and followed.

As he rounded the corner, she rounded another, and Sam marched quickly up the slight incline, his back groaning with pain.

He waited a moment, pressing himself to the wall and ran a hand through his wet hair. Having been in the military so long, Sam wasn't used to having long hair. It didn't bother him as such, but the feeling of wet hair tickling the side of his face was alien to him.

From the street ahead, he heard an Italian yell something in his native tongue, most likely a crude cat call at Alex as she walked alone.

Sam shook his head.

If only they knew. Alex may have been naïve, but she would certainly be able to handle a drunk idiot.

Slowly, Sam ventured round the corner in time to see Alex stood, fist raised, in front of what looked like an abandoned car repair shop. She glanced back and Sam slowed his walk, trying his best to stumble like a drunk returning home.

The blanket of rain and scarce lighting helped.

Alex thudded her fist against the door and after a few shunting noises, the door opened. Sam saw the large man at the door, watched Alex step in and the door close.

He hurried on, passing the few motorbikes and nice-looking cars outside. His training to absorb every detail took over and he noted the pristine condition of the vehicles.

Undoubtedly, they belonged to the crew that were recruiting Alex.

But for what purpose, Sam wasn't sure.

As silently as possible, he pressed his ear to the metal door, trying desperately to hear anything from the inside.

Minutes passed, each one feeling like an hour.

Maybe she was right?

Maybe they were going over the details of the job and Sam had just overreacted.

A large crash and the mixture of human and metal clattering to the floor echoed loudly inside.

Something didn't feel right.

Sam knew that if he was wrong, he would be in for a rough time. Most criminals didn't like intruders, especially one they didn't know. But as the faint noise of someone rooting through a toolbox filtered through to him, the need to intervene took control.

He looked around at his surroundings, nothing but a few cars and some old signage. One of the signs was broken, the metal bar that ran across the top had snapped due to years of rust and neglect.

Sam wrapped his hand around the loose end, twisted and ripped the pipe clean off. His shoulder ached, but he ignored it. He had felt worse pain.

The two scars on his chest from Project Hailstorm.

The scarring and burns from his time in the small village of Chikari.

Sam Pope was built to survive.

Tightly gripping the pole, Sam stepped up to the door and slammed his fist against a couple of times. With the rain pouring down, Sam took a step to the side and took a deep breath.

The sound of footsteps grew louder and then the loud clang of metal as the bolt was moved.

The door swung open.

Sam stepped into action.

CHAPTER FIVE

Luca's teeth didn't stand a chance.

As the pole collided with his jaw, his mouth was reduced to a mushy pulp of blood and tooth. As the cracked remnants of his smile burst forth in a spray of blood, Luca stumbled backwards, the sickening crack catching everyone in the workshop by surprise.

Sam swept in, glancing the pistol tucked under Luca's arm and instinctively reached out and caught the hulking man before he hit the ground. His hand slid into the jacket and quickly reunited him with a firearm.

It felt right in his hand.

Like a part of his body had been returned to him.

With his other arm, he used Luca's deadweight momentum to spin him round, pulling his arm tight and locking him in place.

Luca was now a motionless, human shield.

With the gun raised in his right hand, Sam scanned the room.

Beyond the few depleted cars that had long since been stripped of any value, he immediately locked eyes on Alex. Her eyes were red with tears. Her chin was red with blood.

Circling her, surrounded by forgotten work benches were three heavies, each one of them decked head to toe in the black uniform of Blackridge.

Beside Alex, an immaculately groomed man smiled cruelly and dropped the hammer he was holding onto the ground. As the clang echoed around the room, so did his sarcastic clapping.

'Impressive,' the man called out, taking a step away from Alex and towards the door. Sam made a show of aiming the gun at him. 'Whoa. You want to lower that thing?'

'Let her go.' Sam's words dripped with menace. With his eyes locked on the ringleader, he noticed the others moving in his periphery.

They were getting into position.

Their hands slowly moving to their sidearms.

The leader took another step, clenching his teeth as if indecisive, and looked back at his hostage.

'I'm afraid I can't do that, Sam. It is Sam, right?' The man had the unfortunate mannerisms of a salesman. 'Allow me to introduce myself. I'm Matt and we…'

'Just let her go,' Sam said again, readjusting the weight of his unconscious shield. Matt continued as if he hadn't heard.

'We were hoping your friend here would help us get in touch with you.' He turned and gave Alex a thumbs up. 'Good job. Now I don't have to break several of your bones.'

'You know who I am, right?' Sam said coldly.

'Indeed.'

'Then you know I'm not bluffing when I say if one of your attack dogs even thinks about reaching for a gun, I'll put a bullet in yours and their heads before they've even tickled the trigger.'

Matt's smile dropped and he ran his tongue across his

teeth, weighing up the severity of the threat. Behind Sam, the cold wind swirled through the door, sprinkling the back of his neck with rainwater. After a few tense seconds, Matt gave the order to stand down.

Obediently, they did.

Matt turned back to Sam, a hint of frustration furrowing his brow.

'How do you think this is going to go, Sam?' He shrugged. 'Do you think we'll just let you walk out of here and not hunt you down in the street? You know the deal. Wallace has already made the necessary calls to keep the heat off our backs tonight. So what's the plan?'

'Alex.' Sam looked past Matt. 'Let's go.'

'Look at me, you mother fucker,' Matt barked, his New York accent taking over. 'I don't fail.'

Alex cautiously lifted herself from the chair, eyeing the rest of the team who snarled at her. Her hesitant steps quickened, and she marched past Matt, who smirked. Alex approached Sam, who uncomfortably shifted Luca's deadweight once more. His back roared with pain under the pressure, but Sam set his bearded jaw. He gritted his teeth and maintained his aim.

'Are you okay?' Sam asked, not taking his eyes off the squadron of armed mercenaries before him.

'Yeah, I'm fine.' Alex spat some blood on the floor. 'I've been hit harder by a lot smaller.'

'Anytime,' Matt offered.

'Out front. Start the car.'

'I don't have the keys,' Alex replied.

'Improvise.' Sam smiled, and Alex nodded, stepping out into the blusterous spring night and out of sight. Matt shook his head. A moment later, the sound of shattering glass drifted into the room and Matt sighed.

'Look, Sam. I'm a reasonable man. Drop the gun and we'll let her go.' Matt took a step forward. 'Sure, Wallace wanted us to put her in the ground but I'm willing to look the other way. Just lower that thing, come with us, and we'll take you to Wallace. He just wants to talk.'

The sound of an engine roaring to life interrupted Matt. Sam smiled as Alex sounded the horn, hurrying him to make his escape. Sam dropped Luca, who flopped uselessly to the floor, his already shattered jaw crunching against the solid concrete with a sickening thud.

Sam clasped his other hand to the gun, steadying his aim and ensuring his shot.

'Tell me, Matt. What's the price on my head?' Sam spoke with a calm that belied his circumstances.

'Why? Are you going to offer to double it?' Matt's response was laced with venom.

'No. I just wanted to know how much you were willing to die for.'

The colour fell from Matt's face and Sam felt a smile flicker across his own. Despite all the bravado and a team backing him up, Matt was under no illusion of how dangerous Sam was.

And they both knew it.

As the rest of the Blackridge members slowly began to advance, Sam stepped backwards through the door, his gun trained directly at Matt's forehead. Behind him, Alex sat behind the wheel of an Alfa Romeo 4C Spider, her hands clasped on the leather steering wheel. The rain splashed against the red bonnet, the droplets sliding down the sleek curves of the sportscar.

With one foot out of the workshop, Sam heard her unlock the passenger door and it swung open.

Sam dashed to the car.

As he jumped in and slammed the door shut, he could see the movement of Blackridge as they gave chase.

He turned to Alex, surprised by her expression.

Sheer focus.

As he saw Matt burst through the door, Sam tightened his grip on the handgun and said one word,

'Drive.'

With an ear-piercing squeal, the wheels spun and in one fluid motion, Alex spun the car out of its tight parking space. As she neared the top of her turn, she slid the car into first and the car shot forward, straightening completely as she pulled her full force on the steering wheel.

Sam heard a shot fire.

A bullet shattered the rear window, but missed its target.

Through the broken glass and the roar of the engine, Sam could hear Matt barking directions and in the rear-view mirror, he could see them leaping into action.

As a few house lights flicked on, Sam could only imagine the fear of the local residents.

A gunshot is unmistakable.

Judging by Matt's boastful notion that Wallace had called off the heat, Sam estimated they had five minutes before the Polizia di Stato would be flooding the streets, their blue cars converging on their location like a wave of justice.

Five minutes.

They didn't have long.

As two motorbikes roared to life behind them, along with the headlights of the silver Mercedes A-Class, Alex took the corner at full speed, sliding through the gears and handling the car with precision. Despite the imminent threat behind them, Sam was impressed at her skills, understanding immediately how she garnered such a reputation.

One that had led her to being recruited for something other than street racing.

That had pulled her into his war and put her life at risk.

As their assailants rounded the corner, Alex pulled onto the clear main road, slamming her foot down and zipping through the empty street. As they shot past a taxi rank, the gentlemen working the night shift looked on in bemusement.

'Where are we going?' Alex asked, her eyes glued to the road.

Before Sam could respond, another gunshot echoed through the street, the bullet clipping the boot of the car. Alex startled, but kept the car steady as Sam flicked his eyes to the mirror.

The woman driving the motorbike had her arm outstretched, the handgun recklessly aimed in their direction. She was gaining on them.

And fast.

Behind her, the other motorcycle followed, along with the A-Class, with Matt sat angrily in the passenger seat.

They wouldn't be able to outrun them all. Not in the middle of a gunfight in the centre of the city.

A few feet from the car, Sam could see the woman lining up another shot.

'Brake now,' Sam commanded and instinctively, like a young recruit obeying her commanding officer, Alex slammed her foot on the brake. The wheels screeched across the wet tarmac and the car slowed instantly. The motorcycle slammed into the back of the car at full force, sending their pursuer hurtling over the top of them before clattering onto the bonnet and to the road in front. The momentum of the car took them forward, the wheels rolling over the woman, the weight of the car crushing her chest and leg, killing her instantly.

The motorcycle spun off to the side of the road, clattering into a parked car, the alarm wailing through the burst of broken glass.

One down.

Alex, shaken from the death she'd just caused, recomposed, rattled through the gears, and powered down the long road that wormed through the city like an arterial vein.

'Just keep going.' Sam assured her. 'You're doing fine.'

She nodded unconvincingly, then yelped with fear as a bullet shattered her wing mirror. The other biker was closing in and as Sam glanced into his own wing mirror, he could see the driver tactfully weaving behind them.

Moving targets were harder to hit.

But not impossible.

Behind the bike, Sam could see Matt's car chasing them down. Despite the man's cockiness, Sam knew Blackridge wouldn't send just anyone after him. It would be someone Wallace trusted. Someone who would get the job done.

There was only one way out of this.

Up ahead, they were quickly running out of road, as it split into a T-junction. To the left was the turning towards the motorway and Sam signalled for Alex to take it.

'I need a clear shot,' Sam demanded and as they approached the junction at a frightening speed, Alex yanked up the handbrake and turned. The momentum of the car drove it forward, the rain spraying up from the tires as they locked, the vehicle sliding to the right. As it did, Sam lifted the gun, drew his eye level with the sight and pulled the trigger.

The bullet blew out the visor of the biker, sending him spiralling off the bike and a burst of blood and glass into the night sky. The motorcycle toppled to its side, slid towards them but Alex slammed down the handbrake, bursting forward up the junction and allowing the bike to slam into the chain-link fence ahead.

Two down.

Alex took the motorway at over ninety miles per hour, the car practically leaping onto the dark, wide road as they took the slight incline. The road was empty beyond the lights of an overnight lorry in the far distance. They were heading out of town, where the police would be too busy dealing with the mess they'd left behind.

The lights of Matt's car joined them on the motorway.

Alex took a few deep breaths, her eyes locked on the slither of road her headlights presented. Sam slid the clip from the gun, counting the four bullets he had left. As a truck barrelled past on the other side of the motorway, the inside of their vehicle was bathed in light and Sam snapped the clip back. As they approached the next exit, Sam could make out an industrial park in the feeble glow of a few street lights.

Four large factories framed a car park, with articulated lorries locked away for the night.

'Take the exit,' Sam said calmly.

'It's a dead end,' Alex replied, the tremor in her voice betrayed her calm.

'Trust me.'

Alex nodded and glanced into the rear-view mirror. The headlights of their pursuers were closer and gaining fast. At the last possible moment, she spun the wheel, the back of the car swinging wildly to the right and she wrestled the wheel to defeat the wetness of the road.

The car behind raced forward and Alex slammed her foot down on the pedal. The car lurched forward, evading the Blackridge attack, and zipped down the dark, bendy road towards the industrial park. Sam spun in his chair, looking out through the shattered window.

All he saw was darkness.

With the motorway clear and the mission at stake, there was no doubt in Sam's mind that Matt was screaming for the car to be turned around.

They would soon be in pursuit.

As Alex sped towards the industrial park, Sam knew they had the upper hand, if only for a minute.

They had better make it count.

CHAPTER SIX

'When are you coming back?'

Natalie 'Nattie' Stone's lower lip trembled as she spoke and it broke Alex's heart. At fifteen years old, Nattie was already destined for big things. Her grades were off the charts and on the few parents evenings Alex had been able to attend, they'd told her how Nattie was already on the radar of some of the country's biggest colleges.

Cornell had been calling.

Columbus too.

While it was embarrassing to step into the parental role, Alex knew they couldn't rely on their mother. Rhonda Stone wasn't a bad woman. When she was herself, she was a kind soul and had a smile that could power the city of New York.

But those days were few and far between.

Her addiction to OxyContin started when Alex was only seven years old. She had fuzzy memories of her dad being around back then, her parents cooing over Nattie in between the marijuana smoke and the rattling of pill bottles. Two years later, when Joel arrived, her dad took off, leaving Rhonda with three kids and an itch she would never be able to scratch,

At ten years old, Alex was changing nappies, picking up supplies from the store, and working her weekends cleaning up hair in the local barber shop. The African American community in the Bronx was close knit, and she was watched over by the locals.

Regie ran the barber shop, and she fondly remembered his pearly white grin peeking through his bushy beard.

As her mother spiralled further down a drug addled rabbit hole, Alex missed more and more of her lessons, skipping out on school to put more money in her pockets and more food in her siblings' stomachs.

It was tough.

By the age of fifteen, Nattie's age now, she'd been expelled for slamming a girl's head against a desk after the girl had uttered a snide remark about her mother.

Alex wasn't defending her mother's honour.

She was defending her own.

Without school, she swept up more hair and soon found herself hanging around with some of Regie's customers. The talks of cars, chop shops, and street races were as common as discussions about the weather.

Her ears pricked up.

Soon, she was behind the wheel of the car weaving in and out of streets, shooting past finishing lines and stacking up enough cash to keep the lights on. Nattie excelled at school. Joel excelled at sports.

By Alex's nineteenth birthday, Rhonda had decided to clean herself up, seeking help from a local support group. They assigned her a sponsor and life took a turn for the better. Alex switched the steering wheel for books, studying to get enough extra credits at a local community college to forge a career as a police officer. She supplemented the money with evening shifts at a diner, hoping to build the life she'd put on hold for the sake of her siblings.

But it didn't last.

It never did.

When she came home on the evening of her twentieth birthday, she found her younger brother in floods of tears. Their mother lay motionless on the sofa, an empty bottle of pills in her hand. It was a minor miracle when they'd been able to revive her, her heart having stopped for over two minutes.

But that was when the social services began digging.

As the evidence stacked up, Alex had to prove she could look after Joel and Nattie, otherwise the state would assume control of their welfare. They couldn't guarantee they would stay together. They would both be lost in the system, their bright futures vanquished by their mother's addiction.

Alex went back to the streets. To the wheel of a car.

That was when she was nabbed by Trevor Sims and blackmailed into joining Blackridge, putting her out in the field as his squadron's driver.

If she didn't go, her siblings would.

Nattie's voice broke, tears flooding down her face.

'You can't go, Ally,' she wailed, wrapping her thin arms around Alex's waist. 'You can't.'

'Hey, I'm just going for a few weeks.' Alex squeezed her younger sister, running her hand through her braided hair. 'I'll be back before you know it.'

'What about her?'

Joel, stood in the doorway, nodded towards the living room of the apartment. Rhonda lay on the sofa, catatonic, her eyes barely open as she stared at the TV. Alex sighed.

'Well, you're just going to have to be the man of the house, ain't ya?' She smiled. 'You reckon you can handle that?'

Joel proudly puffed up his broad chest. As the star quarter back for the high school football team, he'd certainly blossomed into a hulking specimen. Like Nattie, colleges were taking notice.

Their futures were so bright.

Alex, gritting her teeth, knew she had no choice. Nattie squeezed her tightly.

'We can't do this without you.'

A tear gently slid down Alex's face and she slowly leant down, meeting her younger sister with a smile.

'You can do anything. Be anything,' she said sternly, then looked to Joel. 'Both of you. Now while I'm gone, you need to make sure you eat well and study. You hear me?'

'Yes, ma'am.' Joel saluted, smirking. Nattie solemnly nodded her head.

'Good.' Alex smiled at them both, masking her heart break. 'I don't want to have to whoop some ass when I get back.'

All three of them chuckled and Nattie once again latched onto her like a koala bear. They were soon joined by Joel, who wrapped his muscular arms around the two of them.

It was just the three of them.

Together.

As they huddled together, Alex knew that if she had to swim the Atlantic Ocean itself, she would return to them.

Whatever it took.

———

Taking a deep breath, Alex focussed her line of sight on the entrance to the industrial estate. The large, square car park was near empty, just a few lorries ferried away in the far corner, in front of a warehouse. A large sign displaying the names of the businesses and their locations stood proudly by the front gate and she knew it was only a matter of moments before it bathed in the lights of their pursuer's car.

As the rain clattered against her windscreen, she peered through the fuzzy glass, the wipers smearing it across the glass.

It was like looking through a clouded filter.

Sure enough, the headlights of Matt's car bounced off the plastic sign, momentarily blinding her.

She blinked it away as quick as she could.

The Mercedes roared around the final bend and then screeched to a halt.

Behind the tinted glass, Matt and his last remaining henchman peered menacingly around the dimly lit car park.

As Sam had instructed, she flicked the lever on the steering wheel, causing the full beam to explode through the darkness like a firework.

She revved the engine.

The standoff lasted only a matter of seconds before both sets of wheels spun on the spot, smoke rising from the concrete before both cars leapt forward, thundering towards each other in a terrifying game of chicken.

Someone would have to give.

Sam lined up his shot.

As soon as Alex had pulled into the empty estate, Sam had told her to pull over. They didn't have long, and their element of surprise was dissipating rapidly. The plan was simple.

Alex would lure them in, skew their vision while Sam stood in the shadows. He didn't like it but putting her in harm's way was the only way out of it.

It relied on Matt's recklessness.

And his own aim.

Only one of those things was within Sam's control.

As the rain engulfed him, Sam lifted the handgun with both hands, his eyes locked on Matt's windscreen as they hurtled towards Alex.

His shoulder ached.

His back moaned.

Sam's entire body had been through hell, but here he stood, ready to fight once more.

Thirty feet.

Twenty-five feet.

Sam closed his left eye.

He adjusted the grip.

He pulled the trigger.

The bullet sliced through the raindrops and pierced a perfect hole in the windscreen. The sudden jerk of the car confirmed it had lodged itself between the driver's eyes, blowing out the back of his skull and killing him instantly. The dead weight would have pushed down on the accelerator and as the car spun wildly to the left, Sam envisaged Matt's fear as he scrambled to steady the wheel.

Alex had already spun the wheel in the opposite direction and Sam took his shot.

With pinpoint aim, he blew out the back tire of the Mercedes. Combined with the speed and sharp trajectory the car flipped, spinning through the night sky and crashing on its side, the momentum causing it to roll a few times, shaking its contents like a baby's rattle.

The windows shattered.

The body crumpled.

Eventually it came to a stop, its tyres facing the sky and resembling a turtle lying prone on its shell.

Alex brought her own car to a stop and took a few deep breaths, her heart trying its best to pound its way clean through her rib cage.

Sam slowly stepped out from the shadows, the gun held down by his side and his finger still caressing the trigger.

He had one bullet left.

As he marched towards the wreckage, Sam shot a glance to Alex, who held up a shaking hand.

She was fine. Shaken, but fit.

Sam marched on and as he did, he could hear the scraping crunching of glass under his foot. Before him, the wrecked car shook slightly, and he watched without pity as Matt tried to slide himself from the wreckage. Blood pumped from a gash across his head and his arm hung loose in its socket. Shards of glass had punctured his stomach, his entire torso stained with his own blood. With the last of his energy, Matt pulled his legs clear of the wreckage, his left leg completely shattered from the knee down, his jeans holding the fragments of his shin in place.

Sam walked on; his expression cold. He stopped a few feet from the dying man and looked upon the pain he'd caused.

Three others were dead.

A fourth would soon follow.

With a deep sigh, he thought back to the broken promise he'd made to his late son.

That he wouldn't kill anymore.

It had been a promise built on the promise of a better future. A future that had been taken from him by the cruel, twisted hands of fate.

The same hands that had pushed him back into the war zone, only this time, the fight was on the streets.

Sam felt his grip tighten around the gun.

Matt, wheezing as the last of the air escaped through his punctured lungs, began to laugh.

'Well… this didn't go…how I thought.' He spat blood to the side and blinked his way through the pain. 'This isn't the end, Sam. It never ends.'

Sam raised his hand slightly, raindrops sliding down his fingers as he aimed the barrel at Matt's head. The dying mercenary closed his eyes, accepting his fate. Alex's hand gently rested on top of Sam's, lowering the weapon.

'Don't, Sam.' Her words were tinged with sadness. 'It's not worth it.'

Alex shivered in the rain, the now freezing downpour masking the adrenaline that was still pumping through her veins. Somewhere in the distance, the wailing of sirens could be heard, screeching into the night like a demonic howl. Sam kept his eyes locked on Matt and after a final, blood-curdling gasp for life, his chest stopped moving.

Alex looked away in disgust. Despite Matt's intentions, watching a human die in cold blood was hard to witness. Sam, unmoved, looked out towards the darkness that surrounded the buildings before them. After a few moments, Alex turned to leave, her hand gently pulling Sam in her direction.

'We need to go,' she said, her voice shaking.

'He's right.' Sam turned to her, his face a picture of concern. 'This will never be over.'

'It is for now.'

'There will be others.' Sam shook his head. 'He'll never stop. Not until he has me.'

'Sam?' Alex's brow furrowed, her voice cracking with anger as the realisation hit her.

'I have to go back.'

'No, you promised me you would come with me. That you would help me get my family back.'

'And I will. I promise you I will, but I have to end this.'

The rain pelted both of them, disguising the tears that were beginning to run down Alex's cheeks. Sam reached up to wipe one away but Alex slapped it away.

'If you go back, you will die.' She shook her head, trying to keep strong. Sam turned her to face him and he looked her in the eye.

'If I don't, then you might.' The sirens grew in volume

as the police hurried towards their location, following the breadcrumbs of their rampage through the city of Naples. Sam pulled Alex in and wrapped his arms around her, hugging her as tightly as he could. 'I'll come back for you, I promise.'

Alex pushed him away, shaking her head. She was right and Sam knew it. Returning to the UK was tantamount to him putting the gun to his head and pulling the trigger himself.

But he cared for Alex.

She'd saved his life, nursed him back to health and worked to get them to safety. All based on a promise he'd made. One he intended to keep.

Just not yet.

Alex took a few steps towards the car and then stopped, turning back to Sam one last time, who stood, rain soaked and full of remorse.

'The war never ends,' she said, almost to herself. 'I don't think you want it to.'

Before Sam could respond, Alex stomped back towards the car, dropped into the driver's seat, and slammed the door. The engine roared to life, the headlights illuminated the falling rain, and then she sped towards the exit, determined to evade the police one more time and do her hardest to get home.

Sam watched the car race towards the exit, before taking the corner and disappearing into the darkness. As the sadness of their departure echoed through his body, he leant down and rifled through Matt's jacket. With a slight remorse for robbing the dead, Sam pocketed the man's wallet. Sliding it into his back pocket alongside his passport, Sam glanced at his handgun and tucked it into the back of his jeans. The motorway behind him was awash with flashing blue lights, giving him his cue to leave. With his new mission taking a stranglehold of his mind, he raced towards the chain-link fence that framed the industrial state, ready to tackle the treacherous path back towards town.

It was time to go home.

It was time to end this once and for all.

CHAPTER SEVEN

Never underestimate the power of a police badge.

DI Adrian Pearce remembered when he first heard that saying. It was nearly twenty-six years ago, two weeks after he'd passed out of the Hendon Training Centre as a fully-fledged member of the Metropolitan Police. Fresh faced and full of enthusiasm, he was soon brought down to earth with a crushing thud.

Although his storied career within the system had hardened Pearce to a number of things, that phrase had stuck with him. Spurred him on.

Throughout his time within the Met, Pearce had dealt with everything the job had to throw at him. Racism, gunfire, dead bodies. All of it had resonated with him, helped mould him into the unflappable detective he became.

But it was that one saying, spoken by the veteran police officer on one of his first beats that would eventually be his calling.

Officer Lawrence Dudley.

A large man with thinning hair who enjoyed the power the position wielded as much as the satisfaction of nabbing a criminal. While not an inherently bad man, he would be a career officer, due to his propensity to cut corners, a trait that Pearce could never fathom.

They had just entered a small sandwich shop amid a busy lunch hour and Dudley had pushed himself to the front of the queue. As uncomfortable as Pearce was, he said little and then watched in dismay as Dudley flashed his badge in lieu of payment.

'*Never underestimate the power of a police badge*,' Dudley had said, stuffing the sandwich into his mouth.

Pearce sometimes wondered if that was the seed that planted itself in the back of his mind and eventually led him to becoming part of the Department of Professional Standards. The DPS investigated the inner workings of the Metropolitan Police, analysing the work of its officers and took them to task when they flouted the rules.

Initially set up to ensure that standards were being met, Pearce soon built up a reputation of hunting his own men. Despite making more enemies than friends, Pearce thrived, and it eventually sent him on a road he could never return from. Just over a year ago, Sam Pope was a quiet recluse, working within the archive department of the Met. With known criminals finding themselves in the hospital, all the breadcrumbs had led him to Sam's door.

Then everything changed.

With the life of an innocent psychiatrist, Amy Devereux at stake, Sam Pope uncovered a horrifying link between the police and a suspected terrorist attack.

People died.

Senior officers disappeared, along with any remnants of Pearce's career. Now resigned to a cupboard for life and busy work, Pearce wondered if helping Sam was one of the most hypocritical mistakes of his life.

They may have stood on opposite sides of the thin blue line, but they believed in the same thing.

Justice.

Pearce couldn't help but smile as he looked at his police badge and the power it had wielded as he'd flashed it to the dismissive receptionist behind the desk as he'd walked into the head office of *The Pulse*. Pearce was old school, sticking to the traditional newspapers as they'd made their transition into the digital age but he was aware of some of the more 'hip' news outlets. *The Pulse* was one of them, a collection of new-age journalists, pumping out a relentless stream of click bait articles, all of them chasing the increasing monetisation of internet addicts. Strewn between their top ten lists and sensationalist headlines, *The Pulse* were widely respected for writing hard hitting and at times, provocative articles, especially on the current events within the country.

Pearce himself had been mentioned in some of the articles, with the character assassination of Mark Harris which underlined his unknowing links to the Kovalenkos.

Now, he was here for a different reason and he looked around at the open-plan office where a number of enthusiastic writers were glued to their laptops. The large floor-to-ceiling windows gave a stunning view over The Strand, their residence almost mocking the historic location where the paper press used to live.

The receptionist, a young blonde lady in a tight shirt, scurried back to the desk, her head set glued to her head like a fighter pilot.

'I'm sorry about that, detective,' she said with a smile as she lowered herself into her leather chair. 'Nigel will see you now. His office is just at the end of the room.'

She pointed lazily and Pearce nodded with a smile, refusing to pull her up on her manners. Her disinterest when he'd first arrived had quickly dissolved when he'd shown her his badge.

Never underestimate the power of a police badge.

Pearce made his way towards the office, noticing the heads that swivelled as he walked by. In an office full of slick haircuts, casual clothes, and trainers, he stood out like a sore thumb. His grey suit was tailored to fit his athletic body, his fitness levels were a source of pride ever since he had passed his fiftieth birthday. His short, grey tinged hair was always well cropped, along with the neat, grey beard that framed his face.

He looked like a detective and he was proud of it.

The door to Nigel Aitkin's office was ajar, his name printed on the plaque, along with his title of 'Chief Editor' was proudly displayed.

Pearce knocked as he entered.

'Detective,' Nigel said warmly, rising from his desk with an outstretched hand. Pearce had done his homework once Assistant Commissioner Ashton had given him this errand to run. Nigel had worked as a chief writer for a number of respected newspapers, with a keen eye for a story and a sharp wit to go with it. He was widely liked by the journalist community and some of his insightful pieces on the poverty within the UK had won him awards.

He had started his own online press just over three years ago and while Pearce admired the man for striking out on his own, he wondered if Nigel regretted the type of content his writers were pumping out.

If he did, it didn't show. A large smile was plastered across his face, his glasses balancing on a thin, pointed nose that suited his sharp face. Thinning brown hair flopped across his forehead and for a man in his mid-forties, he seemed full of energy. Unlike his employees, Nigel still dressed smartly, although the suit had been downgraded to a shirt, chinos, and a smart Chelsea boot.

Pearce took the hand graciously.

'Mr Aitkin,' Pearce replied.

'Please, call me Nigel.' He motioned to the seat as he

returned to his own. 'Please sit. Can I get you a drink? Tea? Coffee?'

'Coffee would be great. Thanks.'

As Nigel buzzed his receptionist and requested two coffees, Pearce scanned the room. It was ingrained in him.

Every detail would be absorbed, filtered, and then if necessary, stored.

The price of being a detective.

He never switched off. It's what made him so damn good at his job but what had wrecked his private life.

But he wasn't here to dwell on his divorce, he was there on police business. As he returned his gaze to Nigel, he was greeted with another warm smile.

'First off, welcome to *The Pulse*,' he said proudly. 'It's not often we get the boys in blue here.'

'Well, you're obviously doing something right, then,' Pearce responded with a nod.

'I'd like to think so,' Nigel said with a deep sigh. 'The day when the newspaper was a source of truth has long since died. Now, with social media infecting everyone's phone, the reliance on the press to hammer through real news is as strong as ever. I like to think that we do our job and do it well.'

'That's very noble of you,' Pearce said, interrupted by the reappearance of the receptionist, who looked less than thrilled to be bringing in two cups of coffee. Pearce nodded politely and then hid his disdain at the foul-tasting drink provided. As she left, he turned back to Nigel, who regarded him carefully.

'How can I help you, detective?'

'I'm here to talk with one of your contributors...'

'Journalists,' Nigel corrected.

'Journalists...Helal Miah.' Judging from the slight shake of the head, Pearce felt the tension. After a few moments and a small sigh, Nigel lifted his mobile phone.

This was a modern office and the idea of a desk phone was laughable. As Nigel sent a text message, Pearce thought about the clunky device on his desk. He still didn't know how to put someone on hold. After a few more taps of the screen, Nigel dropped the phone on his desk. He looked slightly perturbed and Pearce decided to press a little harder.

'Is everything okay?'

'I had a feeling a day like this would come.' Nigel shook his head. 'I've told Helal a few times that his pieces are becoming too provocative and…here he is now.'

The door to the office opened and Pearce stood. Helal walked in with a true sense of confidence, his head high, he shoulders straight. With his neatly cut, slicked hair and neatly trimmed beard, he was well groomed. The denim shirt, black chinos, and Converse shoes completed the outfit of a man completely comfortable in the modern world. While not the tallest, Helal's firm handshake told Pearce he feared nothing.

It was an admirable quality.

One which would make this difficult.

'How can I help?' Helal shrugged, casually walking to the wall and leaning back against it, his arms folding across his chest.

'Helal, this is DI Adrian Pearce from the Metropolitan Police.' Nigel formally introduced him. 'He has requested to speak to you.'

'Oh really?' Helal's brown eyes flickered with excitement. 'Are you here for an interview?'

'Excuse me?' Pearce said, taking his seat.

'I know you. You're the Sam Pope detective. I've mentioned you a few times in my articles. You were the one who exposed Mark Harris, weren't you?'

'Mr Miah, I am not here to grant you an interview, nor do I want to be involved in any pieces you are writing.'

'That's a shame.' Helal looked around the office, pondering when the day would come when it would be his. Born and raised in London to Indian parents, Helal loved the city as much as he loved putting his fingers to the keyboard. Through his years of investigative journalism, he knew that powerful organisations worked hard to keep things behind closed doors. The fact that a detective had shown up, a mere day after he'd published an article questioning the Met's ability to police safely wasn't a coincidence.

It was a confirmation.

'I'm here about the article you wrote.'

'Who's watching over us now?' Helal interrupted, drawing a scowl from his boss. 'Quality, wasn't it?'

'I didn't read it.' Pearce lied, knowing he needed to tip the balance of power. 'But some people did and…'

'Let me guess…' Helal cut him off again. 'Certain higher-ups are upset that the truth is coming out.'

'Truth?' Pearce raised his eyebrows. 'I wouldn't call sensationalist pieces supporting the work of a vigilante as truth. I'd call it click bait.'

'Not according to my sources.'

Pearce smiled to himself and slowly pushed himself out of his seat. He towered over the journalist and locked his eyes onto him. He had been in enough interview rooms to know that his stare could be quite unnerving. This time however, Helal rolled his eyes and turned to his boss.

'Am I in trouble?'

'I don't know,' Nigel said. 'But I did tell you that this article could land you in the shit.'

'It's a free fucking press.' Helal spat, his arms out in dismay. 'If we let the police dictate what we can and can't write, what the hell happens to free speech?'

'Save me the crusade,' Pearce said firmly. 'I'm not here to slap your wrist or to tell you what you can or can't write, despite what some of my superiors would like. I'm here to tell you to be careful.'

'Are you threatening me? Because believe me, I get threatened an awful lot.'

'I don't doubt that.' Pearce smiled. 'But your article has rattled some cages that are best left alone.'

'Never,' Helal said defiantly. 'If I've got certain people pissing in their pants, it's because I've written something close to home. It's what I do.'

Pearce took a step towards Helal, who readjusted his feet, doing his best to stand straight. The man had a backbone, that was for sure, and Pearce couldn't help but admire that. But accompanying that with a smart mouth was a recipe for trouble. Sat behind the desk, Nigel had his head in his hands, as if the whole interaction was a personal slight on his company.

'Just be careful,' Pearce said calmly. 'Otherwise the next person who comes to see you might not be as accommodating.'

'Are we done?' Helal asked dismissively. 'Because I've got a hot date with a cute source.'

'I mean it,' Pearce said coldly. 'There are some stones certain people don't want overturned.'

Helal took a step closer to Pearce.

'Then they shouldn't hide things. I don't write these stories for the glory. I write it because people we trust to serve and protect us have a hell of a lot of skeletons in the closet. Now, I don't condone Sam Pope or any act of violence but if he's prepared to risk it all to do the right thing, then so am I.' Helal looked at his boss, who had a face like thunder. 'The world could use more truth. Then maybe I wouldn't have to write these pieces in the first place.'

Pearce stopped himself from responding. Despite the sensationalist way he saw himself, Helal was right. Powerful people did things in the dark and all he was doing was a shining a light on it.

And potentially painting a target on his back.

'Just think about it,' Pearce finally said, before turning to a desperate looking Nigel. 'Thanks for the coffee. I'll see myself out.'

Pearce shot one final glance at Helal, who gave him an empty smile. As he stepped back into the office, he looked out at the rest of *The Pulse* reporters, whose heads poked up from their screens like startled meerkats. As he scanned the room, each one dropped their glance as his eyes rested on them.

The power of the police badge.

Leaving Nigel to read Helal the riot act, Pearce headed for the door, wondering how long it would be before Mr Miah penned an article about police intimidation.

CHAPTER EIGHT

Amara Singh had failed.

With a resounding sigh, she lifted herself from the leather sofa that took centre stage of her living room and stretched out her back. The feeling of uselessness flowed through her like a current and she wondered once again if she should take up her parents' offer of therapy. For years, she'd always seen the idea of seeking help as a sign of weakness. But now, with her life crumbling around her, she wondered if maybe it would help.

It certainly couldn't hurt?

As she trudged across her flat, she rolled her eyes at the mess. It used to be immaculate, with everything neatly stored away, the shelves sparkling and the only evidence of a human came when she passed through. Now, as she sat at home most days, she'd allowed her standards to slip.

Everything had slipped.

It was nearly five o'clock in the evening and she was still lounging in her pyjamas. Her usual routine of going to the gym, keeping herself in peak physical condition, had fallen by the wayside two months ago, when her superiors enforced an 'extended period of absence.'

They were doing their best to push her out of the Metropolitan Police Service.

This was not how her life was supposed to go.

Six months before, she was seen as the rising star of the organisation. While her aptitude tests, arrest record, and performance as an Armed Response Officer were off the charts, she knew her gender and race had opened doors that had caused resentment from others. But she'd never allowed the snide comments or the sexist remarks stop her.

She'd been focussed.

She'd achieved.

She did not fail.

Then, in the midst of Sam Pope's one-man war on organised crime, she was put in charge of the task force created for the sole purpose of bringing him in. It was an opportunity she'd jumped at, personally recommended by the Assistant Commissioner herself. It was an honour, one bestowed upon a prodigy that should have been her crowning moment.

But somewhere along the way, the lines began to blur.

As a deplorable mayoral candidate pressured her to find Sam, her obsession to catch him had blinded her from the reality.

Sam Pope was not a bad guy.

He was a criminal and she would never waver from the belief that someone should never take the law into their own hands. But while her superiors were concerned with the negative press, he was out, hunting for missing teenagers who were being shipped abroad into the sex trade.

The lines definitely blurred.

As she thought about that harrowing night in the Port of Tilbury, she remembered how close she'd been to death. Set upon by two of Andrei Kovalenko's thugs, she'd fought valiantly, throwing well-trained punches, and dished out as good as she gave. But she soon found herself on her knees, the rain lashing against her as a gun was pressed against her forehead.

As she remembered the feeling of accepting death, Singh felt her knees weaken.

She'd been seconds from death, the thug had wrapped his finger around the trigger.

But Sam Pope had saved her.

Without hesitation, he'd killed both men, before telling Singh exactly where to find the missing girls. That was the moment when it clicked for her.

Sam Pope was not a bad guy.

With an army of armed henchmen baying for blood, Sam ran back into the war zone, doing his best to draw them away. His life or freedom weren't his priority. The safety of the innocent was.

Singh steadied herself against the kitchen unit, looking with disgust at the mountain of dirty dishes and mugs that decorated her sink. She knew she would need to pull herself up, get her life back together at some point, but right now that felt a long way off.

In the aftermath of the Kovalenko empire falling, Singh found herself on the outside. Rumours were rife that she'd helped a known vigilante disappear and her loyalty to the badge was thrown into doubt.

How could they focus on Sam when he'd just saved those girls from a fate worse than death?

As the investigation began on her own conduct, she'd formed a bond with another ostracised detective, DI Pearce. A man who she'd warmed to and thought of as a friend. As her investigations into Sam Pope's past intensified, Pearce had begged her to be careful.

She knew she should have listened.

In hindsight, she should have sat quietly for a few weeks, been an obedient little lap dog and soon all would have been forgiven. Her career may have stalled but another opportunity would have come her way.

But she'd kept digging.

Redacted file after redacted file had turned up nothing on Sam's military past until an errant scribbling on one sheet of paper would paint a target on her back.

Project Hailstorm.

Singh took a bottle of water from her bereft fridge and unscrewed the cap, taking a calming sip as she remembered the midnight visit of General Ervin Wallace. Singh had prided herself on fearing no one. She'd burst into dangerous situations with a calm and authoritative manner, taken out armed criminals, and faced death.

But the menace the man had exuded had been palpable.

His large bulk, piercing stare, and dominating nature had told her from the moment he'd entered her flat that she'd rattled the wrong cage. His thinly veiled threat had been obvious. Whatever connection the man had to Sam, it was a dangerous one and despite Pearce's protests and every warning triggering in her head, she had to know.

She had to know exactly which side of the blurred line her loyalties lay.

It had cost her everything.

Pearce had betrayed her, going above her head to Ashton who had promptly suspended her. A known associate of Sam, Paul Etheridge, had been brutally tortured in his own home.

And her own safety had been put in jeopardy.

Her flat had been ransacked and ever since then, she knew she was being followed.

Whatever reach Wallace had, it was vast. Singh knew she was under the microscope and her extended absence was most likely a request of his.

Whatever she'd found, the man wanted it to stay hidden.

Every rational thought in her mind told her to step away, that the rabbit hole she'd been tumbling down would only get deeper.

It had almost certainly cost her career.

Her friendship with Pearce was dead.

And now her mental health was suffering.

Despite all that she'd lost, she knew she couldn't step away. Not when she'd seen what Sam was willing to sacrifice for the good of the innocent. From what she'd pieced together, General Wallace was hiding behind his iron fist, abusing his power, and influencing an institution created for the safety of the public.

If she couldn't bring him down through the legal channels that he controlled, then she would do it on her own.

As she thought about the repercussions of what she was putting into action, she could feel her hand shaking, the bottle of water sloshing wildly and spilling.

After this evening, there would be no going back.

Singh hopped into the shower, the warm water crashing against her toned body and immediately relieving the tension that had a stranglehold of her muscles. She stood for a few moments, allowing the water to engulf her entire body, the sound of the water hitting the tiles drowning out the worries that were dominating her mind.

After a few more minutes, she turned the water off and wrapped a towel around her body and headed for her bedroom. It had been a while since she'd shared her bed with anyone. With her unsociable hours and relentless drive, a steady boyfriend had never been a priority. To her parents' dismay, she had little interest in the family life. While her sister had provided them with the grandchildren they craved, they'd never understood her refusal to follow suit.

They had respected her career, but since the turn of the year, while she was being ushered towards the door, she could feel the disappointment in their voices when they spoke.

Amara Singh had failed.

Half an hour later and Singh was walking towards the front door of her flat, her small heels clicking across the wood flooring. She had on fitted jeans and a nice, black button up top, wrapped in a leather jacket. Her hair was straight and the minimal make-up she'd applied would certainly turn heads. She was as attractive as she was tough but she hated the idea of being thought of as a pretty face.

But she needed to blend in tonight.

To disappear.

As she opened the door, she could still see the markings of where Wallace's men had broken into her flat, reinforcing her need to fade into the London night life.

They would be watching.

They were always watching.

With a deep breath she stepped out of her flat and made her way through the block, stepping out into a surprisingly mild spring evening. Adjusting her bag over her shoulder, she scanned the street, noticing the black SUV parked a few cars further down.

Inside, a man sat, dressed in black, his attention drawn to her.

For a professional, he was pretty sloppy, and Singh walked briskly towards Canons Park Station, the streets of North London filled with traffic. Her tail tried to follow, but with the rush hour traffic proving too impatient to let him pull out, she glanced over her shoulder to see him exit the car and begin to follow her by foot, his hands stuffed in his black bomber jacket.

She picked up the pace.

As she rounded the corner, she saw the entrance to the

station and clambered the few steps and disappeared into the station.

She only had a few seconds.

Quickly, she pulled a red scarf from her bag and wrapped it over her head. Singh then slid her jacket off and hunched over the ticket machine situated just on the inside of the doorway. Directly in front of the door, the ticket barriers awaited, before leading to two platforms which led to the Northern Line trains.

She'd timed it perfectly.

A train had just arrived, and a swarm of city workers were slowly descending the steps, like a pack of lifeless zombies trudging towards their next feed. Behind her, the pursuer entered the station clearly panicked that she'd slipped through the crowd and onto the train that sat patiently on the platform. With a sense of urgency, he barged through the crowd, hopped the barrier, and bounced up the steps two at a time, ignoring the angry yells of the attendant.

Singh smirked, before turning and exiting the station and approaching the Uber she'd booked before she'd left the apartment. She greeted the man with a smile and dropped into the back seat.

This time, she hadn't failed, and the sense of victory was enough to make her question what she was doing.

She'd always been a phenomenal police officer, working her way to a position where she could really make a difference. As a Detective Inspector, she was already on her way.

But this, if it ever got back to Ashton, would end any hope of a return.

As the car crawled through the traffic towards her meeting, she relived every moment of her spiral. Her relentless pursuit of Sam Pope, the shoot-out in Paul Etheridge's home, the siege on the Port of Tilbury.

The very real threat of General Wallace.

The betrayal of Pearce.

Living in fear since then that everything she'd worked for was about to be ripped away from her for trying to do the right thing.

With regret, she knew there was no way back. Unless she did something monumental, the career she'd given her life to, was over.

At least this way she could go out on her sword, knowing that despite the corruption and clear illegality of her dismissal, she'd still done the right thing.

With a chuckle, she realised she was walking the same path as Sam Pope, just she wasn't armed to the teeth with military grade weaponry.

As she stepped out of her cab and entered the bar, she scanned the booths. She recognised her 'date' from the profile picture used on *The Pulse* website that proudly topped all his articles.

As she approached Helal Miah, he looked up at her, slightly taken aback by the gorgeous woman walking towards him and then he offered her a charming smile.

She wasn't armed with weaponry.

But with information.

With a deep breath, she sat down in the booth and nodded, ready to tell him everything.

CHAPTER NINE

The sexual encounter was one of inevitability.

As Wallace thrust powerfully into Assistant Commissioner Ashton, he grinned. Her moans of pleasure gave him vindication as a man, but the feeling of dominance was what he craved. Propped up on his powerful arms, he didn't even look at her as he thrust as hard as he could.

Ever since he'd stormed into her office, he knew Ashton had been thinking of this moment. A combination of her attraction to power and the possibility of having Wallace's backing when the top job came up was an alluring cocktail.

One which Wallace would have been happy to sit on.

At first, having her use her officers like his own personal police force had been enough.

But as the situation with Sam began to unravel, he could feel the control slipping through his fingers like sand.

Wallace was always in control.

Always.

Grunting, he felt her slide her hands across his broad back, her fingertips gliding through the sweat.

He was under no illusion why he'd called her to his

apartment. It had been three days since he'd dispatched a hit squad to Naples in Italy, where one of his ghosts had made contact with Alex Stone. She was immaterial, an unfortunate cog in a dangerous wheel that was spinning rapidly towards disaster.

Matt Brecker was one of his top assets, as charming as he was deadly. Wallace had given the go ahead for Matt to assemble a small team and to beat Sam's location out of the poor girl. The last time Wallace had seen Alex, she was lying in the underground room where he'd murdered Carl Marsden, an act that still caused him pain.

Marsden had been a good man.

But he stood in the way of the bigger picture.

The information he'd gained and subsequently passed to Sam would not only bring about his own downfall, it would paint a large target on Wallace's back. A target that some extremely powerful and dangerous people would quickly take aim at.

But Sam had slipped through the net.

The USB stick was gone and Matt's progress had been his only breakthrough in three months.

Earlier that morning, Wallace had been informed that Matt and his team had been killed.

An apparent car chase through the city of Naples in the middle of the night, with Matt's team of henchman killed with horrifying proficiency. Blackridge operated on an anonymous basis, which meant it took nearly two days for his team to pick up the deceased's records from the Italian government.

Matt had been found in an industrial estate just outside of the city, his body broken from the apparent wreckage of the car nearby. There was no sign of a collision, however a bullet was found lodged in the blown tire.

Wallace knew only one man capable of making a shot like that.

Sam Pope.

Wallace gritted his teeth and pushed harder, his slight gut slapping against Ashton's naked body as she writhed in a mixture of pleasure and discomfort. There was no passion to the intercourse, just a pure, animalistic fury. With every slam of the headboard, Wallace felt the notion of power and control flow back through him. He quickened his pace, the anger of losing control of the situation fuelling his need to assert his dominance.

They both groaned.

Ashton let out a squeal of ecstasy.

As they finished, Wallace tilted his bald head back and roared powerfully, like a lion asserting its dominance over his pride. Shaking slightly through euphoria, he rolled off Ashton and sat on the side of the bed, letting his heart rate regulate.

The bedroom they'd desecrated was as new to him as it was to her. His ops team had traced several contactless payments made on Matt's debit card in the previous twenty-four hours, totalling over a hundred euros. Which meant Sam had filtered enough money to leave Italy.

Either to escape.

Or return.

Pulling rank, Wallace had made the decision to retreat to an undisclosed apartment in Surrey, heavily guarded by his own private security team. It was one of the governments safe houses, used to stow away high-risk individuals. Wallace had wielded his power and took the keys. It was safer to be off the grid.

But the feeling of cowardice had led him to call Ashton personally before sending a car to pick her up. She'd arrived, dressed immaculately in a black dress, undoubtedly expecting a night of fine conversation and charm. Wallace had made it clear he was in a foul mood from the offset, but her attraction to his position had made it an easy encounter.

She'd gone to the bedroom, undressed, and then called him in.

There had been no kissing. No foreplay.

It had been almost transactional.

But the feeling of control was fleeting and Wallace lifted himself from the bed and wrapped a dressing gown around his naked body.

'Can I have a shower?' Ashton asked, the bed covers held against her chest to cover her modesty. Her words were tinged with regret.

'Of course,' Wallace responded, a feeling of guilt threatening to take over. She was an admirable woman, who had worked hard for a tremendous career. While her attraction to him had been unrequited, he would make sure he wouldn't let it hinder her prospects going forward.

'Are you okay?' Ashton asked sheepishly, sliding herself from under the sheets. 'Was everything okay?'

Wallace grinned.

'It was great,' he replied, reaching for his box of cigars. 'I need some air.'

Ashton nodded meekly, understanding that their one-time tryst was firmly over. As she headed towards the en suite bathroom, Wallace walked back through the expensive apartment and slid open the door to the balcony. The chill of the spring evening hit him like a splash of cold water, the wind riding up his gown and causing him to shiver. He looked down at the cigar cutter, reminded of the torture his friend, Marsden, had gone through. Trevor Sims had ordered the removal of several fingers with a similar device.

Wallace smiled as he remembered putting a bullet through the man's skull.

Lighting the cigar, he let the thick smoke cascade

around him as he contemplated the next move. While there was every chance Sam would disappear, he knew it was unlikely. The man had an outrageous moral code, one that would never let him rest if there was a wrong to put right.

Wallace had killed Marsden.

Sam would want answers.

While the threat of revenge was enough to make Wallace hide, it was the USB stick that had caused his once unbreakable aura to crack. The device was out there, in a location that Sam would most likely know. While the documents were protected by the very best that cyber security had to offer, it still made him nervous.

Wallace had put as much in place as he could.

Amara Singh was being followed.

Pearce was under surveillance too.

Etheridge, the man that his ghost, Mac, had brutally tortured, had disappeared off the radar entirely.

Wallace sighed as he thought of Mac.

There had been no contact since that night in Rome, where Mac was run down by, he assumed, Alex Stone. The man had lived and breathed the idea of revenge on Sam, an idea that Wallace had carefully nurtured ever since he recruited him. While he felt the man's pain for not seeing the mission through, Wallace knew that Mac's obsession with Sam was not what he needed.

Not for this.

This would require someone of a stable mind, which made their proficiency all the more terrifying.

It would also require personal investment.

For the first time in decades, Wallace felt his hands shake with fear as he reached for his mobile phone and made the call he'd promised he would never have to make.

———

The tyres of the coach hit a pothole in the road and shook the entire vehicle causing Sam's forehead to collide with the large, Plexiglas window. He awoke with a start and a frown, his eyes blinking him back into consciousness.

A few hours of undisturbed sleep had been most welcome, even if his dreams were littered with the memory of his son's death.

That and the vast number of criminals he'd put in the ground.

He remembered them all.

From the horribly scarred brute in the High Rise, to the fight to the death with Oleg Kovalenko atop a large tower. Even the first bullet he'd fired in Amy Devereux's apartment, hitting a masked man between the eyes and setting him off on his path of justice.

It had been a long road home, but the coach had turned off the M25 and as Sam's vision restored completely, he smiled warmly as they passed a large sign.

Welcome to Farnham

Craft Town.

It had felt like a lifetime since Sam had been in this part of the UK, waiting patiently with a cup of tea while his friend, Paul Etheridge, mocked up his fake passport and complained about his impending divorce. Sam had felt bad, as his shoot-out with the armed police within Etheridge's house surely hadn't helped. But Etheridge had made it clear it was the straw that had broken the camel's back, and that the loveless marriage had long since dissolved.

He was a wealthy man and a young woman like Kayleigh hadn't exactly been in it for the passion.

But since paying for Sam's ticket to Kiev and passing on the intel of where to find Carl Burrows, Etheridge had gone off the radar. Every phone call Sam had attempted had gone to voicemail and Sam couldn't help but feel nervous.

Marsden had entrusted him with a USB stick that he'd given his life for.

Had Sam put Etheridge in danger by sending it to him?

He had to know.

Sam looked around at the rest of the coach, noting only a few other passengers. A small group of Chinese tourists were huddled near the front of the coach, their eyes taking in the beautiful scenery lit up by the street lights. The mild spring evening giving them a nice view of the quaint town. Based in the Surrey Borough of Waverley, it held a number of wonderful tourist attractions such as Farnham Castle and bordered the Surrey Hills.

To Sam's right, a middle-aged man slept while his teenage son was engrossed in his tablet, watching the latest hit show on Netflix.

Sam let out a sigh. His entire body ached.

He had been through the wars.

But he had a feeling it was far from over.

After leaving the dead body of Matt Brecker in the industrial park on the outskirts of Naples, Sam had made his way back to the city on foot. Full of regret for how things had been left with Alex, he'd taken Matt's debit card and purchased two packets of cigarettes from a twenty-four hour newsagents. He had then headed back to the apartment he'd called home for three months and got a few hours rest, before making his way to Naples city centre. There he'd visited a number of different supermarkets, racking up thirty euro's worth of cigarettes each time.

As the midday rush of tourists begun to filter through, Sam casually zeroed in on a group of English men outside a bar, asking one of them for a lighter. As he puffed the cigarette, he allowed his genuine disgust to take control and then told them he was supposed to quit.

He offered them four packets at a discounted price.

Sensing a bargain, they eagerly handed Sam the cash.

A few hours later, Sam repeated the act with an elderly Scottish couple, who took the deal and wished him luck with his attempts to kick the filthy habit.

Sam did this throughout the afternoon until he'd racked up a hundred and eighty Euros. Sam dumped Matt's wallet in a bin, walked to Naples station, and bought a one-way ticket to Rome.

Less than two hours later, he was back in the capital, the memories of his car crash and possible reunion with an old friend flooded back to him.

It couldn't have been him, could it?

Mac was dead. He had died in an air strike over a decade ago.

It had haunted Sam ever since.

Mac's death

The death of Dr Farhad Nabizada, who had saved his life.

His boys, Tahir and Masood. Orphaned.

They were all scars that Sam bore and as he paid for a train ticket to Paris, Sam was relieved to be leaving the beautiful city of Rome. Just over three hours later, Sam arrived at Paris Terminal. It was the early hours of the morning and Sam checked his money.

With only seventy euros left, he bought a ticket for the ten-hour coach ride back to London and then found a coffee stall. The warm caffeine was like heaven as he gulped it down and the accompanying croissant was the first thing he'd eaten in over a day. As the coach pulled away from Paris Terminal just after midday, Sam decided to rest.

He awoke as they came to a stop in the Channel Tunnel, and his counterfeit passport worked a treat.

Jonathan Cooper.

That's who the border control welcomed back to the UK, not realising they'd just allowed the UK's most wanted vigilante back on their shores.

As they weaved through the rush hour traffic of the M25, they crawled through the stop-start roads of London until they arrived at London Victoria Coach Station.

Sam had felt fresher.

He hadn't showered since his few hours in the apartment. His long hair was greasy from sweat and his stubble was becoming itchy and unruly.

But he was almost there.

Almost at his destination.

After exchanging the last of his euros into sterling, he boarded the coach for Farnham and fell straight to sleep.

Now, as the coach slowed to a halt, his legs ached as he stepped out into the brisk, spring evening and stepped around the group of tourists who were arguing over the directions to their hotel.

Sam knew where he was headed.

He pulled the collar of his jacket up, stuffed his hands in his pockets, and walked the mile and a half to Etheridge's street. As he approached, he scanned the road, ensuring there were no stakeouts. It would make sense that Blackridge would keep a lookout on a known associate of Sam's in a desperate attempt to find him.

But the street was clear and as Sam drew closer to Etheridge's house, his heart sank.

He could see why.

A large 'Sold' sign stood proudly in front of the mansion. Sam walked slowly to the electronic gate of the property and clutched two of the poles with each hand.

He had no more money.

Nowhere else to go.

No other moves.

Despite his refusal, defeat began to dominate his thought process and he leant his head forward, resting it gently against the metal bars.

He was so tired.

As his mind raced to find a way to contact Adrian Pearce, he was oblivious to the stuttered steps of the hooded man behind him. By the time Sam's instincts had kicked in and he knew he'd been ambushed, it was too late.

He felt the barrel of the gun press against the back of his skull.

'Hello, Sam.'

CHAPTER TEN

It had been a long road for Etheridge, too.

Six months earlier, he'd just signed a lucrative deal with a Japanese mega brand to rebuild their entire digital security platform. His company, BlackOut, was leading the way in cyber security and companies were lining up to sign exclusive contracts with him. While he thought of himself as a reasonably modest man, he couldn't help but smile as the clients came knocking and the company's bank account swelled. As the founder and CEO, he was living the life of a millionaire.

The sports cars.

The trophy wife twenty years his junior.

The six bedroom mansion in the picture-esque countryside.

Fast forward a couple of months, and an old acquaintance had shown up at his door.

Sam Pope.

Having begun his career in the military, Etheridge had excelled with his technical wizardry, even if his physical prowess was lacking. As a talented bomb disposal expert, he'd joined Marsden's elite platoon and soon bonded with the ruthlessly efficient soldier.

Then, one fateful night on the Turkish border, Etheridge slipped and fell. With his leg shattered and the enemy closing in, his life had flashed before his eyes.

In a matter of seconds, Sam had eliminated the approaching assailants, the sight of his scope ensuring the bullets from his rifle sent them all to the afterlife.

Sam had saved his life.

So when the UK's most wanted vigilante turned up at his house begging him for help, he had to return the favour. A missing girl was at stake and Etheridge, using his intimate knowledge of security systems, was able to help Sam not only locate her, but bring her home safely.

Sure, it cost him his marriage.

The Armed Response Unit of the Metropolitan Police had engaged Sam in Etheridge's own home, only to be left incapacitated.

Sam had shot to wound.

After a few rigorous interviews by the desperate detectives hell-bent on catching the man, Etheridge was off the hook. Sam had found the young girl, Jasmine Hill, along with three others, all on the cusp of a horrific future in the Eastern European sex trade.

He forged Sam a passport, gave him some cash, and sent him on his way to Kiev to finish the job. As he awaited further contact, Etheridge was soon visited by a stranger, dressed in black and with one goal.

To find Sam Pope.

The pain he put Etheridge through was unlike anything he'd felt. Worse than the broken leg he'd suffered all those years ago. The man, burnt and disfigured, had water boarded him in his own office, bringing him to the brink of death time and again, but Etheridge had shocked himself.

He had not talked.

But his computers did.

Sam's fake passport triggered an alert on his system, giving the sadistic attacker his location. The man in black had gotten what he wanted, but it wasn't enough. Without batting a charred eyelid, he'd pressed a handgun to Etheridge's surgically repaired knee and pulled the trigger.

The pain had been instant.

The burning sensation roared through his body like an explosion as the bone and cartilage was eviscerated. Blood loss and shock caused him to lose consciousness and as his vision faded and his torturer left, Etheridge had accepted his death.

When he awoke in the hospital later that evening, he found DI Adrian Pearce sat next to him. The friendly detective had visited him with a fellow detective, Amara Singh, for Etheridge's expertise. When they asked him again, he bluntly refused.

A few days later, after extensive surgery and a few trips to physio, Etheridge had been fitted with a permanent knee brace which would hinder his mobility for the rest of his life. Pearce had kindly taken him back to his mansion, where to no surprise, Kayleigh had already taken a bag and left.

He was expecting the divorce papers any day.

After refusing Pearce's offer of help one last time he'd stumbled into his house and sat at the vast marble breakfast bar that framed the island in the centre of his kitchen.

Something had clicked.

As he looked around the home he'd held as a symbol of his success, he felt disgust. None of it mattered.

The cars.

The expensive sofas.

The 4k TVs dotted around the house.

All of it meant nothing.

Coming so close to death had changed something within him.

What should have sent him running for the hills had done the opposite. While Sam had been willing to run into a gun fight to save a young girl he'd never met, he'd been too obsessed with making money. With living a life of luxury. While his accomplishments in the business world had been incredible and made him a wealthy man, he felt empty.

He had used his considerable knowledge and skills to widen his bank account.

That was about to change.

Over the following few months, he'd readily signed the divorce papers, wilfully allowing Kayleigh to take a large settlement that would no doubt feed her materialistic itch. He had also decided to sell his controlling shares in Black-Out, which were eagerly gobbled up by the other stiffs who sat at the executive table.

Within a few weeks, he was free of it all, with a bank balance capable of funding a small country and the brain of a man capable of weaponising it.

He put the house on the market, and it sold within a day.

Being a prodigy behind a keyboard meant piling a number of names behind numerous shell companies was child's play. He sold the house to himself effectively, before purchasing a small flat in Tenerife.

A little record manipulation not only moved his own life to another country but showed him just how easily he could shock the system if he needed to.

Even to the most trained eye of the government or whatever nefarious outfit came looking, he'd given it all up after his assault and had retired to the Canary Islands to live a life of luxury. He even made weekly transactions to a local supermarket in Tenerife, before having the deliveries diverted to a local charity.

He was no longer a concern or an interest.

But, still based in his home, he upgraded his software, spending a small fortune on the best computers money could buy. His office which was once a place for him to mull over corporate contracts, was now a control centre, the walls covered in screens and with his own data centre powering it.

He was in every system without them knowing it.

He was a ghost in the machine.

All he needed was a purpose.

A mission.

Then, just like the man in black had, an opportunity had come knocking.

As soon as Jonathan Cooper's passport had pinged up on his screen, he'd quietly left the sanctuary of his control room and stepped out into the brisk, spring evening.

The millionaires' road he lived on was as peaceful as ever, with the large houses all locked away behind their automatic gates and their expensive luxury cars.

Opposite the house, he melted into the shadows of the large hedge that framed his neighbour's house.

A few hours later, he felt his arms shake with excitement as Sam approached the gate of his house, looking forlornly at the misdirecting 'Sold' sign that stood proudly before resting his head against the metal.

Etheridge had stepped forward, ready for his dramatic entrance and quietly approached Sam from behind, the unloaded gun in his hand.

———

Etheridge's story had hit Sam like a punch to the gut. While he knew every war had casualties, he'd never intended to put his friend in harm's way. It had been a desperate act to find a young girl. By associating himself with Etheridge, he had painted a target on the man's back, one which highly trained people had taken aim at.

Sam had felt sick.

As the eerie silence had settled between them as they sat at the breakfast bar in the now sparse kitchen, Etheridge had decided to break the silence.

'You look like crap.'

They had chuckled and Etheridge had insisted that Sam clean himself up, directing him to one of the pristine bathrooms. Sam had graciously accepted, his guilt weighing down every step as he trudged to the bathroom.

As Etheridge handed him a towel, he also handed him a pair of electric clippers with a smile.

Sam had chuckled, but the grim reality hit him in the face as he saw his reflection.

His beard was scraggily, despite his best efforts.

With a click of a button, Sam glided the electric razor across his sturdy jaw, the hair tumbling down to the sink below like brown snow. After a few moments, his face felt fresher than it had done in months, and he ran his hand across the stubble.

He turned the setting on the razor to grade three and then pushed it slowly through the thick hair on top of his head. For a few moments, he looked hilarious, with random tufts of hair flopping over his increasingly shorn skull. A few moments later, he dropped a grade on the clippers and ever so slightly shortened the back and sides. It was hardly stylish, but it was neat and tidy.

Sam hadn't had his hair this short since he was in the army and he couldn't help but smile at the familiarity of it. As he let the shower heat up, he helped himself to a string of floss, attacked his teeth with it and finished off with some mouth wash.

Feeling slightly cleaner, he dropped his clothes to the floor and stepped into the shower, the hot water crashing against him like a warm cuddle. Five minutes later, he emerged, feeling the freshest he had in a long time.

He wrapped the towel around his waist and looked at his body. While he'd lost a little muscle mass in his three-month recovery, he was still in decent shape.

He looked at his scars.

The damage he'd endured during his time in Chakari over a decade ago. The knife wound from his fight with Mark Connor in the High Rise. The bullet wounds in his thigh, shoulder, and stomach ever since he began his fight with the Kovalenko's.

All of them were permanent reminders.

As where the two white scars on his chest, staring up at him like a pair of pupilless eyes.

His body had been through war.

And he was about to go into another.

As he stepped out of the bathroom, he nearly tripped on the clothes that Etheridge had left for him and he welcomed the clean underwear, jeans, and T-shirt as he pulled them on. The T-shirt was a little tight, but it would do.

Grateful for everything, he followed the light shining from Etheridge's converted loft, through the hallway where he'd engaged in a gun fight with the police.

Just another crime to add to his ever-growing list.

As he stepped in, he raised his eyebrows. Etheridge had certainly been busy. When Sam had last been in the same room, he'd been presented with a few screens and some expensive kit. Now it looked like an underground government facility. Several screens lined the walls, all connected to a beast of a computer which Etheridge commanded through his wireless keyboard and mouse. In the far corner, a large batch of servers hummed, different lights twinkling like a Christmas show.

The high back leather chair spun round, and Etheridge sat, his hands clasped together.

'I've been expecting you, Mr Pope.'

Sam chuckled.

'Shouldn't you have a white cat?'

'I'm allergic.' Etheridge smiled and then reached under the desk and pulled open a small fridge. He retrieved two bottles of cold beer and flicked off the caps, handing one to Sam.

'To peace,' Etheridge said dryly. They clinked and Sam took a large swig, the cold alcohol tasted superb. Etheridge took a gulp and smacked his lips. 'It's been a while since I've had one of these.'

'Really?'

'Yup,' Etheridge said proudly. 'Made a few changes.'

Sam nodded his agreement. Last time he'd seen his friend, Etheridge certainly had the look of a man who enjoyed his excess heavy lifestyle. But the chubby beer belly had gone, replaced with a leaner torso. His arms were firmer and the fluffy remnants of hair he'd desperately held onto had been cropped back.

He was a new man.

Focussed.

After a few more silent sips of beer, Sam spoke.

'Paul. I'm sorry for everything that happened to you.'

'What?' Etheridge slapped his knee brace. 'This thing. Best thing that ever happened to me.'

'Seriously. You helped me out and it nearly got you killed. I can't imagine what you went through.'

Etheridge took a long, thoughtful swig of his beer and then placed it on his desk. He took a deep breath and leant forward, regarding Sam with a stern look.

'I'm not going to lie, Sam. It hurt like hell. The man

who did this, he was like nobody I've ever seen. But while I was recovering, while they were checking if I could even walk again with this knee, I realised I wasn't worried. Not about my marriage. My business. All of my expensive shit. None of it mattered.'

He shook his head and continued.

'What matters is the fight. Now before you try to talk me down, Sam, I know I was never much of a soldier. But I'm a good man. I watched you go to war for a young girl you'd never met because it was the right thing to do. From what you told me about what happened in Italy, you've started a fire with Wallace's fucking hit squad to try to save a good man. Because it was the right thing to do. I can't fight out on the streets like you can, but I have the knowledge and the resources to help you. To do the right thing. So what do you say?'

Sam leant back against the doorframe and downed the rest of his beer. He looked at his friend and clenched his jaw.

'It was never meant to go this far. I promised my son I was done killing people, but when he was taken from me and the law did nothing, it changed me. I came this close to ending it all but a good man pulled me back from the brink. Then, when I started taking down the criminals the police couldn't, when I saved those girls, I started to get a little piece of who I was back.' Sam felt his voice break slightly. 'I know I'll never see my boy again. That I've broken my promise to him. But I couldn't save him, so if I can save another, then I will.'

Etheridge awkwardly pushed himself up out of his chair, steadying himself on his dodgy leg and extended a hand.

'Then let me help you, Sam.'

Sam hesitantly took a breath and then clasped the hand and shook it tightly.

'Okay, on one condition. You stay right here. I won't have you taking another bullet for me.'

'Trust me, I am more than happy with that condition.' Etheridge chuckled and dropped back into his seat, swivelling back towards his screens. 'So, what's first?'

'We find Wallace.'

'Okay, and then what?'

Sam's eyes narrowed with fury.

'We bring it down around him.'

CHAPTER ELEVEN

As he drummed his fingers on the desk, Helal stared at his screen. The article had flowed from his fingertips like an unstoppable wave, his trademark dramatic flair dancing across his words.

It was a sensational story.

One he almost fully believed.

And that was the problem.

In the near two decades he'd been writing articles and working his way up the journalistic ladder, he'd always followed one strict principal.

He had to believe in what he was writing.

There were plenty of hacks who were more than happy to bash out a two thousand word click bait article and collect their wages. It didn't matter if it was an article body shaming a young celebrity, or a needless list about a popular TV show. Some of the newer 'journalists' were chasing clicks, which meant more money. It was the way the world had been heading for a long time and Helal had seen the trend emerging way before Nigel and had helped him to somewhat steer the ship upstream.

Sure, the office was filled with the younger generation,

fixated on 'pumping out as much content as possible'. They were a vital cog in *The Pulse* machine. Their empty, shallow articles generated enough money for Nigel to fund the real writers, the ones who put the world into word and laid it out for the public to see.

Helal knew his articles didn't make him popular with some places. He was banned from every football ground in London for his expose on the shifty dealings between owners and agents.

He had been given a police escort for a week after he exposed a racist element to a political party.

Death threats had been made.

His name had been dragged through the mud.

But it had never bothered him. Because he'd believed every word he'd written.

This. This felt different.

His last article had landed him in hot water and had clearly irked the chain of some pretty powerful people within the Metropolitan Police. The detective, Pearce, had been polite enough, but it was going to take more than a stern plea from a nice man to get him to back down. Helal knew the only reason they wanted him to stop was because he was right.

But this…he wasn't so sure.

Amara Singh was an engaging woman and it had taken every part of Helal's resolve not to turn the drink into something more casual. She was one of the most attractive women he'd ever met, but her tenacity was what really struck him. Clearly, for a young lady who had achieved so much by her mid-thirties, she refused to back down from most challenges.

And from what she was willing to share with him, that was still the case.

She knew she was jeopardising her career, even her own safety.

Singh had told him all about the late-night visit from General Ervin Wallace, a man revered by the national press like the second coming of Winston Churchill. While he shared the same lack of hair and burly physique, that was where the similarities ended. In Helal's opinion, Wallace was a war monger and he questioned whether Singh was right to provoke a beast who has shown many times he was all too willing to strike out.

But she was adamant.

Adamant that the government were hiding something. That there was a secret project, one which tied Wallace and Sam Pope together and one that Wallace wanted kept hidden.

Her life had been turned upside down.

She was being forced out of the job she'd fought for her whole life.

She had to lose a tail just to make it to see him.

Whatever it was, it was big.

Helal glanced at the clock, shook his head at the unruly hour that presented itself and poured himself another glass of Scotch. The liquid burnt his throat as he knocked it back and before he could second guess himself any further, he clicked send.

The article slid off his screen, as the file was transported to his boss's inbox, awaiting further approval before it could reach the rest of the world.

It was a shocking article.

At times, maybe farfetched.

It would definitely ignite a heated discussion with Nigel the next day.

As Helal slinked off towards the bedroom of his two-bedroom flat in West London, he hadn't realised that by pressing send, the words 'Project Hailstorm' rushed through a tracing program and placed another target on his back.

———

'Please remain seated until the plane has come to a complete stop.'

A hopeful request from the young air hostess fell on deaf ears as the unruly British public instantly unclipped their belts and began jostling for control of the overhead bins. As the cabin crew tried their best to stem the flow of passengers reaching for their possessions, Ahmad Farukh watched with a pitiful sneer.

The British had always baffled him with their delusions of grandeur. The innate arrogance that they were a great nation, built on strong moral foundations and with a dry sense of humour. In Farukh's eyes, it was a nation built off the backs of others, oppressive as it was cowardly and every British person whom he'd introduced to his noose crumbled sooner than any other.

Once confronted with a force that didn't fear them, nor care about them, the British wilted like a dead flower.

Sat in an aisle seat, he turned to the young man who anxiously looked around the plane, eager to retrieve a bag that wasn't going anywhere.

Zero patience. The western world was always in such a rush, which is why he'd despised his only visit to London nearly a decade ago.

Since then, he'd stayed in the Middle East and Africa, moving from job to job, collecting paycheque after paycheque. While he questioned his loyalty to his own country for abandoning the army, he did use the money he collected as an assassin to fund several community projects in his home town.

He had pumped more back into Afghanistan than most and as far as he was concerned, everyone had done something worth being executed for.

He looked around the plane.

Several of the passengers were grossly overweight, sure signs of gluttony and excess. There were several couples, many of whom had cheated on their partners or engaged in some unlawful sexual act.

Everyone had something justifiable.

Everyone deserved to die.

As he watched the procession of impatience filter off the plane and into Gatwick Airport, he unclipped his belt and hauled his large frame into the walkway. Behind him, the young man scampered up, as if his seat was on fire. Farukh shook his head and then marched down the plane, his broad shoulders almost clipping the overhead storage bins. His thick arms, covered in his black coat, brushed the chairs as he strode through the aircraft.

'See you soon,' the young cabin officer said, his eyes sparkling.

Farukh ignored the man's polite goodbye and stepped out onto the steps, the bitter cold of the English weather slapping him in the face with a frozen palm. It was a world away from Turkey, where the unrelenting heat had caused his brown skin to tan a shade darker.

The wind lapped at his thick beard and he pulled the woollen hat from his jacket and slid it over his thinning hair.

He followed the crowd through the usual rigmarole of entering the UK, watching with pleasure as the computerised passport checker kept failing, inciting an instant rage from a generation of people who are used to instant gratification.

He travelled with just the bare minimum. A wedge of cash which he'd changed into sterling, his passport, and his papers.

The passport was a fake. Top quality.

His identity needed to stay hidden, as he was certain it would flag every international military force in the world.

Travelling by plane was a risk he didn't like to take, but he'd received a call he'd hoped would never come. As a man of few words, Farukh had made sure that he'd always been as good as them.

His word was binding.

So when an old acquaintance had failed as spectacularly as he had, Farukh had assured him he would fix it.

It was more than just their names they needed to keep hidden.

It was a skeleton too big for the world to ever know about.

As Farukh passed through the luggage collection and the duty free, he emerged out of the airport and immediately lit a cigarette.

The nicotine flowed through his lungs and he watched from the corner of his eye as the two men approached. They carried themselves with an undeserved sense of importance and Farukh shook his head in disappointment.

'Mr Ahmad,' the man began. 'Your car is over here.'

'I do not need car,' Farukh said coldly, take a long, hard drag of his cigarette.

'But General Wallace is expect—'

'Tell Wallace I find him in my own time.' Farukh flicked the cigarette into the man's chest, catching him off guard. 'If you follow me, I will kill you.'

With his words hanging in the air like a thick smog, Farukh marched away from the two Blackridge operatives and headed towards the motorway. The Hangman of Baghdad disappeared round the corner and lost himself in the country.

———

Just stop, Sam.'

Theo's voice echoed through Sam's head and he turned to face his friend. The entire sky was blue, not a cloud in sight. The field they were stood on was mowed short, a few daffodils poking through the greenery.

'I can't,' Sam eventually said, taking a step towards him. 'Why?'

'Because someone has to fight back.'

'Why must it be you?' Theo took a step forward. It had been just over a year since his friend had been brutally murdered, giving his life to save Amy Devereux. Sam had missed him terribly, and he wished himself to walk quicker.

But as he did, he knew he would regret it.

He always regretted it.

The dream was a recurring one. Sam would walk aimlessly through empty fields, the world still and quiet around him.

A world he no longer felt existed.

Then, as the silence threatened to last forever, Theo would always appear. He would always step out from nowhere, his welcoming smile as bright as it had been when he lived.

He would ask Sam to stop fighting. To try to make peace with what had happened.

Sam could never accept it. Would never accept it.

As they walked towards each other, Sam would watch as Theo would start to disintegrate, the mortal wounds he suffered would begin to ravage his body and before he could save his friend, his body would hit the ground, ripped to shreds by the explosion of a grenade.

As Sam would mourn him, he would turn his head round, to look at the street which had now appeared. A car slammed into the lamp-post and Miles Hillock fell out of the door, drunk and battered. His head bleeding, as people raced to help.

Sam could see his ex-wife, Lucy, screaming as if she'd just stepped on a rusty nail.

Her heart was breaking, the piercing cries accompanying the rupture.

In front of the car, the broken body of his son, Jamie lay, his arm twisted in a ghoulish way.

His eyes wide open.

His life over.

As Sam tried to walk towards his son, he could hear Theo once again asking Sam to stop.

To forgive himself.

To grieve.

Sam dropped to his knees, the sky opening up and showering him in freezing droplets of rain.

The surrounding scene began to wash away, the rain pushing the memories of his family and his happiness away like a broken drain pumping down the kerb. Feeling tired, Sam slowly closed his eyes, the pain of all his injuries beginning to rage through his body like an unstoppable force.

The knife attacks.

The bullet wounds.

As he flattened himself on the cold, wet ground, Sam closed his eyes and readied himself for death.

'Not yet, Daddy,' Jamie's voice shot through the dark.

Sam's eyes opened.

———

Sam shot up in his bed, his T-shirt stuck to his body. The cold sweat he'd become accustomed to had drenched the sheets and he slid out from them, taking a few moments to stretch out his lower back. While he kept himself at his physical peak, the pitfalls of approaching forty were beginning to appear.

Slowly, Sam peeled the sodden T-shirt from his toned body and hung it over the chair that was tucked under the desk. The spare room Etheridge had offered him was spacious, with a few basic furnishings dotted around. It wasn't the Ritz, and it certainly wasn't in tune with man Etheridge was only a few months before.

The pain and torture he'd gone through had changed him, that was for sure, and Sam could see it by the lack of showmanship or flagrant displays of wealth. In its place, a steely determination and the want to do the right thing.

Sam approved.

He popped open the wardrobe and thankfully found a few more T-shirts. He slipped one on, the sleeves a bit tight around his muscular shoulders, and he made his way onto the landing. The memories of his gunfight with the police flashed in his mind like a freezeframe in time. It always irked him he had to open fire on the police themselves.

Most of the boys in blue were genuinely trying to do a good job. But months ago, faced with an armed response team standing between him and the chance to save a teenage girl from a fate worse than death, Sam didn't even need to think twice.

He shot to wound.

It was also the night he first came face to face with Amara Singh and despite everything that had happened in the months since he last saw her in Tilbury, she would wander through his mind on a daily basis.

Sam shook her from his mind and ascended the stairs to the hub where Etheridge was sat in front of a wall of screens, the mixture of coffee and sweat pulsed in the air like a heartbeat.

It was a little overwhelming and Sam coughed, causing Etheridge to spin his chair, his unshaven face twisted in a smile.

'Morning,' he said. 'You look like shit.'

'Thanks.' Sam chuckled.

'How d'you sleep?'

'Like shit. You?'

'Haven't.' Etheridge spun back to the screen. 'Whatever Marsden has on this stick, whoever locked down these files really didn't want anyone to look in.'

'Really?'

'Yup. Like a digital Fort Fucking Knox.'

Sam laughed and looked beyond the desk to the window. The sky was clear but grey and a wind swept the debris of leaves from the gutter of the loft conversion. But at least it wasn't raining. At the desk, Etheridge's fingers clicked wildly on the keys, like a concert pianist reaching his crescendo.

'Can you crack it?' Sam asked.

'Does the Pope shit on alter boys?' Sam's silence caused Etheridge to turn. 'I mean yes. Give me a few more hours.'

'Cool,' Sam said, heading towards the door.

'Where are you going?' Etheridge called out, more out of politeness than interest.

Sam smiled.

'To see an old friend.'

CHAPTER TWELVE

Sometimes, it helped to stop and appreciate the little things.

It was a saying that made him feel like an old man, but these days, Pearce was feeling his age more than ever. At fifty-two years old, he was certainly on the wind down, and had been able to retire for over a year. But the thrill of the job, the grip it had on him was, at times, all he had. His marriage had disintegrated over a decade ago, his ex-wife, Denise, leaving him for a man who gave her the love and affection she deserved,

Pearce had loved her dearly, but his true dedication was to his work. He understood why she left and when she kissed his cheek for the final time, he knew it would be a life sentence.

He would never retire.

They would have to boot him out, give him some quickly thrown together speech about his commitment and loyalty and then present him with whatever they could buy with the whip round.

That unwavering commitment to the job, to the difference between right and wrong and the justice system had never once faltered.

But then Sam Pope came into the picture.

While Sam's actions had drawn Pearce's attention, the man unearthed links between the police and the underworld that had given Pearce sleepless nights. As a DI who headed up the Department of Professional Standards, seeing those he reported to taking a cut off the top had made him sick.

That commitment soon wavered.

The last year had been a blur. One he'd never seen coming.

He'd made friends.

He'd lost them.

He had seen a broken man fight back against those who feed off the innocent who wasn't afraid to rattle cages that were always left alone. But if you throw a stone into a lake, it creates ripples.

Sam's actions had done just that.

Pearce had been pushed to the side, with Ashton and other senior figures doing their best to push him towards the door.

Amara Singh, a woman he'd grown fond of, had questioned his loyalty and was now as good as fired.

Theo Walker, Sam's best friend and a man who did as much as he could for others, was brutally killed in his own home.

There had been so much death.

So much blood spilt.

While Sam had done it for the greater good, the after-effects were still shaking lives into a state from which they would never recover.

And Pearce felt old.

As if maybe the commitment wasn't there anymore. Not when he knew that those who called the shots were not always as trustworthy as they seemed. Not when the institution he had given his life to would place stopping Sam Pope above finding the teenage girls he was tearing through the city to find.

Maybe it was time to take that step back after all.

As the sun shone down on the concrete playground just outside of Bethnal Green Youth Centre, the decision was becoming harder to turn down. The centre, which had flourished in the past few years, had been the brainchild of Theo Walker once he'd retired from the armed forces. As a fellow black man, Pearce respected Theo's brave plan to take under-privileged children off the streets and push them to make better choices.

Encourage their learning.

Mould their passions.

It was a noble cause from a noble man and as sickening as his death had been, Pearce wasn't surprised it came in a heroic way.

Ever since then, Pearce had volunteered as much as he could. While he didn't have Theo's raw charisma, he was still able to banter with the kids, with a lot of them giving him stick for his profession. But he knew they respected him and the more weekends he'd spent with them, especially those who didn't get to celebrate Christmas due to their home situation, Pearce had felt a stronger connection.

For the first time in a long time, he actually felt like he was doing some good. It had been a feeling he'd felt for most of his career. Whenever he'd outed a corrupt officer or found an issue with a case, he'd felt like he'd made a difference.

But after Sam shook the whole Met to its core, he'd been marginalised.

The local council had contacted him about running the youth centre on a full-time basis, for a marginal salary but easy hours.

It was becoming increasingly tempting.

As he mulled over the decision, three teen boys raced past him, all of them hunting a stray football. The five-a-side match had become a weekly staple, with enough youngsters turning up to run an eight-team tournament. All of them respected Pearce's house rules.

No swearing.

No fighting.

No negativity.

At first, it had been tricky. A few fights broke out. A bit of gang culture threatened to rear its ugly head, but it was soon stamped out. Now, as the sun beat down and Pearce's stomach thought about lunch, he watched with pride as two teams played some excellent football, while the others watched on, chanting and cheering with excitement.

Sean Wiseman, the young man who had stepped away from one of the worst gangs in London, volunteered at the weekends. He had volunteered as ref, but was already running out of breath, much to Pearce and the other boys' amusement.

'He looks like he could use a rest.'

Pearce spun on the spot; the recognition of the voice caused him to smile.

Sam Pope.

On the other side of the fence that ran around the youth centre grounds, Sam stood, one hand gripping the chain link.

'Jesus. I thought you were dead.'

'Almost.' Sam smiled. 'But not quite.'

Pearce nodded and smiled again. Despite the mayhem of the last year, he knew that Sam was a good man. A good man who was pushed down a dark path and was now doing whatever he could to scramble back to the light.

'It's good to see you, Sam. Nice hair cut by the way.' Pearce flicked a glance back to the pitch as Sam ran a hand across his newly cropped hair. 'I'm assuming you haven't come here looking to help out, eh?'

'Sadly not.' Sam looked around at the building, the immaculate state of the garden and the mural painted along the brick work in honour of Theo's memory. 'He would be happy his work is continuing. Thank you.'

'Don't thank me. It's the least I could do.' The ball shot past them both, with one of the boys in pursuit. 'We both know what this world can do to people. It can chew them up, spit them out, and expect them to be okay with it. Whatever we can do to get to those before that happens, we do it. These boys, some of them might not make it off the streets. But if one of them goes on to become a doctor or a lawyer, or has a nice family life, then I would have done my part.'

'You're a good man, Pearce,' Sam said warmly. Pearce turned back, looking Sam in the eyes.

'So are you. Don't lose that, okay?'

'What do you mean?'

'I mean I know what happened in Italy. We've been on red alert to find you by the Assistant Commissioner. You lost a dear friend.'

'I'm not back for revenge,' Sam said coldly. 'I'm back to finish this thing for good.'

'And how does this end, Sam? Are you going to blow up the Metropolitan Police? Or are you going to kill Ervin Wallace? He's been controlling Ashton like a puppet and using the Met as his own little private police force. The moment Singh started sniffing around, talking about secret projects, she was done for. They shunted her out and she points the finger of blame at me.'

'Wallace went after Singh?'

Pearce shrugged.

'She said he visited her one night, threatened her. Told

her to stay away from you and your past. She didn't, so I stepped in. I had to keep her safe.'

'You did the right thing, Pearce. You always do.'

'Yeah, well she hasn't spoken to me since. I've heard a few murmurs that her apartment was broken into, that Wallace is still keeping tabs on her.'

Behind Pearce, Wiseman blew a hard, shrill whistle and then comedically collapsed to the floor, while the boys rolled about laughing. They all rushed towards the doors to the centre for lunch and Sam politely shook his head before the offer came.

'It was good to see you, Pearce.' Sam spoke sincerely. 'I wanted to thank you for saving my friend, Paul. If it wasn't for you, he'd be dead.'

'Like I said, Sam. How does this end?' Pearce held his fist against the metal fence. 'A time will come when someone isn't there to save them. You know that better than most. This is too far gone, Sam. It needs to end before people like Paul, or people like Singh, really do get hurt.'

Sam nodded solemnly and then raised his fist and tapped it against Pearce's. A sign of genuine friendship in what had resembled a war zone.

'It will. I promise.'

Both men nodded one final time and just as Sam turned to leave, the heavy breathing and leaden footed steps of Wiseman approached. His face was flushed, his breathing stunted, and his T-shirt was stuck to his body.

But he looked a world away from the wide-eyed, terrified numbers man working for a gang.

He looked happy.

'Hey…Sam…' He panted. '…I just wanted to… thank…you.'

'What for?' Sam shrugged.

Wiseman took a deep breath, his hands on his hips and regained his composure.

'You saved my life.'

'I shot you,' Sam said, his words heavy with guilt.

'You put me on the right path. You showed me that some people are inherently good. You turned this city upside down to find that young girl. No matter what the police say, or what the papers say, you're a damn hero. The world could use more people like you.' Wiseman suddenly looked embarrassed and arched his neck towards the centre. 'I better check on the kids.'

As Wiseman jogged off, Pearce turned to a thoughtful looking Sam.

'He's training to be a social worker.'

'He's come along way,' Sam said quietly, touched by the impact he'd had on the young man's life.

'You're a good man, Sam,' Pearce said. 'So, finish what you need to do and then try to make peace with it all.'

Pearce slapped the chain-link fence a few times before turning and heading back to the centre, ready to join the raucous noise of a gleeful lunch. Sam watched him disappear into the centre and then stuffed his hands into the pockets of his bomber jacket.

'I'll try,' he uttered, before lowering his head and marching back towards the station.

———

While Sam had been enjoying the Saturday sunshine, Etheridge had been glued to his desk. The luxurious loft conversion did offer a splendid floor to ceiling window, which meant natural light flooded through the room like an unstoppable force and the air conditioning unit had kept him cool.

But he hadn't moved.

Across the screens that presented themselves like a news station, a number of algorithms were running, desperately trying their best to crack the security protocols attached to the USB stick.

It had been semi-successful, with a few less important folders soon wriggling free from the cyber security, but for the most part, Etheridge had been impressed.

He had made millions being able to break, and therefore fix, a company's online security.

Blackridge.

Almost uncrackable.

He had been at it for over eighteen hours and the slog of the mission, along with the lack of sleep, were starting to pull down on his eyelids. He reached for the coffee he'd freshly made and took a large gulp, just as the sound of Sam's footsteps echoed up the stairs. Moments later, Sam pushed open the door and was greeted by a very tired, very smiley Etheridge.

'Afternoon,' Sam said stoically.

'Welcome back.' Etheridge's hand shook as he raised the coffee, instantly explaining to Sam that he was on a caffeine high and careening towards a crash. 'Good news or bad news?'

'Excuse me?'

'I've got good news and I've got bad news. Which one do you want first?'

'Good news.'

'Well, the good news is, I know how to open the USB stick and I have the necessary equipment.'

'Brilliant. Let's do it,' Sam said eagerly, sliding his jacket off.

'Bad news is, it's only functional with a fingerprint scan.' Etheridge sighed. 'I have a scanner and can set up a direct link between it and the Blackridge network to verify it. But I can't build a fingerprint. I'm not god.'

Sam chuckled and stretched his back. Etheridge turned back to his screens, understanding the scrawling that flickered across the monitors. To Sam, they looked like scribbles.

But then Etheridge was an elite hacker.

If it came to hand-to-hand combat, or putting a bullet in a sex trafficker from three hundred yards away, Sam rose to the occasion.

Etheridge clicked away on the keyboard and then slumped in the chair.

'Do you need another coffee?' Sam joked. Etheridge flipped him the bird.

'No, I need a fucking fingerprint. But to get a fingerprint, we need to find a Blackridge operative with sufficient clearance. And how the hell do you find a task force that exists in the shadows?'

A light bulb pinged above Sam's head.

'You give them what they're looking for.'

'What do you mean?' Etheridge turned to him, his eyes narrowing.

'Are you able to set up an untraceable line?'

'Do bears go to church?' Again, Sam stared silently at him. 'Of course I can. Why?'

Sam took a deep breath. He hated the idea of it, but they needed to move quickly.

He pushed his guilt aside.

'We need to call Amara Singh.'

CHAPTER THIRTEEN

General Ervin Wallace had never appreciated a weekend.

In his line of work, which was to protect the country, there were no days off. When he was in the armed forces, out on tour, they never took breaks because they had 'got to the end of the week'. The culture of his country, to get boozed up at the end of a week sat behind a cushy desk embarrassed him.

He worked effortlessly for their freedom.

They were pathetic.

But ever since he'd gone into lockdown, Wallace had more free time than he'd anticipated.

The very real threat of Sam's return had led him to call upon an old acquaintance that he'd tried to resign to the past.

Desperate times. Desperate measures.

But now, as he sat on the balcony of the safehouse he'd accosted in his bid for survival, he stared out over the fields below. The spring sun had risen over the trees and cast his beautiful country in a magnificent gold shimmer.

This, he thought, this was worth fighting for.

Not the miscreants who didn't understand the meaning

of the word sacrifice. The maggots who spout about how great their country is but would turn on each other the second shit hits the fan.

They were not worth the buckets of blood he'd spilt.

But this country was.

The evening before, he'd invited Assistant Commissioner Ashton over once again, their meal laden with awkward conversation verging on apologetic. Wallace could sense her fear of failure, which made her more accommodating when they made their way to his quarters. Again, the sex was more transactional than passionate and Wallace had arranged for her to be taken home early in the morning.

He had assured her that the discretion was for the protection of her sparkling career.

He was sure she believed it.

All he wanted to do was make a batch of Colombian coffee, light a cigar and sit on the balcony, trolling through the online papers.

It was then that his fist crashed ferociously against the glass table, shaking the pane, and spilling his latte.

His tablet rocked before falling forward onto its screen.

Wallace took a long, hard pull on his cigar as he launched to his feet, pushing out the thick, grey smoke in an endless plume towards the sun.

He rested his meaty forearms on the balcony railing and shook his head.

Helal Miah.

The fucking irritant.

The article had gone live that morning, an exploratory piece on Wallace's career, with several serious accusations and links to some insidious deeds that Wallace had worked his hardest to keep off the books.

But nothing was ever fully off the books.

Someone knew. Someone always knew.

With a rage shaking through his body like a vibration, Wallace returned to the table and lifted his tablet, glad to see there was no damage to the screen. He scanned through the article again, bewildered at the level of detail the man had gone into.

Whoever his source was, they knew something.

Maybe it was Sam?

Wallace immediately laughed away the idea. Sam was blinded by his own self-righteousness, but he would never paint a bullseye on a civilian.

Whoever it was, Wallace needed them silenced.

Another thick cloud of smoke wafted from the balcony and Wallace pondered his next move.

He could call Ashton, tell her that Pearce's efforts to quiet Miah had been pathetic.

Perhaps he could check in with his team and see if they had had any luck locating Sam?

Or Farukh for that matter.

The idea of such a violent man walking freely in his country made Wallace uneasy, like a sudden attack of sea sickness. But Farukh, while as barbaric as they came, wouldn't attract needless attention. The man was a ghost.

Not one of Wallace's.

He was his own man.

Thinking of his own assets, Wallace wondered about reaching out again to locate Mac, the man who had come so close to finishing off Sam Pope and rendering all of this pointless. The man had lived and breathed his vengeance for years, blaming Sam for the horrors he suffered through two years of captivity by the Taliban.

But that chance of redemption had been snatched away.

And with it, Mac had disappeared too.

Dangerous. Unhinged. Untraceable.

Wallace knew it was another mess to clear up, but it

was quickly tumbling down the list of priorities. Mac was a potential problem.

Wallace was dealing with absolutes.

As Wallace took a deep inhale of his thick cigar, a voice he'd feared echoed behind him.

'You still smoke those shit?'

Wallace dropped the cigar, turning abruptly and doing his best to hide any fear. The gentle shake of his hand and the sweat building on his line addled forehead betrayed him instantly.

It had been a long time since he'd seen Farukh.

The years had been somewhat kind to him. His hair, now tinged with grey was thinner, arching over his dome like a dull, wispy rainbow. His thick beard hid the cruel smile that sent shivers down Wallace's spine.

Age had played the same trick on them both, their once impressive frames now bulking out, as the metabolism slowed.

Whereas Wallace looked like a big man in a neat suit, Farukh was a different type of menacing. He wore a black jacket and T-shirt, both of which were wrapped tightly against his solid mass. Jeans and boots.

The man carried little else, except for the box of cigarettes which he retrieved from the inside of his jacket. Without asking, he stepped out onto the balcony and took Wallace's lighter, sparking the cigarette to life. Wallace shot a concerned glance to the front door.

'Don't worry. Your doorman is alive.' Farukh took a puff and chuckled. 'Asleep. But alive.'

'How did you find me?'

Farukh smiled, his yellow stained teeth were crude and sharp, like a Rottweiler ready to pounce.

'I find people. It is what I do.'

'It's what you used to do. Nowadays, not a month goes

by where I don't get fed a report of another high-profile target found hanged in a remote location.'

'I have to eat,' Farukh responded, dismissively.

'Quite.' Wallace stubbed out his cigar. 'But I need you to find someone.'

Farukh, unblinking, took a long pull on his cigarette. The smoke filtered through the patio door and into the spacious kitchen, irritating Wallace. But he stayed silent.

'You need me to clear up mess. Mess you promise never happen.'

Wallace sighed.

'I know. Believe me, I have done everything to keep this contained. Hell, I even killed a dear friend of mine.' Wallace shook his head as he remembered pulling the trigger and sending a bullet into the body of Carl Marsden. 'But it wasn't enough.'

'What is name?' Farukh said, flicking the cigarette off the balcony. He gazed out over the sun-drenched fields and was surprised to find such beauty in a disgusting country.

'Sam. Sam Pope.'

Farukh turned, his eyebrow cocked.

'Pope? The sniper?'

'You remember him?' Wallace could feel his palms sweating. As a man who had faced war with a grin on his face, he found himself scared of the man before him.

'I remember what you did.'

'Yes, well, that is part of it. He needs to be stopped and he needs to hand over the information.' Wallace tried to wrestle the authority back. 'Otherwise it will be over for both of us.'

Farukh lit another cigarette before taking two steps closer to Wallace. Both men stood tall and proud, their chests out. A silent dick measuring contest. With a cruel grin, Farukh took a puff and blew the smoke directly into Wallace's face.

'I will find him. This Sam Pope. I will make him give me the stick. I will kill him. I will kill those who help him.'

'Good,' Wallace stammered.

'But I want that stick destroyed. All files wiped. And I never want to hear from you again.'

Wallace nodded greedily.

'Absolutely. You have my word.'

Farukh took one step closer, seemingly growing in stature as Wallace shrank.

'If not, then I will hang you for your country to see.'

As the threat hung heavy in the air like the tobacco laden fog, Farukh turned and marched back through the apartment, merrily puffing on his cigarette without any hint of respect for Wallace's abode. As the door slammed shut, Wallace realised he'd been holding his breath and he let out a large exhale. As the air flooded through his lungs, he was able to stop his hands from shaking.

He was clammy. Sweat had drenched him.

There was very little in the world that scared him.

But Farukh did.

The Hangman of Baghdad.

Wallace smirked as he imagined the fate that awaited Sam, and all those who dared to oppose him.

———

'Can I buy you a drink?'

The man flashed a perfect white smile, his strong jaw sprinkled with stubble. The question snapped Singh back into the world, her mind wandering down several paths.

She hadn't been home since her drink the evening before, instead dropping by her sister, Priya's house in Barnet.

Three years older, married and with two beautiful daughters, Priya was the spitting image of the perfect child in the eyes of their parents. She had a stable family life with her husband, Ravi, a highly successful lawyer. Their home, a four-bedroom detached house, was as pristine as the outfits her sister always wore.

Even to pop to the shops, Priya looked like she was about to hit the catwalk.

But none of that had ever appealed to Singh, and she knew it never would.

While her parents were resigned to only having one pathway to grandchildren, she did feel some sense of pride from them when it came to her career.

The public praise she'd received for her work on project Yew Tree, as well as her handling of some potential terror threats, had filled her family with pride.

The brutal beating she'd suffered at the Port of Tilbury had shaken both her parents, but they'd showered her with praise for her determination to find those missing girls.

She hadn't told them that she had worked with Sam Pope, the man she'd very publicly been put in charge of catching.

Now, with her career in the mud and being slowly stomped to a pulp, her parents saw nothing but failure.

For so long, she never failed.

Now, as she looked at the empty glass in front of her, it was all she was achieving.

She offered the man a smile.

'No, thank you.'

'Shame.' The man shrugged. He had the arrogant aura of a man who made too much money. 'I could have shown you a good time.'

'I doubt it,' Amara retorted. 'Money can't buy you brains.'

The man went to respond, smirked, and casually strode back across the bar, looking for another pretty woman to harass. What annoyed Singh most was that he would most likely be successful. She looked at her watch, noting that it was probably time to find a hotel for the night.

The article had gone out that morning.

Singh had enjoyed her chat with Helal, finding him to be a charming man with a genuine ability to listen. He was engaging and just as passionate about getting the truth out there as she was about exposing it.

But now that it was, she'd felt a sickening puddle begin to pool in her stomach.

It was one thing to kick the hornets' nest.

It was another thing entirely to slather yourself in honey and dive in headfirst.

Blackridge had been tracking her ever since she'd typed the words 'Project Hailstorm' into her computer. The visit from Wallace, the unsubtle threat to her safety. Since then, every door had been slammed shut and every shoulder had turned cold. She was sure Ashton was screwing Wallace, the ridiculous schoolgirl crush was the easiest case she would ever crack.

Pearce had also dobbed her in, but as time had passed, she felt bad for the way their friendship had ended.

He was a good man and probably did put her safety first.

But it was too far gone now.

She was being followed.

Her home had been invaded.

Her safety had been threatened.

As she signalled for the bartender for another gin, she thought about Sam. How all this had started with him and would most likely end with him.

By looking into his past, she'd jeopardised her future.

The gin arrived swiftly, and she lifted it in a mock cheers.

To Sam Pope. The only man to change her life.

As she took another sip, she wondered how long it

would be until they would trace the source back to her. What would happen?

Would she go to jail?

Or worse?

With regret an option she could no longer lean on; Singh was startled from her thought process by the buzzing in her leather jacket. She fumbled it open and pulled out her mobile phone.

It was a number she didn't recognise.

Most likely Wallace, telling her he had a sniper aimed at her head and he was calling to hear her last words.

Or Ashton, telling her they had the place surrounded and to come out and surrender.

Something told her not to answer, that it would only lead her further down the rabbit hole. She took a swig of her gin, realised she'd passed the point of no return a long time ago and clicked the accept button.

She should have listened to herself.

'Amara.' The voice shocked her straight. 'It's Sam. We need to meet.'

———

In an unknown location, deep below a derelict building in the centre of a small town, a number of servers were humming loudly, the entire Blackridge network buzzing with activity. For all the dirty work the operatives got through, the computer experts furrowed away underground were just as vital.

Every wiretap.

Every intelligence report.

Every location beacon.

They all went through 'The Hub'.

The beating heart of Blackridge.

On that Saturday evening, a young man who had been

recruited personally by Wallace out of Cambridge on the promises of espionage and adventure, found himself sat in the dark room, the heat of the monitors and the power of the servers causing his back to dampen with sweat.

Apart from the odd reconnaissance report and the one time he provided real-time information for an operative hunting down a target, the job had been oversold.

But that evening, he hit the jackpot.

The audio file had been downloaded from the tap on Singh's phone and he'd run it against three separate voice recognition applications. Despite being in a shitty location, Blackridge had a near limitless budget and the equipment was enough to make his shorts tighten.

All three different programs verified the voice.

It was Sam Pope.

With his fingers trembling, the young man scrambled to put his headset over his thick, sticky hair and he pressed the direct line to Wallace.

His heart thumped with excitement and he almost lost his voice as the cantankerous voice of Wallace demanded the update.

The young man licked his lips, cleared his throat, and spoke as clearly as he could.

'We have him, sir. We have him.'

CHAPTER FOURTEEN

The very idea of running a covert operation on home soil made Wallace nervous. Less than twenty-four hours ago, stood on his balcony, cigar in hand, he'd received a very real threat from the Hangman of Baghdad. It had seemed like the entire situation was slipping through his meaty grasp like particles of sand.

But then he received the call he'd been waiting for.

Sam Pope had resurfaced.

With Assistant Commissioner Ashton at his beck and call, he would have preferred to have gone through the appropriate channels. Have her pull together the remnants of the failed taskforce and have them ready to pounce. Let the police do their job and bring Sam Pope to justice.

But this wasn't a run-of-the-mill operation.

And Sam Pope wasn't a run-of-the-mill target.

Questions would be asked and the last thing Wallace wanted was the very few people he answered to asking them. No, this needed to be like majority of all other Blackridge operations.

Off the books.

Sat on the balcony of his remote safe house, Wallace

felt the headset digging into his skull, listening with intent as the minimal task force moved into position. Three operatives had embarked on London Liverpool Street Station, all of them in their positions, ready to act at the first sign of Pope.

The Hub were logged in, using their considerable authority to seize control of the CCTV equipment of the station itself and were furiously surveying the scene.

Sam had given Singh strict instructions to meet him at one o'clock that afternoon.

It would be busy.

It would be full of people.

Clever, Wallace thought. The more people around, the harder it would be for his team to intercept. But his operatives were the best of the best, all of them recruited the same way Sam had been all those years ago. These were trained soldiers, all of them looking for the bigger thrills and the fatter paycheques.

Leading the team was Roland Brandt, one of Wallace's ghosts. Brandt had been recruited seven years ago, after spending twelve years in the Kommando Spezialkräfte, an elite German special forces squadron organised under the Rapid Forces Division. Brandt was as ruthless as they came and if Wallace directed him to put a bullet in both Sam and Singh's heads, he would do it without hesitation.

But he needed Sam alive.

Singh, she was collateral damage, but he figured he could throw Ashton a bone and let her prove that Singh was in collusion with the wanted vigilante. Both would rot in prison and Wallace would get his hands on the stolen files.

Two birds with one stone and hopefully, enough to remove Farukh from his life forever.

As Wallace sipped the large glass of Scotch that sat beside his laptop, he felt his heart rate quicken. He had carte blanche to run his operations across the world, eliminating terrorist targets, and dealing in the dirt that the UK government didn't want to be a part of.

He had never failed them.

But this was personal.

He was trying to cover tracks he'd thought were long since covered and by carrying it out, in the midst of the British public would certainly land him under the microscope.

That could not be a possibility.

The entire morning had been spent trying to locate Farukh, with a number of his staff sending messages of the operation to all the possible contact numbers they had for the man. Emails, texts, phone calls – even remote, isolated message boards on encrypted websites in the vain hope that he would pick them up.

There had been no response.

Wallace took another swig of his Scotch and then lit a cigar.

It was ten to one.

'This is General Ervin Wallace,' he barked into his headset. 'We cannot fuck this up. Sam Pope is a wanted vigilante with government files that we believe he is trying to sell. The man is a turncoat and must be stopped.'

'Understood.' Brandt's robotic voice cackled through, his German accent thick and menacing. 'STK?'

Shoot to kill.

Wallace smirked. Brandt's ruthlessness had always impressed him and while he would have loved to have given the order, he had to put his personal vendetta to one side.

'Negative,' Wallace commanded. 'Our target is meeting Amara Singh in the middle of the concourse. Once we have eyes on her, I want all operatives to maintain their positions until visual is established.'

Sarah Masters, one of the other field operatives spoke up.

'In position, sir.'

The final member of the three strong team, Will Cook echoed her message. Wallace watched the multiple cameras on his screen, all of them laid out like a grid. He could see Brandt stood by the ticket machines to the left of the escalators, his muscular frame shrouded in a leather jacket. Somewhere within, it concealed a firearm that his itchy finger was undoubtedly craving.

All three of them wore earpieces, along with heart rate monitors, their vital signs displayed in a small window on Wallace's screen.

He had eyes on everything.

'We have a visual of Singh.'

A voice cackled through from The Hub, one of the analysts speaking in a nervous tone.

'Eyes open,' Brandt barked, as he tried to blend into the pandemonium of one of the UK's busiest train stations on a beautiful Sunday afternoon. The footfall was massive, with the station linking to a number of major UK cities, bringing a large number of tourists and day trippers to the capital city.

There were plenty of witnesses.

Enough people to blend in.

Several chances for this to go wrong.

Wallace nervously ran his hand across his mighty brow, the skin slick with sweat. He pulled a cigar from the gold-plated case on his desk and snapped the end off with the cigar cutter which still bore the bloodstains of his dear friend, Carl Marsden.

It reminded him of how out of control the whole situation had got.

Good men had died.

The national security of the country was at stake.

The very real threat of Farukh hung over him like one of the bodies of the man's victims.

'I repeat,' Wallace barked as a thick, grey plume of smoke snaked into the bright, spring afternoon. 'We cannot fuck this up.'

'Understood,' Brandt answered immediately, his voice calm.

Wallace's eyes flickered around the screens and he felt himself hold his breath, as the digital clock at the bottom of his screen flicked to one o'clock.

———

The knot in Sam's stomach tightened.

London Liverpool Street Station was a hive of activity, the foot traffic absorbing the concourse as the city went about its business. Stood on the upper level, he watched as people filtered in every direction. Directly in front of him, he could see the steps which led down to the London Underground, connecting the commuters with the rest of London through the Metropolitan, Circle, and Hammersmith & City lines. As droves of people made their way underground, Sam cast his gaze across the rest of the station.

The high ceiling was made of thick, glass panels, allowing the spring sunshine to bathe the public in its warm glow. Underneath the walkway that Sam stood, entrances to the national rail line platforms were in full effect, with station staff checking the tickets of those heading in and out of the city. With connections all over the country, the station was one of the busiest in the country, if not Europe itself. In the centre of the main concourse, a vast, computerised screen hung, divided into nineteen boards, all of them providing information on a specific platform.

Trains were running late.

Some had already arrived.

The volume of the station echoed around the impressive structure like an orchestra, a calming beauty compared to the isolation Sam had endured in Italy.

He thought of Alex Stone.

Where had she gone?

It had broken his heart to leave her. They had forged a bond, not off the back of the one night of passion, but of their reliance on each other. They had saved each other's lives, literally, and had survived together. Alex had nursed him back to health, when the ghost of his past had come close to claiming him.

He had made her a promise.

While he intended to keep it, he knew he had to break it to keep her safe. Hopefully one day she would understand and when the time came that he could reunite her with her family, he hoped she would forgive him.

If he didn't end it, she would never be safe.

Lodged in his left ear, the high-tech earpiece crackled.

'Sam. How's it looking?'

Etheridge was back at base, headset on, and his permanently damaged knee resting comfortably on the leg support. He had hacked into the station CCTV system, laughing at the pathetic security system they had in place. For such a valuable gem in the London economy, the transport service's digital protection was alarmingly bad. He made a note to offer his guidance, using his expertise to enhance their platform but there were bigger things in hand.

They needed to bring down Wallace.

They needed to open the files.

They needed to know the truth.

Sam looked around, drawing a wry smile from a pretty woman as she walked past.

'It's busy,' he responded, shyly looking away from the woman and lowering his head. He wore a black baseball cap and a navy bomber jacket, with Etheridge ordering him some new clothes online and paying for express delivery.

It paid to partner with a man who had a serious bank account and no real need to spend it.

Under the jacket, he wore a black T-shirt, along with jeans, and black trainers.

Sam was never one for fashion and he knew his basic look would help him blend in with the moving crowds. Etheridge had already confirmed that there was another hack into the security system, joking that Blackridge were about as a subtle as a sandpaper suppository.

Sam had rolled his eyes at that one.

As he scanned the station, his eyes fell on the large digital clock attached to the far barrier.

Three minutes.

Sam lifted the coffee he'd bought from one of the many outlets dotted throughout the station, appreciating the warm caffeine as it flowed down his throat. Although the station's primary function was for transport, it had an impressive number of food and clothing outlets dotted on both floors, with a number of chain restaurants and high street brands pitching their flags. There were plenty of places to hide, but most importantly, plenty of small alcoves where discretion would be afforded.

It would be needed.

Sam pushed himself away from the railing and slowly meandered down the walkway, gazing blindly at the shop windows of the stores that lined it, immersing himself in the crowd.

Blackridge were there.

The call to Singh had been used to fish them out and Sam knew that they would have their field agents patrolling the station, all of them champing at the bit to bring him down. They all wanted the gold star from Wallace and after a few encounters with some of their teams, Sam knew how keen they were for violence.

They were built in Wallace's image.

They would all fall in it, too.

But Sam felt uneasy, the idea of pulling Amara Singh further into his world had kept him up all night. The phone call had been brief, telling her he was alive and that he needed to speak to her urgently. While it had been nice to hear her voice, the expletive laden rant she began reminded him of how volatile she could be.

Be that as it may, Singh was a fighter.

She'd been with him in the Port of Tilbury and had risked her own life to save Jasmine and the other girls. She'd put the needs of others before her own career and if what Pearce had said was true, it had been costly. She was on Wallace's radar, one of the most dangerous places she could have landed, and it was his fault.

She'd done some digging.

And it was that which Sam used to lure her to the station. He had told her he needed to speak to her about Wallace and 'Project Hailstorm'. That was all it took.

She agreed immediately.

Sam could hear the nerves in her voice and secretly, he echoed them. It had been a long time since Lucy had left him, moving on with her life as a way to deal with the pain of losing their son. She was remarried and on her way to starting a new family. While his tryst with Alex had been memorable, it blossomed into a true friendship. But there had been something about Singh, from the moment he'd evaded her at Etheridge's house to watching her flip him the bird through his sniper scope.

In another life, perhaps.

Sam shook his head clear and felt the guilt rising within

him. One of his first missions as the designated shooter was in his early twenties. He was seen as a sniping prodigy within the armed forces and, under the tutelage of Carl Marsden, soon found himself on covert operations way beyond what his experience should have attained.

The mission was a simple extraction within the Amazon jungle, where two French diplomats had been taken captive. With the risk of an uprising, the UK and US armed forces had dispatched an elite team to bring the man home.

But he'd been used as bait.

Three of the team had died, with a rogue sniper putting Sam to shame and several bullets into several of his comrade's skulls.

The diplomats, an innocent couple who had done nothing other than uncover information that needed to remain hidden, were dead before they even got there.

The failure of the mission had stayed with Sam. Marsden had told him it wasn't his fault, that he couldn't have eyes everywhere.

But Sam felt uneasy.

That unease grew, as the ear piece sparked to life once again.

'Sam, she's here. It's go time, buddy.'

Sam took a deep breath, finished the last of his coffee, cursed his decision not to bring a gun and waited for their mission to begin.

CHAPTER FIFTEEN

The entire journey into London Liverpool Street had felt like a bad idea. With a reduced service running on Sundays, Singh's journey into city had taken longer than usual. She'd hopped on a train at Barnet station, traversing the Northern Line to Kings Cross before hoping onto the first train through to Liverpool Street. The trains were heaving, a few Sunday afternoon football matches had drawn a worrying number of drunken louts to the city centre like moths to a pointless flame.

Singh had never understood the mass appeal of football, especially from her times as a police officer, managing the raucous crowds and seeing people fighting over the ridiculous notion of football rivalry.

Was it really worth violence?

Especially when she'd been pulled into a world of gunfire and pain. It had rocked her entire life, the past few months shaking her career and her moral compass like a baby's rattle. For so long, she'd been steadfast in her commitment to the justice system. And while she still knew the difference between right and wrong, she was sure that

Sam Pope operated in a small, grey shaded area that existed between.

Singh tapped her Oyster Card on the barrier and was granted passage into the Liverpool Street Station. She weaved her way through the large swathes of tourists and hopped up the steps onto the main concourse. With trepidation, she made her way towards the large screen in the centre of the station as instructed, carefully scanning the station for any sign of Pope.

———

Etheridge had watched her walk up the steps to the main concourse and took a deep breath.

There was no going back now.

While he fully believed that putting Singh in the firing line was the only way forward, his finger guiltily hung over the enter button of his keyboard.

Along with Pearce, Singh had saved his life when they found him unconscious in the very room he was sat.

Beaten, tortured, and losing an almost fatal amount of blood, she'd helped Pearce load him into the car before she made her getaway. Sam's mission had smashed her world into pieces, and he watched with regret as she nervously surveyed the station.

It was Etheridge's responsibility now.

He had to keep her alive.

He was the eyes.

He was the voice.

With a deep breath, he clicked the button, scrambling the CCTV monitors for everyone other than himself. He knew that Blackridge would have already clocked her, instructing their field agents to keep their distance and to shadow her every move. Etheridge had made light work of the Blackridge radio frequency, but the agents were clever.

They gave little away regarding their location.

The vague response of *'in position'* was all that was said when Wallace barked impatiently for progress.

The moment they saw Sam, then they would engage.

Judging from what happened to Marsden, who Etheridge had privately mourned, they wouldn't hesitate to use whatever means necessary.

Etheridge quickly pulled up his phone infiltration software and blocked all transmissions from Singh's phone.

The line was secure and he dialled the number.

———

Singh answered on the first ring.

'Sam, where the hell are you?'

'Amara, it's Paul Etheridge.' He heard her responding but cut her off. 'We don't have loads of time. Wallace has a team in place at the station, with eyes locked on you.'

'Oh shit,' Singh exclaimed, trying to mask the worry in her voice.

'I've scrambled the CCTV, but you need to follow my every word. Do you understand?'

'Where the fuck is Sam?' she demanded, her fist clenching the phone and threatening to crack its plastic casing.

'Do you understand?!' Etheridge repeated.

'Yes.'

'Okay, do you see the empty outlet on the far right-hand side of the station, next to the Coffee Cove?' Etheridge had his hand ready on the side of headset, ready to switch feeds. Singh nodded. Etheridge sighed. 'You have to speak up.'

'Yes,' Singh barked, irritated.

'Head there, now.'

Singh obliged, keeping the phone pressed against her

ear as she began to stride towards the abandoned shop. Etheridge scanned the CCTV and instantly caught a glimpse of a burly man in a black leather jacket, on the other side of the upper floor begin to move, his eyes locked on Singh.

'Keep heading there. I'll be back in one minute.'

Before she could fill his ears with expletives, Etheridge flicked the feed of his mic, transitioning back to Sam's earpiece.

'Sam, your level. Four o'clock.'

'Already on it.'

———

Sam had clocked the Blackridge agent before Etheridge's instruction and he walked briskly around the upper walkway, trying his best to not draw the attention of the agent on the other side. The man was well built, definitely an ex-soldier, and carried himself with clear intent.

This wouldn't be easy.

Luckily for Sam, most of the foot traffic was below them, with the family on the upper level fortunately turning towards the escalator before Sam approached.

On the upper level, directly above the Coffee Cove, there was a small alcove, leading towards a staff only staircase. With the CCTV scrambled, Sam knew that unless one of the station security happened to be coming up that stairwell, he had a clear minute or two to make his move.

He rounded the final corner, a mere five metres or so from the agent who finally looked up.

Agent Will Cook was unprepared for the ambush, and Sam wrapped his forearm around the man's neck and allowed his own momentum to send them hurling back into the alcove.

They were out of sight of the public.

Cook was a broad man, and as he propelled them backwards, he slammed Sam into the brick wall, driving the air from his lungs. Sam relinquished his hold and coughed, wheezing for air. The earpiece dropped from Sam's ear, clattering to the ground with the cries of Etheridge going unheard. Cook, as deadly as Sam expected, spun on his heel, and launched forward, swinging a solid fist at Sam's head.

He ducked.

The shattering of bone was sickening as Cook hit the solid brick behind.

Before he could yell in anguish, Sam shot a vicious uppercut into his jaw, shattering it instantly. Shell shocked, Cook swayed on the spot, lazily flinging his other hand at Sam.

With a swift step to the side, Sam hooked his own hand underneath and wrenched upwards. He clasped his hands together, locking Cooks in a brutal choke hold. Still reeling from the jaw shattering uppercut, Cook struggled tamely and Sam, still struggling for breath from the collision with the bricks, hauled him towards the *staff only* sign. With a sharp kick backwards, he shunted open the door to the stair well and pulled Cook through.

A hard right hand caught Sam in the kidney and he released Cook, who dropped to his knees. Another hard fist caught Sam in the chest, before a third splattered his bottom lip into a bloody mulch.

Sarah Masters leapt forward with a brutal knee strike, hoping to capitalise on her ambush. As she did, Sam managed to grab her leg and haul her off balance, slamming her hard into the metal railing that ran through the stairwell like a vein.

The landing area was a small square of concrete with a set of concrete stairs on either side of the metal. Masters had raced up to meet Sam, clearly having seen him accost her comrade moments before. As she gingerly got to her feet, she removed her black jacket, revealing muscular arms, slathered in tattoos.

She reached up for the knife attached to her bicep and whipped it from its sheath, before lunging towards Sam who had just cleared the ringing from his ears.

He weaved to the left, the blade slicing through the air a few inches from his ear, before Masters sliced back towards him. Sam managed to raise his arm, countering her momentum with his own powerful forearm. Masters relinquished the knife, dropping it but catching it swiftly with her left hand and again lunged forward, hoping to disembowel Sam. Sam stepped back, colliding with the wall and once the knife missed, he grabbed Masters' wrist, wrenched her towards him, and dropped to his knee.

The sound of her face colliding with the solid brick wall was sickening and Sam wasn't surprised to feel her limp body fall on top of him. Blood was pumping from her nose and eyebrow and he would bet his watch and wallet on her missing some teeth.

Sam dropped his shoulder and let her roll onto the concrete. As he lifted himself to his feet, he reached for the knife. After a quick inspection and an impressed nod, Sam slid it into the inside of his bomber jacket. Cook, unable to speak, moaned in pain as he tried to get to his feet. Sam shook his head as the man feebly raised his only functioning hand, challenging Sam to continue.

'Really?' Sam asked, shrugging. Cook, his jaw hanging slack, lunged pathetically. Sam easily sidestepped, pulled the arm in, and drove a knee straight into the man's gut, before driving an elbow to the back of his skull.

Cook was out like a light.

Sam spat blood from his busted lip, stretched out his aching back and then pulled an envelope from the inside pocket of his jacket. Inside, it contained sheets of transparent plastic which Etheridge had procured from a stationery shop.

Quickly, Sam dropped to his knee and systematically pressed each hand of the unconscious duo against a separate sheet, ensuring their fingerprint smudged clearly.

Neither of them moved throughout the process.

'Paul, I've got two sets.' He raised his finger to his ear, realising then that the earpiece was gone. 'Shit.'

Sam scrambled to his feet and stepped out of the stairwell to where he and Cook hit the wall. Scanning the floor, he felt his heart rate calm as he found the earpiece quickly. As he lifted it and turned, a small, portly station security guard stood. With his hand on his radio, his jaw dropped at the carnage through the doorway, he stared at Sam with fear in his eyes. Sam looked at the motionless bodies, as well as the blood on his knuckles, before returning his gaze to the security guard. Slowly, he raised a finger to his lips. The security guard nodded his understanding, before turning nervously and walking back towards the main walkway.

Sam let out a deep breath.

That was close.

He put the earpiece back in.

As soon as he heard Etheridge's cries of panic, he darted through the door, leapt over the prone mess that was formerly the Blackridge field team and bounded down the steps three at a time, hoping to god he wouldn't be too late.

———

'What the fuck is happening?' Wallace exclaimed, his fists slamming against his glass balcony table and rocking its contents. The ashtray, now full of disposed cigar ends rattled. 'Get me some fucking images!'

Wallace was furious. Just as his team had got into place, the CCTV feed dropped. Considering the amount of government money he'd spent to build his operations hub, he doubted it was to do with faulty wiring.

Someone had scrambled the system and what infuriated him most, was that nobody in his team seemed able to reverse it.

Wallace had expected the best.

He made damn sure he paid enough for it.

Failure was not an option and he made a note to march into the secluded location once it was all over and personally end the careers of the hapless team working the operation. He had long passed the point of playing nice.

He needed Sam Pope.

He needed that USB stick.

Not only to protect his career and his reputation, but after the very clear warning from the Hangman, his life. Thinking of Farukh sent a shiver down his spine, then caused his knuckles to whiten as there had still been no response.

Wallace hated not being in control, but at that particular moment, he felt it filtering from his fingers like dust in the wind. A few moments later, he heard from Brandt that Singh had made her way to the far side of the station and the fearless German commanded Cook and Masters to follow. With the reassurance granted by Brandt's terrifying efficiency, Wallace had afforded himself a brief comfort, lighting yet another cigar and pouring another glass of Scotch.

His lungs and liver be damned.

As he sat back down, his discomfort quickly returned.

The heart rate monitor in the corner of his screen quickly told him things hadn't gone to plan. Clearly, Cook and Masters were unconscious.

Sam Pope.

Wallace slammed another meaty fist onto the glass table, sending a crack shooting through the pane. A few cigars toppled from the overstuffed ashtray and he hurled his glass tumbler as hard as he could against the balcony wall. It shattered, not unlike his confidence in the mission.

Luring Sam into the open was not going to work.

They had to smoke him out.

Wallace slammed his headset back on.

'Brandt,' he barked. 'Fucking answer me.'

'Sir,' Brandt crackled, his voice emotionless.

'Masters and Cook are down. It's time to stop pussy-footing around and bring Sam in.' Wallace puffed his cigar. 'Get Singh. By any means necessary.'

'Copy that,' Brandt replied. 'Any, sir?'

Wallace dropped back in his chair and squeezed the bridge of his nose with clammy fingers.

He had a potential clean-up job on his hands.

But needs must.

'Affirmative, Brandt,' Wallace eventually said. 'Any means necessary.'

———

Brandt removed the earpiece from his ear, tired of the weary orders of a man slowly losing his grip. While he'd been handsomely rewarded for being one of Wallace's top assets, Brandt knew his skill set would see many offers laid at his doorstep.

There were many shady corners of every government that needed someone of his capabilities and he'd already made up his mind that once Sam Pope had been eradicated, he would step away from Blackridge.

It was time to move on.

But he couldn't help but smile at Wallace's order.

Any means necessary.

As all his ducks began to line up, he couldn't help but let a broad smile crack across his strong jaw when he laid his eyes on a worried looking Amara Singh as she strode back across the station, her phone plastered to her ear.

She was clearly shaken, her panicked lips giving an earful to whoever was on the other end of the phone.

Sam Pope?

Perhaps.

It didn't matter.

As she hurried her way towards the far end of the station, Brandt turned on his heel and followed. She turned right at the main tunnel to the outside, walking down a deserted walkway towards the staff elevator. Brandt had memorised the layout of the station, as was customary for any mission he undertook.

It was a dead end.

He was almost disappointed at how easy this would be.

As he turned to follow her down the walkway, he reached into his jacket, pulled out the Glock pistol and purposefully made his way towards Amara Singh.

CHAPTER SIXTEEN

Sam ran as fast as he could.

Bursting through the security door, Sam shot out onto the main concourse, drawing a few panicked looks from nearby civilians. Given the track record of instances in London train stations, he understood their concerns, but now wasn't the time to quash public panic.

Not when there was a genuine threat nearby.

'Where is she?' Sam spoke, his finger to his ear so the block out the cacophony of noise that enveloped the station. Commuters were loudly discussing their plans, announcements were echoing from the sound system, and trains were roaring their engines as they departed.

Sam needed to hear Etheridge.

It was life or death.

'Far corner. Nine o'clock.'

Sam propelled himself forward like an Olympic sprinter, barging past a group of lads who threw a few curses his way. Heads turned as a man with a bloodied mouth darted through the station, a few families cowering away. They were sure to alert security, if they hadn't already clocked him and Sam appreciated all the mornings he'd spent running through the cold streets of Naples.

He rounded the corner, a long corridor leading down to the staff elevator.

There was no sign of Singh or the Blackridge agent.

Etheridge had no visibility.

Sam could feel his lungs screaming as he pushed on, hoping to god that he wasn't too late.

———

Singh had walked down the deserted corridor of the station, the hysteria of the main concourse drowned out by the eerie silence afforded by the narrow walkway. A few empty billboards lined the wall, a reminder of a time when the corridor was part of the functioning part of the station. Now, all that remained were scraps of previous adverts, a remnant of something important.

A horrible metaphor for her own career.

Although her heart was racing through a mixture of fear and adrenaline, she zeroed in on her training. She wasn't a damsel in distress. She was one of the finest young detectives the Met had ever seen, with an extensive background in combat.

But she'd seen the ugly side of Sam's world and was smart enough to know that a team run by Ervin Wallace wasn't to be messed with.

Wallace had already made it pretty clear to her that he would go to extreme lengths to keep the truth buried and she was certain that he would have no hesitation in burying her with it.

As she continued down the corridor, Singh heard the clomping of boots behind her. A quick glance told her she needed to hurry.

The man was about six foot three, his dark hair parted

neatly at the side. His freshly shaven face was stoic, his eyes locked on her like a homing missile. While he was broad, he wasn't particularly stocky, but he carried himself with the movements of someone highly trained.

Highly efficient.

The man pulled a Glock from the inside of his black jacket and Singh felt sweat slide down her neck.

Highly dangerous.

She rounded the small corner at the end of the corridor and her heart sank.

A dead end.

To the left, in a small alcove, was a rusty old elevator and she frantically tapped her thumb on the button. To her relief, the green light surrounded the button and somewhere above, she heard the agonised churning of an old pully system.

'Do. Not. Move.' The man's words were deep and powerful, slathered in a thick, German accent. 'Drop the phone.'

Singh obliged, hoping that Etheridge could still hear as it slapped against the concrete. Slowly, she began to turn.

'I said don't move,' Brandt repeated, taking a step closer before crushing the mobile device under his weighty boot. Singh flinched at the crunch and began to question how many times she was going to look down the barrel of the gun before she realised how dangerous this game was.

In front of her, the lift dinged, and the doors struggled apart, revealing a surprisingly large elevator. A service lift designed for carrying large quantities of stock for the shops and the transport of defunct equipment. The thought crossed her mind to leap into the lift, hit the button, and slide through as the doors closed like a modern day Indiana Jones.

But she knew the man would fill her with holes before she even crossed the threshold.

'Move. Into the lift.' Brand stepped forward and prodded the gun into her spine. Singh tensed but then quickly obliged, stepping into the lift which suddenly felt a lot smaller. She finally turned to face her captor, who remained as expressionless as a mannequin.

'I am a police officer…' Singh began, scolding herself for even trying.

Brandt didn't respond. He took a few steps towards the elevator, only turning as he heard the final footsteps but by then it was too late.

Sam had pressed himself against the wall as he approached the end of the corridor, tip toeing to hide the sound of his impending arrival. After Brandt had forced Singh into the lift, he knew he had to time it just right. There was no way Wallace would send an amateur to lead the team and judging from what Etheridge had been witnessing, the emotionless man was completely in charge.

As Brandt took a step toward the lift, Sam lunged, with the large German turning at the final second and raising the gun. Sam threw a fist, catching Brandt on the wrist and dislodging the gun from his grasp. Brandt shot his other arm out, wrapping his vice like grip on the scruff of Sam's jacket and hurling him towards the wall. Sam hit it hard, and then raised his arms to block the barrage of blows that Brandt swung, each of them propelled with the proficiency of a boxing champion.

Sam was equal to it, absorbing the impact on the muscles of his arm.

A sickening thud echoed in the corridor and Brandt stumbled forward. Sam, not one to look a gift horse in the mouth, charged forward, slamming his shoulder into Brandt's solid midsection and ran with him, using his momentum to send them both careening into the service elevator. Singh followed, the handgun still in her hand, the handle dripping with blood from where she'd pistol whipped her assailant.

Brandt hit the metal wall hard, the entire carriage shaking and Sam whipped up, ducked a right and cracked Brandt with a sickening elbow to the side of the head, drove a knee into the man's midriff, and then spun him swiftly by the right arm, guiding him face first into the metal bar that ran the perimeter of the lift for support.

The impact shattered Brandt's nose, which exploded down in a sickening wave of blood and cartilage.

With one final swipe of his arm, he drove his elbow into the back of Brandt's skull, shutting his lights out.

For now.

The doors to the lift finally shut, and as they ascended, Sam reached across an impressed looking Singh and pressed the emergency stop button.

The lift shunted to an unconvincing stop.

Sam turned back to Singh.

'Look, I am so sorry we...'

Singh slapped Sam across the face as hard as she could.

'You prick.'

'I deserve that,' Sam agreed, pressing his tongue to the inside of his cheek.

'I thought you were dead, Sam,' Singh ranted. 'After what happened in Tilbury, I figured it was you who killed the rest of that disgusting family. It had your handiwork all over it. But then you just disappeared. Nothing. No sign of you anywhere and for the last few months, your old boss has been making my life a living hell.'

'I know.'

Singh stared at Sam, who offered her an apologetic smile. As she handed him a tissue from the pack in her jacket pocket, he began to tell her what he'd been through over the last few months, dabbing the blood from his face as he spoke. He told her about being forced into a mission with a threat to his ex-wife, and his need to get to his mentor before Blackridge.

Singh listened in disbelief, her eyes widening as Sam told her how he fought Buck to the death in a small, abandoned, underground facility in the outskirts of Italy, while his mentor lay dead beside them. He lifted his T-shirt, showing her the healed bullet wound that scarred his stomach, missing his spine by inches.

'Jesus,' Singh exclaimed. 'That was lucky.'

'It was exact.' Sam felt a chill run down his spine. 'Shoot to maim.'

'Huh?'

'The person who shot me, he didn't want to kill me with this shot. This was to put me on my knees.' Sam shook away the awful memory.

'Who was it?'

'My mind is playing tricks on me, telling me it's a ghost from my past that I long since buried.' Sam offered her a shrug. 'But it's just another bridge to cross.'

'And all this? Wallace? Project Hailstorm?'

'It's all on the USB stick with Etheridge. But to get it, we needed Blackridge agents, to try to steal their access.'

'So, you used me as live fucking bait?' Singh fumed.

'I need a fingerprint,' Sam said, his voice straining as he squatted down beside Brandt and lifted his limp, lifeless hand.

'You're going to cut his finger off?!'

'God no.' Sam shook his head and pulled out the envelope. 'I'm just taking a copy of his prints. I'm not a savage.'

Singh smirked at the joke, but quickly hid it with a scowl. Sam didn't notice as he quickly went through the same process with Brandt as he had with the rest of the team, collecting the prints on the plastic sheets before storing them safely away in his pocket. Once he'd secured them away, he reached over to press the button once again, to complete their journey, but Singh stepped in his way.

'Do you have any idea what I have been through in the last few months?'

'Was it worse than recovering from a bullet wound?'

'Fuck you,' Singh snapped. 'My life was perfect before you came into it. I had the job of my dreams and everything was perfect. Bringing you in should have been the best moment of my career.'

'Then why didn't you?' Sam took a step closer to her, his brow furrowing with frustration. 'You knew I was at the top of that tower. Why didn't you send a team up to arrest me?'

'Because you saved my life.' Singh could feel her eyes watering and cursed herself for it. 'I should have died in that Port, but you saved me. You killed a lot of people that night, and a lot more since, but ever since you saved me I've struggled to find any compassion for those you have put in the ground.'

'I'm sorry for everything, Amara. I truly am. But I need to end this. There is a woman who saved my life, who will never be safe until Wallace and Blackridge are torn to the ground.'

Singh wiped her eye with her sleeve, shaking her head in frustration.

'Why, Sam? Why do you have to be the one to do it?'

'Because this is my fight. It's not yours. It's not anyone else's,' Sam said coldly. 'Once it's done, you'll have your life back.'

'The only way I will ever have my life back is if I bring you in myself.' Singh looked up at Sam, who stood less than a foot from her. She looked down at the gun still in her hand and smirked.

Sam leant in and pressed his lips against hers and Singh dropped the gun, her hand reaching up and running through his recently shaved hair. The kiss was as passionate as either of them had ever experienced, with months of fear, excitement, confusion, and anger bursting forth as they stumbled back into the wall of the lift, with Singh pinned against the metal. They kissed for a few moments longer, with Sam resting his hand on the curve of Singh's face before gently moving his mouth away from hers.

The moment lingered between them as they considered how different life could have been.

How, down different paths, they may have walked one hand in hand.

But the fight wasn't over.

Some people didn't get to live the lives of others. There were those who had to fight. Those who had to make sacrifices.

Those who did the right thing.

Agonising as it was for Singh, she pressed the button on the lift, kick starting it back to life and giving Sam the silent permission to leave and finish his war once and for all.

The doors pinged and the two of them stepped out into a similar looking corridor only on the upper floor. As derelict as the one downstairs was, this one was worse. Clearly nothing more than a cut through for staff, the lighting fixtures were rusty, with a few lights flickering a slow death.

At the end of the corridor, leading towards the bright sunshine that the station was basking in, was a large man. Sam stopped in his tracks, placing a protective arm in front of Singh and moved her behind him. She couldn't help but feel a flutter as Sam stepped between them like a barrier.

The man was heavyset, with thinning black hair on top of his heavily bearded face. His skin was brown, clearly of an Arabic decent and his frame filled the leather jacket almost to breaking point.

The man's eyes bore through Sam, as if searching for his soul.

Slowly, the man began to remove the leather jacket, giving Sam every indication that there was only one way out of the tunnel.

'Let's go back,' Singh said quietly, her eyes widening as the man began to walk towards them.

'You need to get back into the lift,' Sam said, not taking his eyes off the incoming threat.

'Sam…'

'Go,' Sam ordered. 'Get out of here and if you can, buy me some time.'

Singh stepped back into the lift, flashing a worried glance as the monstrous man closed in on Sam, who cracked his neck and stretched out his shoulders, limbering up.

The hulking figure approached.

The Hangman of Baghdad.

As the doors closed, Singh held her breath, terrified for the safety of the man she was in love with.

CHAPTER SEVENTEEN

Sam carefully considered the large man as he approached, noting how the man was very clearly unarmed. The intention was clear.

The man wanted to fight.

Which meant he was good.

Farukh held the weight and height advantage and judging by the glint in his eye, Sam could tell that this was what the man enjoyed. Sam gently cracked his neck, loosened his shoulders, and raised his fists, ready to take the big man on. As the doors to the elevator closed behind him, Sam took a step forward and threw his first punch. With a speed that caught Sam by surprise, the man ducked, drilled Sam in the ribs with a concrete like fist and then thrust his thick, black boot into Sam's chest.

The impact was sickening and Sam stumbled back, colliding with the wall behind. The man hardly moved, his arms relaxed by his side, almost goading Sam to take another shot.

In his ear, Sam could hear Etheridge complaining that he had no visual on his location, but he knew that Wallace had scrambled the armed police towards the station and that Sam was running out of time.

Sam flicked the earpiece from his ear.

He had already run out of time and escape routes.

He didn't need reminding.

Sam took a deep breath, looked beyond his bearded attacker towards the bright light of the station and the hint of an exit.

There was only one way to it.

'Let's do this,' Sam muttered to himself and pushed himself from the wall and towards the man. Sam swung a hard right to the head, but as Farukh lifted his arm to block, Sam swerved and drilled it into the man's ribs. It was like punching a cement block and Farukh swatted his arm down, locking Sam in place. He spun Sam on the spot, then thrust his meaty skull forward, smashing his thick forehead into Sam's face.

Dazed, Sam stumbled on the spot and Farukh twisted his arm, before kicking him in the back of the knee. Sam dropped down like he was praying and Farukh placed the bottom of his boot on Sam's spine and mockingly pushed him forward. Sprawled on the floor, Sam was realising pretty quickly that he was outmatched.

As he slowly lifted himself from his chest, blood dripped from his nose, the impact of the headbutt drawing blood. Reaching all fours, Farukh drove a vicious kick into Sam's ribs, flipping him over onto his back, before lifting and then driving his heel down. Sam rolled out of the way, stamped his right foot back and knocked Farukh's balance off.

With his attacker wobbling, Sam pushed himself back to his feet and threw a couple of hard hooks, both of them rocking the man's mighty, beard encased jaw.

They seemed to irritate more than incapacitate and on the third punch, the man ferociously blocked it with an elbow, then grabbed Sam by the scruff of his jacket and hurled him into the wall. Sam hit the brick hard and fell to the tiled floor, slowly dragging himself towards the walkway ahead.

Behind him, he could hear the calm steps of Farukh, his military boots clapping casually behind. Whoever this man was, he was not part of Blackridge. Something told him that he was much worse. But what was his investment in Sam?

If he was working for Wallace, why?

Sam struggled to piece the dots and as he continued to drag himself across on his body like an injured snail, he could hear the man chuckle.

'You were supposed to be challenge.' The man tutted. 'Like everything to do with this country, you are nothing but disgrace. Now tell me, where is USB stick.'

Sam pushed himself to his feet, his body aching from the punishment the man had dished out. His face was dripping with blood and his ribs felt like they'd been run through a blender.

'Who are you?' Sam asked, each word causing his split lip to sting.

'My name is Ahmad Farukh. You know this name?'

Somewhere in the back of Sam's mind, he did. While he couldn't place the how or the why, he knew that the man wasn't known for his good behaviour.

'Why are you helping Wallace?' Sam demanded, taking small steps as he walked backwards, edging his way closer to freedom. While his hopes of escaping had already diminished, Farukh humoured him by allowing him to continue.

'I don't help Wallace. I want stick,' Farukh said calmly. 'For it, I am willing to kill you quickly if you're helpful. Continue to fight me, Sam, and I will ensure the pain is such that you beg for death.'

Sam took a second to contemplate his options. His body wasn't capable of outrunning Farukh, that much was sure. The man had systematically targeted his legs, back and shoulders, ensuring Sam's freedom of movement was compromised. Whatever red flag the name had set off in Sam's mind, the man's actions had clearly backed them up. Over the past year, Sam had been through enough battles to know when he was outmatched. He had fought Mark Connor in the High Rise, the two of them dismantling the apartment before Sam had lodged a knife in the man's eye and pushed it through to the brain.

In the abandoned tower overlooking the Port of Tilbury, he'd fought Oleg Kovalenko to the death, eventually hanging the simple behemoth with a hook through the jaw. Buck had fought with all the ferocity of a marine in the underground bunker in Rome, but Sam had been armed then and was able to put a bullet through the man's skull.

All of those fights had pushed Sam to his limit.

But Farukh had every intention of pushing him beyond. Sam took a deep breath and his shoulders slumped.

'Fine.' He eventually relented.

'Good. Hand it over.' Farukh held out his hand, the knuckles a faint memory after years of fighting.

Sam reached into the inside of his jacket, his face resigned to defeat.

It was the only option he had.

It was a Hail Mary, but it was at least a fighting chance.

His fingers clasped around the handle of the thin blade Masters had attacked him with and in one swift movement, he drove it clean through Farukh's palm, the blade bursting out the back of the hand with a visceral spray of blood. With one fierce shove, Sam drove the man's hand down to his own thigh, pushing the blade through the jeans and into the thick muscle.

Farukh grunted with pain as Sam stepped back, hobbling as fast as he could towards the walkway and the possibility of escape.

That's all it was.

A possibility.

Farukh pulled the hand clean from his thigh, his jeans stained with blood and in one sickening act of grit, pulled the knife back through his hand. He slammed the blade down onto the ground and then stomped after Sam, ignoring the roaring pain of his wounds and the blood that gushed from them both.

Sam stepped onto the walkway, just as Farukh grabbed the back of his jacket.

He spun Sam on the spot and drove a hard elbow into Sam's throat, doing his best to crush it. Sam coughed blood, the air struggling to slide through and he stumbled back against the railing, the concourse behind him. Nearby civilians screamed in terror as the two bloodied men emerged from the corridor, and as Farukh stepped forward, Sam took his final throw of the dice.

He threw a leg out, driving his trainer into the fresh wound that adorned Farukh's thigh.

It was like kicking a bee's nest.

Nothing but rage erupted from Farukh, who drove forward, grabbed Sam by the scruff of his jacket and hurled him over the railing, letting him drop the fifteen feet to the unforgiving concrete below.

———

Singh had to clench her hands to stop them from shaking.

As the doors had shut and she descended in the elevator, she second guessed whether she should rush back to the top and help Sam.

But he'd made it clear to her.

This was his fight.

He had apologised as honestly as he could for dragging her into his world, and while her mind raced due to the kiss they'd shared, she knew she had to return to reality at some point. The man was a vigilante, paying no respect to the law that she'd dedicated her life to. While the system was doing its best to push her out and mark her as a criminal, she knew she couldn't afford to give them any further reason to.

After a few moments, the lift shunted to a stop and Singh looked down at the motionless body of Brandt. The man had pointed a gun at her, with every intention of using it and thankfully, Sam had been there to save her.

Again.

She'd returned the favour of course, cracking the gun across the man's skull to give Sam the advantage.

Her eyes lit up.

The gun.

Singh dropped to her knee and retrieved the handgun, and as she stood, the doors slid open.

A team of six security guards and two police officers greeted her. Carefully, she slid the gun into the back of her jeans and retrieved her badge from her back pocket.

One of the young officers, keen to impress the security guards, stepped forward.

'Don't move,' he said cockily. Singh responded by shoving her badge in his face.

'I'm a fucking detective,' she barked. 'DI Amara Singh. Stand down.'

The young officer crumpled like a house of cards and as she stepped out of the lift, the other officer cut her off.

'What the hell happened here?' He gestured to the

prone body of Brandt.

'This man tried to attack me in the lift. Something to do with a drug ring we busted last year.' The lie came to her pretty quickly. 'Fortunately, he was bigger in size than in brains.'

The security team chuckled, and the more experienced officer regarded her with a careful eye.

'Okay. You two, get him some medical attention.' He turned to the younger officer. 'Stay here with them until the ambulance arrives.'

'Good work, officer,' Singh said firmly. The officer offered her a smile, one she didn't fully trust.

'Assistant Commissioner Ashton has just arrived with an armed response unit in tow. We have reason to believe that Sam Pope is in the vicinity.'

'Right, well... I better help the search...' Singh began. The officer grabbed her arm and wrenched it behind her, luckily avoiding the handgun.

'I think we should go and see her together, don't you?' the officer said. Clearly, he was aware of the rumours linking Singh to Pope and with the likely event of Wallace tipping off Ashton, her presence at the train station wouldn't be seen as a coincidence.

Most likely, it would be the final nail in her coffin.

Resigned to her fate, she marched with the officer who seemed to be basking in the glory of his discovery. Sadly, she understood the feeling, his smugness at climbing the hierarchal ladder echoed her own ambitions less than six months before.

The only way she would ever clear her name with the police was if she brought Sam in wearing cuffs.

As they moved from the corridor and across the concourse, panicked screams filled the upper walkway and the officer stopped, spinning round and relinquishing his grip on Singh's arm. Singh followed his gaze to the railing above, where Sam Pope was leaning, his face bloodied as he held the metal barrier for support.

Then, to Singh's horror, the hulking man she'd glimpsed before grabbed Sam by his jacket and hurled him over.

The station fell silent as Sam tumbled down, dropping about eight foot onto the roof of a sweet trolley, decked out like an old school wagon. He landed with a sickening thud, before rolling to the side and dropping onto the hard, unforgiving concrete.

As panic began to spread through the crowd as the bloodied man grunted with pain and began to stir, Singh saw her only chance.

She grabbed the gun from the back of her jeans, lifted it into the air and pulled the trigger.

Nothing shot fear through a crowd faster than the sound of gunfire and within seconds, the station was in a frenzy. Sam scrambled to his feet and Singh made sure he was moving with the crowd, as they rushed towards the exits, the escalators, and stairways to Liverpool Street crammed with people. Sam managed to move within the crowd and he vanished.

The armed response began to flood in through the side entrance, rifles at the ready, with Ashton's hopes of catching Sam vanishing by the second.

Singh knew the attacker would be long gone, and decided to follow suit, pushing the officer as hard as she could in the back, propelling him into the panicked crowd and watching as he crashed to the floor.

She felt bad, realising that the few ties she had left to the police were about to be severed, but she slipped into the terrified stream of people making their way to the exit and as she made her way to the street, she realised she'd gone too far now.

There was no way back.

CHAPTER EIGHTEEN

'*The scene at London Liverpool Street Station today, was one of terror. A sunny afternoon in Spring, turned into a nightmare for those commuting into the city.*'

Wallace sighed at the dramatic introduction of the news report, watching on TV as the cameraman tried his best to capture the business of the station, as well as the stunning weather coating it all in a bright sheen.

The man was trying to channel his inner Spielberg, while the reporter was doing his best to add some gravitas. CCTV footage of a figure lifting their arm in the air and a sudden flash, accompanied by thunderous clap followed.

'*A gunshot, triggered by this assailant, sent panic through the station, one which has seen five people admitted to hospital with severe injuries. Amongst the five, a senior police officer, who was trampled underfoot and is suffering with several broken bones and a concussion. All of those injured are in a stable condition and expected to make a full recovery.*'

'Whoopie-fucking-do,' Wallace slurred, slamming back another glass of Scotch and ignoring the burn as it fell down his gullet. He followed it with a thick, clogging breath of cigar smoke.

His safehouse had become his prison and he realised that for a man who feasted on fear, he was now a slave to it. A man of his stature and power, who had brought entire countries to their knees, was holed away in a remote location, all because of one man.

Sam Pope.

As his fists clenched, it felt for a moment that the tablet, propped in its carry case on the table, was reading his mind as the news report continued.

'Mobile phone footage submitted from a few anonymous sources caught sight of a struggle on the upper floor of the station. A confrontation involving two men, one of whom can be seen to be bleeding heavily from the face. In an act of unprecedented violence, the man is thrown from the upper level, thankful for the sweet cart below to break his fall.'

The image is frozen on the screen and using state-of-the-art technology, it is enhanced.

'Rumours abound that the man in question is Sam Pope, the wanted vigilante who was last reported to have brought down a people trafficking ring. A further sweep of the building found three unconscious people, all belonging to the same private security firm, Black-ridge. They have been contacted for a comment, but so far, all contact has been unsuccessful.'

Wallace slumped in the chair opposite the tablet, his mind racing. Again, it felt like the tablet itself was running his own inner monologue out loud.

'With the first sighting of Sam Pope in months, what does this mean for the city of London? What are the links to Blackridge? Who was the unidentifiable man who tried to kill Sam Pope? These are questions that will probably burn on for a while, until the Metropolitan Police, Blackridge, and our own government, can provide answers. Aseem Chaudary, BBC News, London.'

Wallace slammed the tablet face down onto the glass table. The crack from his earlier display of frustration had grown and he grunted as he made a note to have it replaced. He would claim it back through the government, another gift, paid for by the good people of Britain.

The way he saw it, he'd sacrificed enough over his lifetime for their freedom. The least they could do was pay for his comfort.

Comfort? He chortled, pouring himself another glass from the decanter and smelling the fiery stench of his Scotch. This was what he'd been reduced to.

Hidden away, drinking away his fears and frustrations, and hoping for a solution. A man of his stature and reputation had never left anything to chance. There was always a plan, always an angle to work. Whether it was infiltrating various terrorist cells, planning the coup of a government, or just executing a known traitor, Wallace had a plan.

There was always a road to his desired outcome, one that he would have meticulously laid out by his experts.

But this?

They had released the most brutal assassin he'd ever come across into the country, hoping he would bring Sam in. It had almost worked, but they were fishing in the dark.

He needed an absolute.

He needed a plan.

First things first, he needed to shut down the media. A quick phone call later and he'd given a clear directive to the communications expert of Blackridge, to give a blanket statement distancing themselves from the operation. As vague as possible, it would at least keep some of the wolves from the door.

But others would be more persistent.

Like Helal Miah.

As if his skull was an empty piggy bank, he felt the penny drop, rattling inside his brain. An evil smile crept across his unshaven face, his teeth, stale and unclean chomped together. Another phone call, this time to his software experts and the plan was in motion. It would only take them a few moments, as they were some of the best in the business. Although, after being outshone by whoever was helping Sam, Wallace wasn't sure that held any weight anymore.

They needed to deliver, especially if they wanted to keep their jobs.

Feeling a little more relaxed, especially as he'd begun to claw back elements of control of a situation that threatened to bring his entire empire to its knees, his tablet pinged.

The email had been sent.

It was a record of Helal Miah's phone record, all the messages and most importantly, the location. On a separate tab, he had the exact same information for Amara Singh.

On a third tab, his analyst had pulled together all the instances of communication between the two. While only a couple of text messages had been sent, the records pinpointed the exact date, time, and location when they met.

Two evenings ago.

It was the day before the 'Project Hailstorm' article was published.

'Bingo,' Wallace spoke, his sinister words creeping from a cruel grin.

There were a thousand reasons why people went to war. Power. Religion. Racism. Freedom. Famine. The list was endless. But for men like Sam, there was only one. The need to fight. Wallace admired, envied, and loathed Sam's boy scout nature, his incessant need to fight for the right thing. It had led them on a collision course that by now, they both knew could only end one way.

But to lure Sam from the mission, Wallace had to make him fight for something else.

Something he cared about.

Amara Singh.

Chuckling at his own twisted genius, he lifted his phone once more and called the Hagman of Baghdad. There was no fear this time.

After a few rings, the phone answered, but there was no voice. No respect. No honour among thieves.

Wallace gave the clear instruction, hung up the phone, took a large swing of his drink and toasted to the memory of Helal Miah.

———

'Stop being such a pussy.'

Etheridge shook his head at Sam, who hissed in pain as he pressed the cloth to his busted lip. Etheridge had invested decent money in a top of the range medikit, not wanting to take any chances after the beating he'd received from the man in black at the end of the previous year.

Sam understood, and was grateful, but pressing antiseptic liquid onto his split lip stung like hell.

Etheridge lifted Sam's shirt and pressed his fingers against his ribs, prodding them gently. On the fourth prod, Sam grunted, and the bone was definitely cracked.

'You certainly took a beating,' Etheridge said.

'You should see the other guy,' Sam said dryly, pushing himself up from the chair and pulled his shirt down.

'I did. He was terrifying.'

'Not going to argue with that.'

Etheridge smiled and pulled two beers from the glass fridge under his desk, popping the caps off with his keyring and handing one to Sam. While his new diet and lifestyle had seen him cut out his daily alcohol habit, something told him his friend needed a beer.

By the look of him, he needed a doctor, but sadly, there wasn't too many people wanting to join the illegal cause they were fighting for. For a moment, Etheridge thought of Theo, a sudden twinge of pain flickered through him like photo flash and he knew good people had died for the cause.

That whatever he and Sam were fighting for, it was worth it.

Theo.

Marsden.

Good people who had died to protect others. Etheridge would honour them all by seeing it through to the end, and that meant giving Sam all the help he could.

'Who was that guy?' Etheridge asked, sipping his beer.

'Ahmad Farukh,' Sam replied. 'I recognised the eyes. Somewhere, I've seen that man before but I couldn't tell you where.'

'A horror film, perhaps?' Etheridge joked and Sam raised his eyebrows in agreement. 'Well, whoever he was, he's working for Wallace. He said he wanted the stick.'

Etheridge slid open the draw of his desk and pulled out a secure, metal box. Taking the key from his key chain, he clicked the lock and pulled out the USB stick Sam had mailed him months ago.

He had tried in vain to hack into it, but the security was top of the range.

They needed a fingerprint to access it.

Sam had pulled thirty of them straight from the company themselves and Etheridge took a chance that the more senior of the team would be more privy to the files.

'What's the plan?' Sam asked, always enthralled by the complexity of Etheridge's knowledge.

'First, I'm going to run a quick scan across all databases to confirm which sheet is Brandt's.' Etheridge began clicking away on the keyboard. 'Once we establish that, I'm going to transfer all fingerprints onto the scanner, until one of them unlocks them.'

'You have program that does that?' Sam asked, impressed. He grimaced slightly, his body reminding him of the beating he'd taken. Etheridge flashed him a grin.

'Yup. It's a delicate process of placing each print on the scanner.'

Sam stared blankly at him, unimpressed. Etheridge chuckled and continued as Sam stepped away to the bathroom. He took a quick shower, allowing the water to try to calm the pain raging through his body. After a few moments, he stepped back out, got dressed, and rejoined Etheridge in the loft. Impressively, Etheridge had already identified which sheet belonged to Brandt and was now going through the arduous process of pressing the prints against the scanner.

On the eighth print, they got a match.

Two of the screens flicked to life, as the unlocked files of the stick suddenly opened on the screen and an avalanche of documents flooded the folder, all of them labelled in a random code of numbers.

It would take a while to crack the code on each one, but Etheridge interlocked his fingers and cracked them, ready to accept the challenge. After flicking through a couple of documents, he typed out an intricate formula in a separate window, inputting the numbers from the document name in, before hitting the enter button.

Each number was turned into a letter, and Sam blinked twice to try to comprehend it.

While he could dismantle and rebuild a sniper rifle with his eyes shut, Sam was a novice when it came to computers, He could do enough to survive in a world that was on the cusp of complete digitalisation, but what he'd just witnessed felt like magic. He patted Etheridge on the back, who seemed chuffed with the approval.

'This may take a while.'

Whatever Etheridge did, Sam wouldn't understand.

But as his fingers tap danced across the keyboard, the large servers in the room roared into life, as Etheridge's genius began to push them into overdrive.

The numbers on the file names began to scramble and slowly, they were replaced with letters.

The process took over three hours, and the two of them shared a couple more beers as Etheridge ordered them a pizza from a local eatery. According to him, it 'shat all over Domino's and Pizza Hut' and while Sam wasn't particularly au fait with either chain, he didn't doubt it. The pizza was incredible and the two of them shared stories of their lives before.

Etheridge asked Sam about Jamie, not wanting to know about the pain of his passing, but the good times before that.

It was cathartic for Sam to recount his little boy talking to him about books. Sam had always struggled with his son's academic prowess but had promised him he would read more to give his son tips.

It was one of the two promises he'd made his son. The other, not to kill anymore, he'd broken.

'But for good reason,' Etheridge pointed out. 'You are not letting him down by doing it, Sam. You are honouring him.'

Sam could feel his eyes watering.

'How?'

'Because he knew his dad was a hero. That you fought for what was right.' Etheridge held out his beer bottle. 'You still are fighting, Sam. And I guarantee you, Jamie is looking down at you with pride.'

Sam took a moment to compose himself, took a deep breath and then clinked his bottle.

'Thank you, Paul. For everything.'

Etheridge shrugged.

'Also, I got a shit tonne of books in this place. Help yourself.'

The two men chuckled, when suddenly, Etheridge's phone gave a satisfying chime. It was linked to his computers upstairs in the loft.

The decoding had completed.

The two men left the kitchen and returned to the loft where the heat emanating from the servers felt like stepping into a sauna. After cracking the large windows and letting in the brisk, night-time air, Etheridge sat down at the base of several screens, and flicked his powerful system into life.

The files were now labelled correctly, and a quick search landed them on a folder marked 'Hailstorm'

'This is it,' Etheridge said, the tension in the room was palpable. 'You sure you want to know what's in this? Once we do, we can't go back.'

Sam reached forward and clicked open the folder. A grid of documents welcomed them and systematically, they opened them reading through each one. As they ventured further into the truth, their eyes widened.

Sam's fist clenched.

The truth of Project Hailstorm laid bare to them.

Sam felt sick.

'Jesus. Fucking. Christ.' Etheridge exclaimed, as they read the mission report.

Seeing the events written down was like lifting a blindfold and Sam suddenly felt woozy, as the memories that had evaded him for so long, suddenly came rushing back.

He remembered.

He remembered everything.

CHAPTER NINETEEN

Seven Years Earlier...

The sun had long since set over the horizon, the ferocious heat that bathed Afghanistan on a daily basis had been unbearable at times. But none of the squadron had uttered even the smallest of complaints. All of them were heavily trained, the best of the best, and Sam knew he belonged among them.

For over a decade, he'd been the UK's most feared sniper, racking up over ninety kills for his country, many of which were high profile targets or covert operations needing his cover. For the most part, his career had been a sparkling journey of success, with medals and praise showered upon him for his skill and bravery.

The horror from three years ago, when he was blown from the mountains overlooking the depleted town of Chikari haunted his nightmares, the final moments with his good friend Matt McLaughlin, his spotter, who was blown away by the blast. Not a day went by that he didn't mourn his friend's memory.

They had never recovered a body and Sam could only hope that the young man had felt no pain when the missile hit.

Apart from another mission gone wrong in the Amazon rainforest,

Sam had a reputation to back up Marsden's recruitment of him into the elite squadron, overseen by the imperious General Ervin Wallace.

The man carried himself with unshakable power, like a prize bull patrolling his pen, and although the entire squadron who had made camp two clicks south of the target were some of the most skilled men the UK and US had ever seen, none of them dare speak out of line.

Wallace was a tyrant.

But he got the job done.

It was why he'd been given the go ahead to create an elite team for missions that were so off the book, they were not recorded. The long-lasting partnership between the UK and America had taken on a new role, one of policing the world without it knowing.

For soldiers like Sam, and the others who were preparing their weapons, it was a duty they had willingly signed up for.

For men like Wallace, it was like a drug.

The power.

The control.

With the resources bestowed upon him by the government, Wallace had created a team that made him one of the most powerful men in the world. The finer details were kept to hushed conversations in dark corners. The official reports would be written with as much information redacted as needed.

The world would only know the bare minimum.

The reports would be useful only as a record of an event.

The soldiers themselves knew what had happened but were never privy as to why. Again, need to know become unknown, and despite his unease, Sam followed his orders as a good soldier did.

The war on terror had been raging for years, with horrifying milestones such as 9/11 and 07/07 a painful reminder that the war never ended.

The fight was never over.

In secret government boardrooms, Wallace was hailed as a hero. A man who had pulled together two of the most powerful armed forces in the world and took the fight to the bad guys.

They had already successfully completed three missions, all of them taking place on the outskirts of Kabul, the Capital of Afghanistan. Several prominent figures in the Taliban militia had been eradicated, and the squadron had lost only one man.

A Corporal Lance Milton.

The American died in an explosion when a fallen Taliban soldier pulled the pin on a grenade as Milton turned his body over.

It was a fateful mistake, one which the rest of the squadron mourned and learned from.

There was no humility anymore.

Every Taliban soldier was to be killed on sight, with a double tap a requirement. The phrase didn't sit too well with Sam. Not only because it was coined by his American brethren, but because in Sam's career, he'd never needed the security of a second shot.

Sam only needed one shot.

Lethal in one.

That's what the smarmy Trevor Sims had said, the repugnant man following Wallace around like a snivelling shadow. While Marsden had left the operation after recruiting Sam, he'd warned him of Sims.

The man was distasteful, racist, and delusional.

But he had no moral compass and his blind ambition made him as loyal as a dog.

Perfect for his role as Wallace's second in command.

As the cold night washed over the dusty wasteland surrounding their camp, Sam watched as an unmarked Jeep arrived, it's lights off and two men inside. As it came to a stop, the driver quickly leapt out, scarpering around to the back of the vehicle and pulling out a large sports bag. From the passenger seat, a large, stoic man stepped, his neat beard framing a strong jaw. His piercing eyes locked onto the driver who handed him the bag and then backed away.

Sam didn't know his name, but the man was tall, stocky, and walked with a purpose. A few murmurs from the rest of the watching crew mentioned the name 'Farukh', but Sam paid no heed.

If he needed to know that man, then Wallace would have made an introduction.

As the man disappeared into the tent where Wallace and Sims were talking strategy, Sam reached into his pocket and pulled out his wallet. Inside, he looked at the photo of Lucy, her smile bright enough to light up the dark dessert. He yearned to return home to her, to their home in Ruislip, where they'd discussed starting a family.

This would be the last mission, he decided. It was time to step back from the never-ending war and build a new life.

Maybe he could help train others to take his place, guide those with the gift of accuracy down a career path such as his own. The thought saddened him, as he didn't want others to face the horrors he had.

To experience the same pain and injuries he had.

His best friend, Theo, had been with him for a few years in the same battalion, his skills as a medic keeping a number of their brothers alive.

But even Theo, the most optimistic man on the planet, had decided to step away. After a late night discussion on a cliff face many miles away, his friend had spoken about giving back to the community and had made good on his word.

Theo was now running a youth centre in London, helping under privileged kids stay on the right path. Maybe that was Sam's next move? Give back. Lucy had suggested becoming a police officer, which did hold an appeal.

Before he could follow that train of thought any further, Wallace stepped into the camp, decked out in his camouflage uniform, the jacket done up to the top and a cap squeezed over his large, bald skull.

'Attention,' he barked, and the entire strike force turned silent. 'Our target is located in the facility two miles north. Abdullah Bin Akbar. One of the Taliban's chief officers. We are expecting a small team, heavily armed. Shoot to kill and do it swiftly. In and out, gentlemen.'

The large man stepped out from the tent, walking proudly beside

Wallace and staring at them all without a hint of hesitation. Wallace continued.

'This is Ahmad Farukh. An Afghanistan Secret Service Officer who has offered us valuable intel on Bin Akbar. He will be riding with me. Any questions?'

No one ever had any questions.

The orders were clear. Storm the base and eliminate all targets.

'Good.' Wallace nodded. 'Let's go.'

The squadron lifted their rifles, secured any further weapons to their persons, and began to march. Sam was one of six men selected for the operation.

Project Hailstorm.

Wallace had picked the name himself, comparing his ambition with a mighty storm that would destroy the Taliban intelligence chain. But the soldiers, in their quarters, had mocked the decision, claiming that Wallace just wanted a cool sounding name for when the mission was over. Sam didn't care.

When the mission was finally over, he would be going home.

Back to Lucy.

To begin their life together again.

The two-mile walk through the dark, uneven terrain was done in silence, with the three American soldiers taking point, while Sam and two others covered them. Further behind, Wallace, Sims, and the terrifying Farukh followed, flanked by two further gunmen. As they approached the facility, Sam began to absorb as much detail as he could.

It had always been part of his training, to take in his surroundings, to memorise as many factors as possible.

It made him deadly.

The stone structure was shrouded in darkness, the shadows covering as much stone as the moon above would allow. There was no sign of light, or life, and Sam began to question whether a Taliban outpost would be left so vulnerable.

Out front, a rusty old car was parked, hardly the transport a wealthy militia would afford.

Something didn't sit right.

In unison, the six soldiers lowered their night vision goggles, and Sam squinted as the building was bathed in the bright green glow. Ahead of him, two of his squadron raced across the stones, keeping low, their M4 Carbine rifles held at the ready. With one covering, the other slid a combat knife into the tyre of the vehicle, rendering it useless.

Beyond the car, an Arabic cry filled the air.

The covering soldier stood tall, rifle clasped against his shoulder, eye on the sight.

He pulled the trigger, and an instant flash rocketed from the end of his gun. The oncoming man dropped to the ground, riddled with bullets.

Shoot to kill. Without hesitation.

The same as the other missions in Project Hailstorm.

Suddenly, a few flashes of white appeared from the darkness of the windows, as bullets flew from the building towards the squadron.

'Open fire,' Wallace demanded, and the other soldiers raised their rifles, unloading the clips without mercy at the building. A few more men raced out, hands in the air, but were met with bullets.

Surrendering or holding explosives, it didn't matter.

Wallace wanted them eradicated.

After a few more moments, the scene fell deathly silent and the two soldiers by the vehicle began to circle the building to the right-hand side, while Sam's squadron took the left. The crunch of gravel underfoot echoed loudly through the eerie silence, and as Sam watched his fellow soldiers round the building, he allowed his curiosity to get the better of him.

Something wasn't right, and Sam had dedicated his life to doing the right thing.

Quickly, Sam clambered through one of the paneless windows of the structure and entered the dark, unknown layout of the building. The corridors were illuminated in a pale green, his goggles affording him sight as he slowly drew his rifle up, taking careful steps towards the exit of the room. In his earpiece, he could hear Wallace demanding an update and knew it was only a matter of time before his absence was noticed.

Outside the building, he heard another burst of machine gun fire and confirmation of two more dead in a thick, Texan accent. Sam stepped into the corridor, the stone walls were bare, and the building resembled a tomb more than it did a terrorist outpost.

There were no soldiers.

No plans. No equipment.

No sign of the Taliban.

Quickly, Sam made his way through the corridor, ignoring the fury of Wallace who was demanding he return to base, as word had got round that he'd gone rogue.

Sam turned a corner, flicking his rifle up and down, ensuring the coast was clear, before he descended the dusty, stone staircase. He stepped off the bottom step, dropped to one knee, and whipped the rifle to his eyeline.

His finger resting on the trigger.

'Please. Don't shoot.'

The man stood ten feet away, his arms splayed out to his side. Behind them, a frail woman cowered, along with two young children. Their faces were wet with tears and Sam stood, lowering his rifle.

These were no Taliban soldiers.

It was a terrified family, trying their best to hide.

'Who are you?' Sam demanded, his mind racing.

'My name is Abdullah Bin Akbar.' The man spoke in broken English, his words stuttering with fear. 'We are unarmed.'

'What the hell is going on?' Sam asked, stepping forward, his hands held up as a show of attrition.

'I find information. Information that Taliban working with governments.' The man looked back at his terrified family, trying to calm them in his native tongue. He turned back to Sam. 'Taliban receive funding from countries to build on campaign.'

'What the hell are you talking about?'

'Please. My family. We go into hiding.' The man began, but suddenly, a deafening bang echoed through the room and Sam felt a searing pain through his back, followed by another before he hit the ground. It only took him a couple of seconds to realise he'd been shot twice, the bullets ripping out through his chest and he hit the stone hard, his breathing quickening as blood pumped from the bullet wounds.

As his vision began to blur, he arched his head up towards the family, watching as Farukh stepped forward, grabbing the two children by the hair and dragging them away from their screaming mother, another gunshot turning the top of her skull to paint. As she dropped to the floor a few feet from Sam, he watched as Abdullah fell to his knees, looking over her. Two large, military boots obscured Sam's vision, and Abdullah flashed him a knowing look, confirming the entire lie that was Project Hailstorm.

Abdullah Bin Akbar wasn't a terrorist. He was a man who had discovered the truth.

General Wallace pointed the gun at Abdullah and pulled the trigger, the bullet eviscerating the man's skull and he fell atop his wife, both of them dead. As Sam's consciousness faded, he heard the sickening sound of a knife piercing skin and shed a tear for the children who were being slain.

Project Hailstorm had been a cover-up job.

Hiding the links between the UK, US, and other governments with global terrorism.

Wallace.

Sam's eyes began to close against his wishes, the life leaving his body and he thought of Lucy, begging her forgiveness for not returning to her and for the part he'd unwittingly played in it all.

CHAPTER TWENTY

Sam and Etheridge sat in silence for the next few hours, pouring over the files in sheer disbelief.

The war that Sam had been a part of for most of his career had been a lie, the betrayal laid out for him in documents only to be seen by those who portrayed it. There was a very real terrorist threat on a global scale. But instead of fighting against it, Sam had been helping lay the foundations for it.

As the tears fell from his eyes, Sam read report after report, his actions leaping from the page. Several targets he'd eliminated during Project Hailstorm had been those trying to expose the truth, all of them silenced by the pull of his trigger.

He had helped to hide the truth.

To allow Wallace, in collusion with other powerful figures from around the world, to build an empire based off the fear of terrorism.

As Etheridge read on, he felt sick, realising that his own government had been duped by a man who had risen to an unassailable level of power.

Wallace was funding global terrorism through Blackridge, with several untraceable payments sent to the likes of the IRA, the Taliban, and ISIS. He had started a revolution in Bolivia, allowing a militia regime to take the throne and through it, had portrayed himself as a hero.

He was fighting a war he'd instigated.

For every promotion or reward Wallace had received for his public fight on the world's biggest threat, he had ensured thousands had died for it to happen.

The man was a monster.

Pure evil.

But the government, the media, and the country held him as a hero, a man who had dedicated his life to keeping the world safe.

Sam pushed his chair back, the legs squealing as they scraped the floor. He stood woozily, the truth hitting him like a ten-tonne truck and Etheridge struggled to his feet to help him.

'Don't touch me,' Sam snapped, clattering into the door and half falling down the stairs. Etheridge watched from the doorway as Sam rushed into the bathroom, dropped to his knees, and emptied the contents of his stomach into the toilet.

He felt sorrow for the man who had lost so much and now had to face the very real reality of his actions.

Sam had always strived to do the right thing. It was what had driven his mission over the past year, using the skills he had to bring an end to pain and corruption. To help those who were held under the oppressive boot of injustice.

But now, the entire backbone of his once proud career had been shattered.

He had blood on his hands.

Lots of it.

Etheridge gingerly lowered himself down the stairs and sat on the last step, stretching out his damaged leg and looking at the top of the range knee brace clamped around it. He was another man caught in the cross fire, his permanent crippling a ripple effect of Sam's actions. While he would never blame Sam, he knew it was just another cross that Sam bore.

The man had been racked by guilt ever since his son had been taken from him, and while he found redemption in every criminal he took off the street, there was no way back from the truth.

Sam had been an assassin for a secretive terrorist movement.

The deaths by his hands had helped set in motion a rise to power of a man who had lied to him. The files made for horrifying reading.

A man known as Yohan Henri, a French journalist had been killed by Sam seven months before the fateful night on the outskirts of Kabul. Henri had been extradited back to the country under the pretence of arrest in China, but the truth was far uglier. The man had discovered a viable link between the French, UK, and Chinese governments regarding questionable payments to an Afghanistan corporation.

Further digging unearthed potential ties to the Taliban.

While he sought safety and protection from his own government, the Maréchal de France, Pierre Ducard, had sanctioned his assassination with Wallace.

Sam had been given the job and as a convoy, transporting the prisoner through Strasbourg, turned through an enclosed road through the scenic countryside, Sam had sent a bullet through the windscreen, eliminating the driver and causing the Range Rover to spiral off the road, clipping a rock and flipping onto its side.

Henri had crawled from the wreckage, only to receive another pinpoint shot through the centre of his cranium, sending him crashing against the wreckage, his brains splattering the picturesque surroundings.

Sam had been congratulated at the time, another war monger eliminated before he could set off his reported plans to attack the centre of Paris.

What Sam had actually done was murder an innocent man who had turned over the wrong stone.

Etheridge waited patiently as Sam heaved into the toilet bowl, the vomit splattering the porcelain among anguished cries of fury.

The list of Wallace's accomplices and partners was petrifying, although Sam had helped his 'boss' to eliminate a couple, those who had been deemed as threats to his position.

Abdullah Bin Akbar was nothing more than a man trying to keep his family safe, after discovering a joint venture between Blackridge and the Taliban which would see a number of car bombs detonated within the city of Kabul, giving Blackridge the authority to interject and eventually hand the keys to the kingdom to the oppressive terrorist regime.

Ahmad Farukh had been one of the Taliban's top generals and a trusted enforcer for Wallace on that side of the world.

Abdullah Bin Akbar and his family's bodies were never found, the stone structure where Sam had been left for dead was burnt to the ground, their bodies nothing but ash. It was only at the behest of two of the other soldiers within Project Hailstorm that Sam made it out alive, the American soldiers refusing to leave a man behind.

The story was concocted that Sam had been shot by Bin Akbar, who then turned the gun on his family and them himself.

The world wouldn't look any further.

The man was painted as a terrorist by the man they

trusted most, and Sam received a heroic send off from the army and the matter was closed.

People didn't truly understand war until they lived in it, Etheridge knew that. It was a world he'd been unsuited for which is why his career in the Armed Forces had finished.

His skills were behind a desk, planted in front of a computer.

But Sam was a soldier.

The war was as much a part of him as breathing.

But as Sam flushed the toilet, washing away the bile and pain, he was symbolically washing away the past. The life he believed he'd lived, the honour for which he'd fought.

All of it gone.

Flushed down the drain by the sickening truth.

General Ervin Wallace's Blackridge was the largest terrorist cell in the world and Sam had been one of his chief weapons. Project Hailstorm had stripped the world back, spread fear through them all and laid the foundations for which Wallace would build his throne.

'You okay, Sam?' Etheridge spoke softly. With a slight discomfort, he hauled himself up via the bannister and shuffled through the hallway to the bathroom door. Sam was sat opposite the toilet, his back against the wall and his head back. His face was wet with tears, his hair damp with sweat. Taking long, deep breaths, Sam's eyes were closed and after a few minutes, he responded.

'I'm a murderer.' His words were racked with guilt.

'No, Sam,' Etheridge responded sternly. 'You're a soldier. One of the best. You were just following orders.'

Sam scoffed.

'Orders? I killed people, Paul. Innocent people who were actually doing what I believed I was. They were trying to save the world and I sent them to their graves because of it.' Sam slammed his fist down against the immaculate, marble tiles of Etheridge's plush bathroom. 'I should have done something.'

'Like what? How could you have known? I've read the files, Sam; they covered their tracks. Hell, they did a better job than even I could do. You are not a murderer, mate. You were just a guy who had the rug pulled like everyone else.'

Sam opened his eyes and turned to Etheridge. The broken stare caused Etheridge to shake, the pain in his friend's eyes was heartbreaking.

'My son died thinking that his dad was a hero,' Sam began, the words choking in his throat. 'He would draw pictures of me fighting bad guys and tell Lucy that I was saving the world.'

'You were his hero.'

'But I wasn't, was I?' Sam wiped his tears. 'I was murdering people. I was letting men like Wallace cover the world in fear and my son celebrated it. Lucy proudly displayed my medals in the home. They both thought so highly of what I did. But it was all a fucking lie.'

Etheridge ambled into the bathroom and theatrically lowered himself down, drawing a small smile from Sam.

'It wasn't a lie, Sam. Everything you have ever done, *you* did for the right reason. Everything you are doing, this fight you're raging, you need to see it through to the end. Marsden died for this information to get this far. Many others have died too, trying their best to show the world what the fuck is going on. So, you need to forgive the sins of your past, because they were never yours to make. You need to stand up, you need to fight, and you need to be the hero that your boy knew you were.'

Sam raised his eyebrows slightly, impressed with the pep talk. Etheridge pulled himself to a standing position via the towel rail and then extended a hand to Sam. There were no quips or jokes, the man's face was as serious as Sam had ever seen.

'Now are you going to fight or what?'

Sam took a few more breaths and looked up at his friend. Thinking about how broken his life was, he mourned for everything he'd lost.

His mentor.

His best friend.

His wife.

His son.

Now his career. Everything had been taken from him, but there were still a few things left. A few people, like Etheridge and Singh who still believed in him.

He had lost so much, but not the one thing that would keep him going.

The fight.

With one final exhale, Sam swung his arm up, clamping his hand around Etheridge's wrist and allowed his friend to haul him up. The room wobbled slightly, the dehydration kicking in and he offered his friend a smile.

'Thank you, Paul.' He gently patted his friend's shoulder. 'For everything.'

Etheridge nodded; their friendship had been forged when Sam had saved his life all those years ago. He was happy to return the favour.

'So…what now?'

'Right now, I need a beer,' Sam said dryly. 'And then we're going to burn Blackridge to the ground.'

———

The article had practically written itself.

Helal Miah had been watching the news all evening, open-mouthed at the chaos that had transpired at Liverpool Street Station. A day after his article had seen an avalanche of traffic hit *The Pulse* website, it was a vindication that something strange was a foot.

Sam Pope was at the scene, clearly in the midst of a brutal battle with an unknown man who had tried to end his life. Discovered among the carnage were three operatives, all of them with links to Blackridge.

They had been beaten badly. Undoubtedly by Sam and Helal had thrown open his laptop and let the words flow. It was a sensational story and one that he knew he was walking dangerously on the cusp of.

Further footage had emerged as the night went on of Amara Singh blasting a handgun into the air moments after Sam had fallen from the balcony. It had caused a mass panic, allowing Sam and Singh to disappear into the crowds and evade whoever the hell was after them.

Blackridge?

The Met Police?

Were they in it together?

The beauty of Helal's journalistic mind was nothing was out of reach. Speculative as it may be, he was beginning to piece together a very dangerous jigsaw, one which he hoped would shake the country almost as much as Sam's crusade. After everything Singh had told him, there were too many coincidences, too many of the same names linking together for there not to be an element of truth to it all.

As the evening turned into night, Helal was strapped to his chair, adding the final touches of drama to the most explosive article he'd ever written, a couple of empty energy drink cans littering his desk.

The article had everything in it.

A detailed look back over Sam's crusade, emphasising the links between the Met Police, Howell, and Frank Jackson. The disappearance of Sgt Colin Meyer not long after. The fall of the Kovalenko trafficking empire and the subsequent withdrawal of Mark Harris from the mayoral race. The emergence of Wallace and his increasing presence within the Met Police, his ties to Blackridge who had been present in Kiev, where Sam had burnt the final embers of the Kovalenkos.

The Blackridge bodies found outside of Naples a week ago while Italy had been the last known location of Sam.

It was all piecing together.

Wallace was hiding something. Blackridge was his shield.

Sam Pope was doing his level best to bust it wide open.

With a satisfying flick of his fingers, Helal signed his name to the article and sent it through to Nigel, knowing his boss would most likely have an aneurism at the wild claims he was making.

They would be liable for a lawsuit.

He could very well lose his job.

But with the same conviction Sam had when he faced the barrel of a gun, Helal believed in his words. He believed in the truth and was damn sure it was being hidden.

Just as he clicked send, there was a knock at his door. He sat upright, a gentle panic vibrating through his body. Hesitantly, he lifted himself from the chair and marched across his apartment, stopping to fetch a cricket bat which had only ever seen a batting cage once in their five-year relationship.

'Who is it?' he called out. There was no answer and slowly, he lifted his eye to the peephole.

The hallway was empty.

Shrugging his shoulders, he turned away from the door, only for the knock to return, this time with added venom.

Quickly, Helal reached for the handle, bat in hand and threw it open, hoping to terrify the young hoodlums clearly playing games.

He was welcomed by a hammer like fist to the face, the impact shattering his nose and breaking his glasses. As the shards of glass and stream of blood fell to the floor, he fell back into the room, tripping over his table, and collapsing to the floor, his head ringing and his eyes watering.

Ahmad Farukh stepped in, taking one final look into the hallway of the apartment block, happy that the coast was clear.

Helal rolled onto his front, helplessly trying to crawl back towards his office to reach for his phone.

It was an empty gesture of survival.

With his face as emotionless as his soul, Farukh shut the door and made his way towards his target.

CHAPTER TWENTY-ONE

Singh took a large sip of her gin and let the alcohol work its calming magic.

Since leaving the station amidst the panic she'd caused, the rest of her day had become a blur. Whether it was fear or adrenaline, or maybe a mixture of both, she'd managed to slip away from Liverpool Street Station and the carnage of the situation. She'd made her way on foot back down towards Farringdon, the trainlines all brought to a grinding halt by the police as they locked down one of the UK's busiest stations.

The public would be furious, their afternoon out in the sunny capital ruined by her actions, but she did what was necessary. Whoever that man was that confronted them by the lift, he was certainly dangerous, evidenced by the state in which she'd seen Sam.

He had been bloodied and beaten and the man had no qualms at all in hurling Sam to his potential death. While the collision with the confectionary stand must have hurt like hell, it was a damn sight better than a full-on drop to the concrete.

Sam was lucky to be alive.

And, as her hand trembled as she lifted her glass, she realised so was she.

As she'd meandered through the backstreets of London, she'd stopped to withdraw three hundred pounds from her account, maxing out the withdrawal limit, but made sure she ventured further. In all likelihood, her peers would link her to the scene of the chaos and would be looking for her.

Ashton would make it a priority.

If she needed an excuse to finally shove Singh through the exit door, she now had one. In fact, she probably had enough to build a case to put Singh behind bars.

Knowing she couldn't go home, Singh continued through the sunshine until it began to descend, walking through the beauty of Russell Square, amazed at the greenery smack bang in the centre of the city. Kids ran gleefully through the fountains, as parents gathered on the grass, joking with each other as they sipped Pimm's and shared snacks.

Normal lives lived by normal people.

For the first time in her own life, Singh envied them. She envied her sister; the tranquil family life she'd settled into was a world away from her own.

Once a promising detective, she was now a wanted woman. Not only had she bitten the hand that fed her, but she'd also enraged an entirely different beast.

Wallace had sent Blackridge to the station to catch Sam and judging by the gun pointed at her face by the agent at the lift, she was now expendable. They would be watching her home like a hawk.

Things could never go back.

Not while Sam's war waged on.

She finished her drink and motioned to the barman for another; the young man offering her a sorrowful smile as he obliged. The Lord John Russell was a small pub just off the Bloomsbury shopping arcade near Euston and afforded her enough of a hiding place for now. The narrow alleyway that ran alongside the pub was packed with locals, all of them enjoying the humid evening and filling the tunnel with drunken banter and cigarette smoke.

As she sat against the old, wooden bar, she'd already rebuffed the lecherous advances of two separate men, both of them offering her a good time but unlikely to follow through.

As she paid for her drink, she felt anger at having to pay in cash.

It was a reminder of her situation, that she had to stay off the radar and it filled her with rage. Sam had used her as bait. He explained to her why, trapped in the small, metal lift with her, but it still hurt.

While Sam may have been a good man, he'd still put her in harm's way.

A means to an end.

As she furiously knocked back her drink, she wondered if that was really what had angered her. That, or the kiss they'd shared. That among all the mayhem, the violence, and the fight that had ruined her life, there was a glimpse of a life she could have had.

What annoyed her most was that she cared about him.

That after everything, from the humiliation he put her through at Etheridge's house, to the beating and near death she suffered in the port, she still cared for a man that her entire life's work had told her she should despise.

With the alcohol now taking full effect, she stumbled from her bar stool and weaved her way through the pokey establishment, sliding past a group of guys who offered her a crass night with all four of them.

She responded with a middle finger, before buckling over the small step and stumbling out onto the pavement outside. The groups of friends, penned in on the benches that framed the doorway, cheered in the sarcastic way all British pub goers did.

She was too drunk to care.

Too angry to feel embarrassed.

As she stumbled back to the cheap bed-and-breakfast she'd already paid for, she stopped in at the off-licence, buying another litre bottle of gin and some tonic water, letting the shop keeper keep the generous change she got from her twenty.

She didn't care.

All she wanted was to get back to her room, drink away the myriad of confusing thoughts swarming in her head and blackout, hoping the next morning would bring about change.

It was unlikely, but it was better than wallowing in the ashes of her life.

As she kicked open the door to her grotty room, she dumped her jacket on the rickety chair opposite the vanity mirror and dropped onto the uncomfortable bed. The room spun, the alcohol playing havoc with her sense of balance and she closed her eyes, taking a deep breath. In the room next door, she could hear the TV, the occupant watching an action movie. The sound of gunfire and explosions wasn't welcoming, given the current circumstances, so Singh reached for a glass from the tray, ignoring the meagre offering of coffee and tea. She unscrewed the gin and poured in a generous helping, before pulling out the tonic. Just as she unscrewed the cap, her phone vibrated in her pocket.

Despite her drunken state, curiosity took over and she pulled up the message.

We need to talk. Privately. Come alone.

It was Helal Miah.

Singh sat upright, her interest piqued, and she slammed the tonic down, spilling it slightly.

Another message followed.

It was his address.

Considering everything she'd told him, his article that had already spread across social media like wildfire and the day's events, she imagined he'd connected some dots.

Maybe he had found something?

Possibly about Project Hailstorm.

With jittery fingers, she typed her brief reply.

On my way.

With the units of alcohol heavily outweighing her better judgement, she slid her arms back into her leather jacket, collected her phone and money, and headed for the door, trying her best to clear her head and work out her route to his location.

———

Farukh placed the phone down on the side table and finally afforded himself a smile.

When Wallace had passed on the details, he wasn't sure the plan would work. There were too many unknown variables for it to run completely smoothly. While he was a man of terrifying action, Farukh was also a man of finer details.

You didn't evade numerous governments and bounty contracts by being reckless.

But the stakes had been raised since Sam escaped him and as a man unaccustomed to failure, he was keen to step outside of his comfort zone.

Helal had offered up no fight. It was easy as swatting a fly. Slowly, he turned back to his captive.

All the furniture in Helal's front room had been pushed back to the walls, providing Farukh with enough space. After he'd floored the man upon opening the door, Farukh had made a show of shoving them all out of the way, circling the fallen man as he crawled pathetically towards the hallway. At one point, Helal had reached out to him in a lame attempt of mercy.

Farukh had crushed the man's hand under his boot.

The bones snapped, and as Helal roared in pain, Farukh had hoisted him to his feet and slapped him, telling him his silence would save him pain.

There was no retaliation. Just the fearful resignation that he was in the presence of a dangerous man.

Moments later, Helal was strapped to a chair in the centre of the room and Farukh had demanded Helal contact Amara Singh. At first, the chivalry was commendable.

Stupid, but commendable.

Farukh responded to it with some sickening punches, each one expertly landing in all of Helal's major organs, all carrying the velocity of a sledgehammer swing. The plucky journalist coughed up blood, begged for forgiveness, but Farukh demanded the same again.

When Helal refused, Farukh brandished two handheld curved blades from his belt. Like two crescent moons, they shimmered under the light of Helal's apartment.

Farukh warned him he was about to seriously hurt him, but Helal foolishly stayed silent. Farukh ensured it, by stuffing a sock in the man's mouth before sliding the blade down the side of his head, severing the top of his ear in three easy slices.

Helal screamed in agony, the sock muffling his cries for help and as the blood poured from the wound, Farukh mockingly held the severed ear in front of his eyes.

Helal relented, telling Farukh where his phone was and the code to unlock it.

Amara was listed under 'Source' and Farukh sent the message, luring her to her fate and Helal felt sick.

Pain and guilt.

A horrid combination. As they waited, Farukh wandered over to the corner of the room and began to inspect Helal's impressive home entertainment system. The large TV stood proudly on the oak stand, along with two games consoles and another small, electronic box that Farukh didn't understand.

What he did see, however, were a lot of cables.

Helal, blinking through the pain, watched in puzzlement as Farukh detached as many cables as he could, before tying them together. He was systematic in his process, pulling each knot taut, before moving onto the next. There was a time where those electronic devices were his most cherished possessions, and he was sure his protective attitude over them was one of the reasons his last girlfriend left him.

Now, his only concern was surviving, but the realist within told him it was unlikely.

He had intruded in a world where he didn't belong.

He had stumbled into a fight that wasn't his.

It was always the innocent who got caught in the crosshairs. As Farukh finished tying the final knot, he turned to Helal, his face a blank slate, framed by a thick, greying beard.

'You know I do not like guns,' he began calmly, feeding the cable back around itself. 'I find them too easy. They make a loud noise but kill easy. Anyone can kill with gun. You just point at the head and pull. One pull. That is it. No fight. No struggle. Simple.'

Helal's eyes widened with fear and he struggled against the straps of his chair. It was no use and Farukh turned to him, showing him the makeshift noose he'd made out of Helal's own equipment.

'But you hang a man, you truly see the fight. You see the need for man to survive.' Slowly, Farukh lowered the noose over Helal's head, allowing it to hang loosely around his chest. Helal, through tears, tried to beg for mercy. 'You can tell a lot about a man from how he struggles. I know you only fifteen minutes, but I know you will try. You won't try for long, there is no fight in you. But to watch a man fight for his dying breath is one of life's beautiful moments. Like a waterfall. Or a childbirth.'

Farukh ran the cable around the door frame, before securing it tightly to the large wardrobe that stood in Helal's bedroom. It pulled the cable a little tighter, the plastic coating pressing against Hela's neck. Farukh returned, stood in front of Helal and once again, afforded himself a smile.

Helal begged for mercy.

There was none.

'Appreciate each breath.' Farukh reached into his pocket and pulled out his cigarettes. 'You do not have many left.'

Farukh lit the cigarette and stared at Helal. As tears flooded down his cheeks, Helal let his mind flow back through any cherished memories he had. A few relationships during the good times. The rare occasion he got along with his dad. The moment he won an award for a hard-hitting piece on poverty within the country. All the cherished moments he would take with him.

He sat in the chair and gently wept, knowing he was about to leave it all behind.

The Hangman of Baghdad watched him intently, slowly puffing his cigarette and preparing himself for another look at man's fight for survival.

CHAPTER TWENTY-TWO

It had been a hell of a weekend and Etheridge stood at the window of the converted loft, the cool spring air filtering through and cooling him down. Being trapped in the room with eight monitors and several servers soon got warm and while Etheridge enjoyed a sauna as much as the next man, he needed some fresh air.

Sam was asleep.

After the startling revelations of Project Hailstorm, Etheridge had decided to change the topic of conversation. They would get to it, he'd promised Sam, but when his mind was clear.

They had a couple more beers, enough to take the edge off the sickening truth and soon, tiredness laid claim to Sam's body. He had been through the wars that day, with his fight through the station not only resulting in his face being busted open but also taking a swan dive off a balcony.

Sam was lucky he hadn't been paralysed.

Or worse.

But as Sam slept through the pain, both physical and

emotional, Etheridge looked out into the dark fields that backed onto his mansion.

Life was certainly different now.

Gone were the days of board meetings and small talk. The endless grind of traffic jams and demanding customers. A trophy wife, who wanted to know how much money he had every week.

Now, he was hiding in plain sight, helping the UK's most wanted man go after its most protected.

He had never felt more alive.

The stiffness in his right knee reminded him the peril he'd faced to arrive at the moment. He was only a matter of metres away from where he was beaten, tortured, and then shot, the bullet shattering his kneecap beyond a full recovery.

But soldiers wore their scars proudly, and while he wasn't on the frontline of the war like Sam, he knew he had a role to play.

He wasn't pulling the trigger on the gun, but he was damn sure going to make sure Sam had everything he needed to be able to.

As he sipped at his coffee, Etheridge thought about the last time he got a full night's sleep. Since Sam had returned two days ago, he'd been working round the clock. It would eventually catch-up on him, it always did, but for now, the regular caffeine and adrenaline was enough to get by.

They were so close.

They had the access to the files, proving beyond all doubt that Ervin Wallace was not only the world's biggest terrorist, but had also used the UK government as a smoke screen to portray himself as a hero.

It was damning evidence, enough to put the man behind bars for the rest of his life.

But the cyber security attached to the files was unlike

anything Etheridge had seen, which frustrated and impressed him in equal measure.

While they'd worked around the fingerprint access parameters, the files had what he'd described as an inbuilt 'anchor directive'. The term was lost on Sam, but essentially, it pinned the file to its hard drive.

Meaning they couldn't transfer the files from the USB stick.

Sam had suggested sending the USB stick to the BBC, allow them to break the news and sit back and watch Wallace get brought to his knees. It would be unsatisfying on a personal level, but justice would be done. Etheridge quickly dismissed the idea on the grounds of the security of the files.

As they couldn't be manipulated, there was no way of proving the legitimacy of them. Wallace's reckless pursuit of Sam was evident enough, but he could easily dismiss them as fakes.

They needed a confession.

Etheridge had clocked the sparkle in Sam's eye as he suggested it, knowing that after discovering Wallace was the man who left him for dead all those years ago, Sam was aching for his chance to face the man.

But it wouldn't be easy.

Etheridge had pulled up all the information he could on Wallace's location, with little of it providing useful. He had moved from his usual abode to a remote location, a government safehouse which was not recorded on any database that Etheridge could gain access to. While he was running a few automatic programs to check other databases for anything resembling a bread crumb, the chances were slimmer than none.

What he did have, was access to government instructions to provide a motorcade for an emergency COBRA meeting first thing Monday morning. With Sam's emergence, the presence of Blackridge, and the mass panic caused at Liverpool Street Station earlier that day, Wallace had been summoned for a discussion with the prime minister and his cabinet to discuss the potential threat.

Sam was being painted as a potential threat, but surely, Wallace's conduct would be brought to light.

That wasn't enough for Sam, and as he yawned, he told Etheridge to plot the exact route and fill him in when he woke up.

Now, as the spring evening developed a slight chill, Etheridge stepped away from the window, lifted his arms above his head and stretched his back out. He had spent a small fortune on making his desk and seat as comfortable as possible, but there was only so much money could buy.

After a few more moments of stretching, he sat back down at the desk, took a swig from his coffee and went back to it.

———

As the train filtered into another Tube station, Singh took a few more deep breaths, leant forward and closed her eyes. Her drunken stupor had slowly alleviated, leaving nothing but a thumping headache and the very real possibility of projectile vomit as one of the final trains on what had been a strange Sunday made its way to the station nearest to Helal's location. As the crow flies, the distance from Euston to Perivale wasn't huge, but navigating the underground tube system, while drunk had proven a harder task than Singh had anticipated.

She'd taken a train two stops in the wrong direction, before cursing herself loudly, drawing the attention of a number of commuters making their way home.

She looked like a drunk which had angered her but as

she stumbled through the station to correct her mistake, she realised she was near to rock bottom.

Luckily for her, a small off-licence, no more than a shutter in the wall, was still open and she bought two bottles of water. She downed one in front of the man, before hurrying to the platform for her train.

Now, as she stepped off at Perivale, she felt her body shake as the alcoholic aftermath took hold.

She was glad she wasn't on a timer.

Helal could wait.

Stepping out of the station, she took a nice, long breath of fresh air, the sharp chill snapping into her lungs and waking her up. She'd planned on getting an Uber, but with a kebab shop open next door to the station, and the prospect of a walk through the brisk evening, she decided against it.

The chips she bought soaked up a large amount of alcohol, the greasy carbs acting like a sponge. She still felt like crap, but Singh was at least functioning as she made her way to Helal's apartment block. As she pushed open the gate, she was pleasantly surprised by the immaculate garden, wondering how much a digital journalist made to afford such a plush residence.

At the door, she scanned the list of names by the buttons, located the one for H. Miah and pressed it, the buzzer echoing sharply through the speaker.

Without a word, Helal unlocked the main door, an ear-piercing sound echoing from the timer before it relocked. Singh stepped in, cursing the lack of elevator to the second floor as she clambered up the steps. While she felt better, her body was drained and she paused a few times, needing to steady her legs.

Hopefully, Helal would have some more food on the go.

Eventually, after what felt like a trek up Everest, Singh

arrived on the second floor, marching down the corridor until she came to Helal's door.

With a shaking hand, she knocked.

———

Knowing you're about to die is a horrible feeling. Helal had come to terms with his imminent death, knowing that his torturer was correct.

There was no fight in him.

In the world which he'd discovered to be a violent and terrifying place, there were only a select few who could fight back. Who could fight for survival. He was sure there were plenty of parents who would run into oncoming traffic to save their children, but to fight for their own survival?

What could Helal have done?

The man who had brutally and systematically tortured him was clearly well versed in it, with a terrifying bulk and strength that Helal would never be able to match. If he had fought back, the man would have beaten him easily and, due to the disrespect or the perceived lack of fear, would most likely put him through much worse.

As it was, this was the path of least resistance.

He had had tried, valiantly, to hold back on the information, to keep Singh's name safe.

But the pain was too much.

The horror too real.

As Helal felt a tear run down his face, the Hangman's voice echoed from behind him, the vile stench of cigarette smoke clinging to each word.

'It is no shame,' he said softly. 'Many men believe they are strong willed. They will not break. But they always do.'

A sharp buzzer broke his speech, indicating Singh had arrived and was hoping to be buzzed up. With the sock still lodged in his mouth, Helal tried in vain to scream out to her, hoping she would hear.

His muffled cries fell to the ground, unheard.

Farukh marched across the apartment and without uttering a single word, unlocked the main door and lured Singh into the building. With one final glance back to Helal, he offered a respectful nod.

Not an apology. Just an acceptance that it was he who had killed him.

Helal tried to struggle but stopped quickly. Once Farukh had sent the text to Singh and placed the noose around his neck, he'd leathered Helal with a few more sickening right hooks, dislodging teeth and cracking ribs.

Freshly beaten, Helal was in no state to resist and the Hangman freed him from his chair, letting the poor journalist flop to the ground. With no furniture for him to reach for, Helal lay in agony, a sad acceptance of his fate.

The horror became real enough as Farukh hoisted him up to his feet by the noose, pulling it tightly across his windpipe and Helal squirmed for air.

'Up,' Farukh demanded, and Helal wept as he took a step up onto the chair, before his other foot followed. He heard the roar of the masking tape as his attacker wrapped it around his wrists, pinning his arms behind him.

He was about to be executed.

His attacker was the Hangman.

Literally.

As his hopes of survival withered away, he watched the burly assailant attach string to the leg of the chair and then rolled it out, until it just about reached the front door. A quick knot later, and Helal's fate rested on the movement of a front door.

As soon as it opened, the chair would move, and his balance would go.

Helal felt the cable tighten around his neck, as Farukh pulled it tighter, ensuring the ties were in place.

They were.

Helal literally had a few moments left.

He quickly thought of his family, uttering silent good-byes to them all. He hoped that he'd helped or heard people throughout his life.

That people would remember that he cared.

He regretted not settling down. Not having a child.

He wondered which places he should have gone to, and who of his previous girlfriends could have been a wife.

As he heard the gentle knock on the door, Helal shed one final tear. He took a deep breath, stood straight, and exhaled.

He was ready.

Farukh stood to the side of the door and with a flick of his mighty wrist, he turned the handle, taking the door off its latch. The suggestion of an invite. Singh obliged, pushing the door open with reckless abandon.

'Hello?' she began, before her eyes widened. The chair was pulled out from under his feet and Helal dropped a few inches, the cable snapping tight around his neck and shutting off his air supply.

His eyes bulged, his throat wretched a silent scream of pain, and he shook as his body hung from the ceiling.

'Helal...' Amara took a step forward before everything went dark. A black cloth sack was slid over her head then wrenched back with enough power to behead her. She stumbled back, her balance gone, and then with a mighty swing, she felt herself propelled into the air.

Farukh slammed her headfirst into the wall, the impact sending her limp.

As he watched her slump to the floor, he took out his mobile phone. He bent down and removed the cloth, revealing an unconscious Singh, whose right eye was starting to swell, and a trickle of blood skirted down from her eyebrow.

Farukh took the picture and sent it to Wallace, before popping the cloth back onto her head. When she awoke, he wanted her to be suffocated by the darkness, it would only add to the fear.

Fear meant she would listen.

Which would make it a lot easier.

As Singh lay motionless beneath him, Farukh reached into his pocket and lit himself a cigarette. Closing the door, hiding his sadism from the world, he turned casually back to the horror playing out before him.

Helal had slowed his struggle, the final strains of life being squeezed from him. He looked to Farukh with an acceptance of death, his eyeballs a bloodshot red. His neck was purple, a few veins pressing against his skin.

Farukh blew smoke into the room, his face blank, as if ending the man's life meant nothing to him.

As far as Farukh was concerned, it was just part of the job. Helal had painted the target himself by typing the words Project Hailstorm and considering the almighty mess Wallace had made, Farukh was leaving little to chance.

Sam may have got away, but he would meet him again.

Then, he would kill Sam and he would kill the woman.

Wallace, he would keep alive.

But there would be no more chances.

Helal jolted one final time, his heart stopping, and the final strands of life left him. Swinging gently from the ceiling, he looked as peaceful as Farukh had ever seen a man.

'*Aljulad bin Baghdad.*'

The Hangman of Baghdad.

Farukh stubbed his cigarette out on the wall and then

made his way to the kitchen. It was going to be awhile before the trade would happen and he was hungry.

He wanted to be at full strength the next time he came face to face with Sam Pope.

As next time would be the last time.

CHAPTER TWENTY-THREE

Control.

It was something General Ervin Wallace had craved ever since he put on the camouflaged uniform of the United Kingdom armed forces and he'd fought, killed, and betrayed for it. Control was power and with that came fear and respect in equal measure.

When people respected you, they listened.

When people feared you, they obeyed.

It was something he had been accustomed to for nearly forty years and now, as Ashton writhed on top of him, the bed sheets wrapped around her waist, her exposed chest bouncing with each thrust, he could feel it returning to him.

The control.

The power.

It had been just after eleven when he received the text message from Farukh. While he didn't want to know the full details of the mission, the bloodied, unconscious face of Amara Singh was enough for him to know that the pendulum had swung back in their favour. Wallace had sent the image on to his operatives working in the Hub, telling them to trace the number on Singh's phone from earlier that afternoon and make contact.

He wanted to be on the other end of the phone when Sam answered, and he wanted to hear the pain in the man's voice when he told him he had lost.

That Singh would be brutally killed unless he handed over the files.

To celebrate his newly returned mojo, he made a call to Ashton, inviting her over under the false pretences of discussing the events of that afternoon. They both knew it was a lie, and as the car arrived to pick her up, she'd wondered if her infatuation with the General was worth the emptiness she felt when he dismissed her after their sessions.

Wallace didn't care.

All he saw was an attractive woman who was pulled in by his magnetic stature.

Throughout the past few months, ever since Sam Pope had decided to try to destroy everything he'd worked so hard to build, Ashton had been a chief ally. While her command of some of her more irritating staff had left a lot to be desired, Wallace had enjoyed using the Metropolitan Police as a more local branch of Blackridge.

But now, with the whole situation under control and what would likely be less than twenty-four hours before he had the USB stick in his hands, Farukh gone for ever, and Sam Pope most likely dead, he had little use for Ashton.

This would be the last time he invited her over to massage his ego, and he contemplated whether he would cut ties completely. He had dangled the carrot of his backing when the Commissioner seat became available and for everything she'd done for him, he would most likely give it.

It would pay to have the Commissioner of the Metropolitan Police at his beck and call.

After a few moments of awkward silence, Ashton excused herself from the bed and made her way to the bathroom, and Wallace could hear the shower burst into life. He took himself to the balcony, looking at the over-stuffed ashtray from the afternoon. He chortled.

How quickly things changed.

Earlier that afternoon he was foaming at the mouth, his rage threatening to derail everything he'd worked for. But now, as he stood, his thick arms resting on the balcony railing, he smiled.

This time, he lit a cigar in success.

Ashton soon joined him on the balcony, dressed and ready to leave. She put an apprehensive hand on his shoulder.

'I hope tomorrow goes well,' she said hopefully, offering him a smile.

'It will.' Wallace puffed his cigar. 'The government want to know what the plan is. By this time tomorrow, Sam Pope will be dealt with.'

'Really?' Ashton raised her eyebrow. 'How can you be so sure?'

Wallace took a long puff and stared out into the darkness. His COBRA meeting tomorrow would be a formality. He would lay out the plan to the prime minister and his cabinet, and while they would baulk at the lengths he'd gone to, they would green light it.

Matters such as this were left to men like Wallace.

The men who were not afraid to get things done.

As he tapped the ash over the edge of the railing, he contemplated telling Ashton his method. How would she react to know that one of her own, DI Singh, was currently in his capture? That she'd been beaten and was facing the very real prospect of death.

The ripple effect of Project Hailstorm coming to light threatened way more than just a few lives.

International relationships would be broken.

The very real threat of retaliation could see the country head to war for the first time in nearly eighty years.

What was one life to save millions?

'This question may seem redundant considering the success rate your team has had so far.' Wallace's tone was nasty. 'But how do you catch a man like Sam Pope?'

Offended, Ashton shrugged before offering her suggestions.

'CCTV footage? Expert analysts?'

'No. You take something he cares about. You take it, you threaten it, and you lure him to it.'

Ashton shuffled uncomfortably on the spot. Wallace was a powerful yet secretive man. She was under no illusions that he did things that crossed the line of right and wrong. His closet undoubtedly had skeletons, more than most, but his position required it.

While she didn't fully trust him, she did trust him to put the country first.

Wallace's phone rumbled and the text message drew a smile to his face. He flashed her a quick glance and a stern nod, his way of effectively drawing their night to a close. Ashton, cursing herself for once again rushing to his bed as soon as he clicked his fingers, marched to the door of the apartment where a driver would be on hand to take her home.

Wallace waited until the door had closed behind her, sneered and then selected the number he'd been sent, knowing the phone would be answered on the first ring.

———

Neither Etheridge nor Sam said anything for the first minute or so after the message had come through.

Somehow, Blackridge had reverse engineered Etheridge's secure line into Singh's phone and located his number. As impressive as that was, the message that was sent through was haunting, drawing both men into a shocked silence.

The image depicted Amara Singh, sprawled on the floor of an unknown room, her right eye swollen, dripping with blood from the cut that sliced her eyebrow.

She was clearly unconscious.

She was in a shit tonne of trouble.

Under the horrifying image of their acquaintance, the message simply said:

Answer the phone when I call.

Guilt had been an emotion that Sam had wrestled with so many times, he considered it a tag team partner. His entire life, ever since he lost his son, had been moulded by it, by the nagging feeling that things were his fault. The blame lay at his door, as he failed to protect his son.

He had spent his whole career protecting others, under the false pretence of peace, but he'd failed to keep his son safe. Ever since then, every criminal he'd put down or every bad guy he'd killed, had helped him claim a little bit of himself back. With the discovery of Project Hailstorm and the atrocious reality of his career, Sam knew he had a lot to make up for, and that the guilt would once again hang from his neck like a pendant.

He felt guilty for the death of his best friend, Theo Walker.

He felt the guilt of Adrian Pearce's career meandering to a disappointing end.

The guilt of the permanent disability that would hinder Etheridge's life forever.

And now Amara Singh. Beaten and held captive by a man who ruthlessly clung to power. They wouldn't have long, and even then, she was as good as dead.

She'd dug too far, drawn into a world that she didn't belong and once again, the blame lay at Sam's door.

He was tired of feeling guilty.

His fists clenched as the phone rang and Etheridge leant forward and clicked the green button and slid the call onto speaker phone.

'Where is she?' Sam demanded, crossing his muscular arms across his chest.

'I take it we are skipping the pleasantries?' Wallace chuckled, revelling in the control.

'We are a long way past that.'

'She has twenty-four hours to live, Sam.'

'This has nothing to do with her.'

'Quite right. This has nothing to do with her, Sam. It has everything to do with you.' Wallace's tone had changed, snapping into a venomous snarl. 'You chose not to hand over the files, you chose to fight back in Rome, and now you are the reason this has gone this far.'

'If you hurt her...'

'What? Sam? You're going to kill me?' Wallace scoffed. 'Let's save the macho bullshit. You want Singh, I want the USB stick. You have twenty-four hours. You can reach me on this number.'

'I know the truth, Wallace.' Sam spoke through gritted teeth. 'Project Hailstorm. All the lies. The bullets you put through me. I know everything.'

'But you can't prove it,' Wallace responded smugly. 'Bury it, Sam. Before it buries you. Twenty-four hours, gentlemen. I'll be waiting.'

The line went dead.

Sam turned and slammed his fist against the wall in anger, before raising both hands to his head. Every possibility was a dead end and his muscles tensed with frustration.

'Check mate.' Etheridge sighed, picking up his phone

and sliding it into his pocket. Crest fallen, he limped back towards his desk, reaching for the USB stick. Sam's eyes lit up.

'Wait.'

'It's over, Sam. He has Singh. He'll kill her.'

'He'll kill her the second he has the USB stick. And me. But what does Wallace value more than the stick?'

Etheridge shrugged.

'Power?'

'Himself.' Sam's eyes twinkled fiendishly.

'I don't follow.'

'You said he had a meeting first thing tomorrow morning, right?'

Etheridge glanced down at the watch strapped to his wrist.

'Well, technically it is tomorrow, so yeah, he has a COBRA meeting in a few hours.'

'You can pull up his journey plans, right?' Sam turned towards the door, and Etheridge connected the dots.

'Jesus, Sam. You're going after Wallace?'

'You're damn right I am.' Sam stopped, looking back, his face as serious as Etheridge had ever seen. 'You're right, Paul, this has gone too far. The only thing that Wallace will trade for Singh's life is his own. I take Wallace, he frees Singh and the rest I'll figure out as we go.'

'What about you?' Etheridge asked as Sam slid his arms into his jacket.

'This is my fight, Paul. Let me fight it.'

'This is crazy,' Etheridge said with a sigh, looking back at the grid of screens that adorned his wall. With access to all the databases he could imagine and the ability to traverse them undetected. With an almost limitless bank account, he had the resources to do anything. Be anything. With a smile, he turned back to Sam. 'I'm in.'

Sam extended his arm and Etheridge clapped his hand around it, cementing their agreement.

'First things first, I need to know which of my safe houses the police hit while I was away,' Sam commanded. 'I'm going to need some fire power.'

Etheridge was already back at his computer, looking over the details.

'You're not wrong. Apparently, the itinerary says that Wallace drives in the middle of a three-car motorcade, with two Blackridge operatives riding with him, and three in each of the others. Jesus, he's got his own private army.'

'He's going to need it,' Sam promised, heading towards the door.

They only had a few hours, but it was their final hope. Without Wallace, there was no saving Singh. They would put two bullets in her the second they had the stick and they would never find the body. If they didn't kill Sam too, maybe they'd put her blood on his hands, but either way, there was no other outcome.

Without Wallace, they had lost.

Sam stomped down the stairs towards the front door, his phone buzzing.

Etheridge had already located a lock-up that the police had yet to discover, and Sam was hopeful it would still be untouched. He needed all the weaponry he could lay his hands on. But that wasn't all.

He knew he had to make a phone call; one he didn't want to make but couldn't think of any other solution.

Etheridge needed to stay in the house. Sam needed him on point, watching the roads and ensuring a clear oversight of the mission at hand.

The phone call was one he was dreading, but as he pulled open the front door to the house, Etheridge appeared at the top the stairs, his face fraught with fear.

'This is suicide, Sam.'

'It's our only shot.' Sam turned back to face his friend. 'I have to save her, Paul. This is my fight. I have to end it.'

Etheridge nodded, a begrudging understanding.

'Say you do get her back, then what? What are you going to do then?'

Sam turned on his heel and marched out of the house, leaving Etheridge with a very clear answer.

'What I do best.'

CHAPTER TWENTY-FOUR

It was hard to measure success before the event.

Wallace had had a few hours' sleep after his successful phone call to Sam, the terms laid out plainly for his adversary. While he had no doubt that Sam and Etheridge would be looking for some kind of way out, he knew he had them where he wanted them.

He had Singh, her life now tied to whether Sam Pope would do the right thing.

Wallace knew him well enough. He had recruited him when he was just a boy, an innocent young man who watched his father pass away, a life spent in the military. He was easy pickings but instead of just being another grunt under his command, Sam had developed into one of the deadliest soldiers the UK had ever seen.

But beyond all that, Sam had never lost the sense of morality, something Wallace had willingly sacrificed years ago. In a way, he envied Sam's commitment to good, but for now, he would prey on it.

Sam wouldn't let Singh die.

He wasn't capable of making the hard sacrifices. It was what Sam never understood, and while the reports of

Project Hailstorm may have made for horrifying reading, there was more to it than that. Yes, Wallace's wallet had grown fatter and the power he wielded made him near on unreachable, but the world was a safer place.

Terrorists, sponsored by the government, were less likely to be a threat.

In Wallace's mind, it made sense. The government looked the other way, allowing the General to police the world, ensuring the country was safe and the breadcrumb trail ended a long way from their door.

But Sam was a threat.

Not just to Wallace's safety and reputation, but to the government. To the international security of the country.

They would want him dealt with.

As the Range Rover turned the corner and began its smooth passage across Tower Bridge, Wallace felt a sense of pride as he looked out over the sleepy city of London. Beyond the odd fitness fanatic, there was nobody on the streets at five in the morning. The roads were clear too, the first buses of the day yet to depart from their various garages and Wallace was enjoying the calming journey.

The sex with Ashton had been enjoyable, the following sleep uninterrupted. Now, in the middle of a three-car motorcade heading to the remote location for the COBRA meeting, Wallace could afford himself a smile.

The coffee in the flask mug was still hot, and he sipped it gently, the piping caffeine stinging the back of his throat as he swallowed. The sun, slowly beginning to peak through the buildings like a child playing peek-a-boo, bounced off the murky waters of the Thames, the reflection basking the river in a stunning glow.

The city truly was beautiful, Wallace thought. Strip back the cars and the hordes of people. Pull it back to its bare bones and it was a tremendous reflection of what the country was capable of.

The country he'd sworn to protect and did so with ruthless efficiency.

It was a stark reminder of what Wallace would have to do. He would give assurances to those in power, then arrange the meet.

Singh for the files. Once they'd been destroyed, Singh would be disposed of and Sam would be arrested. Hell, he would even let Ashton have the credit. It would be the making of her and while Wallace had little interest in another sexual encounter with the woman, she was just another pawn he was moving into place.

Wallace would be in the clear.

Sam would be dealt with.

Singh would be gone.

No more headaches. No more problems.

A large grin spread across his freshly shaved face, as he thought about returning to his home, to the normalities he was accustomed to and the success he would taste.

He always won.

As the Range Rover passed through the tunnel of the stunning towers that leant themselves to the bridge's name, shadows bathed the vehicle. The mighty suspension bridge was locked in place, allowing an easy passage across the Thames and Wallace peered out at the magnificent tower ahead. He could understand the appeal to the tourists, the floods of people who flock to the iconic landmark on a daily basis were usually spellbound by its beauty. He didn't blame them and as the car passed through the other tower and back out into the sunshine, Wallace felt a renewed sense of British pride.

Through the windscreen, he could see the car ahead. He noticed the small, round object bounce in front of the car. It took a second for him to realise it was a grenade, but before he could say anything, the entire bridge shook. The grenade exploded, decimating the front of the motorcade in a fiery ball of scrap metal and flailing limbs.

The blast sent a shockwave back, shattering the windows of the two cars in pursuit and slashing the skin of the passengers. Wallace's driver slammed on the brakes, pulled on the wheel with all his might in an attempt to avoid the fiery remains of the front car.

The car behind slammed into theirs and the entire motorcade came to a violent halt.

———

Sam had watched from the side of the tower as the cars had pulled onto the bridge. He hadn't slept all night, his venture out to his safehouse in Greenwich had taken up most of the evening, but he was happy to find his storage bin uninterrupted. Ever since he'd gone missing after taking down the Kovalenko empire, his flat and a number of his safe houses discovered. After Theo's death, Sam had dug up what they'd called his 'rainy day fund', a bag of high-powered weapons that was buried in Theo's garden. After Theo's funeral, Sam had committed himself to a life of fighting crime and one of the plus sides of taking on organised crime is they were armed.

Throughout a number of his raids, Sam had amassed a fine collection of rifles and handguns, enough to ensure he had a number of weapon stores dotted around the city. The one in Greenwich was one of the smaller ones, but still, three grenades, a Beretta 92 pistol, and an SA80 Assault Rifle.

A small arsenal.

But in Sam's arms, it was enough to bring down an empire.

There was no point returning to Etheridge's, so Sam made his way to a twenty-four-hour coffee shop at a petrol garage and got himself a couple of coffees and a sandwich. It didn't taste particularly great, but it was enough to keep him going.

Etheridge called him, gave him the details of where he needed to be and when.

Tower Bridge.

Five past five.

That gave him just over an hour.

It wasn't much to prepare, but there was no other choice. Wallace held all the cards and even if they followed his instructions, Sam knew that Singh wouldn't survive.

The only way to keep her alive was to raise the stakes.

To go all in.

They needed Wallace, and as Sam rolled the grenade onto the road an hour later, he was damn sure going to get him.

As soon as he rolled the explosive onto the street, Sam dove back and ducked behind the base of the tower, his fingers pressed to his ears. The ground shook as the car exploded, the roar echoing through the tower and undoubtedly waking the city.

A panic would spread, and the entire capital would be flooded with wailing sirens, flashing blue lights, and every policeman.

Sam didn't have long.

With the SA80 rifle locked to his shoulder, he stepped out from behind the tower, just in time to witness the third 4x4 of the motorcade slam into Wallace's car. The collision spun the car out of line and both of them came to an abrupt stop.

The driver's door of Wallace's car burst open, a Black-ridge officer, decked in a black polo shirt and jacket stumbled out, blood streaming from the gashes on his face.

A handgun flailed in his hand.

Sam squeezed the trigger, the rifle sending a three-shot

burst through the man, all three bullets puncturing his chest and sending him spinning to the ground, a burst of red mist dropping with him.

From the third car, both back doors flew open and Sam saw the handgun just before the agent pulled the trigger.

Sam spun on his heel, dropping to his knee in one fluid movement, and raised his rifle.

He squeezed the trigger.

The three bullets shattered the glass of the car door, embedding themselves in the woman's skull and sending her sprawling to the concrete, a trail of her blood and brains following. From the other side of the car, a man spun out, handgun raised but Sam rolled to the side, out of the man's sight, just in time for the driver of the third car to push open his door.

Sam rolled through, swiftly back onto his feet and he lunged forward with a brutal kick, slamming the open door back into the driver's head, and knocking him off balance. The window, shattered from the collision, was lined with thin, razor-sharp shards of glass, and Sam reached through with his gloved hand, grabbed the back of the man's head by his hair and pulled his head through.

Ducking the line of sight of the other gun man, Sam dropped down, dragging the man headfirst onto the broken window, slicing open his throat and feeling the warm flow of blood stream down his arm as the man gasped for life.

He was dead within seconds.

Sam pressed himself against the car, waiting for the final gunman to reveal his location. As he listened for the footsteps on the cracked glass that littered the now devastated road, he could hear the sirens wailing in the background.

The cavalry was on their way and Sam needed to move.

Fast.

Just as Sam zeroed in on the footsteps, the door to Wallace's car flung open and another agent stepped out, gun aimed squarely at Sam, who had miscounted. The man, clearly concussed from the collision, fired wildly in Sam's direction, the bullets rattling against the car and Sam spun to the side, released the rifle which clattered to the concrete and drew his Beretta.

The handgun was light, smooth, and slipped seamlessly into his deadly grip.

He squeezed the trigger once, blowing a hole through the man's forehead and sending him sprawling back into the door of the car.

Before Sam could admire his shot, an arm swung over his head and around his throat, the muscles tightening as he was dragged backwards from his stance. The final gunman had snuck up on him and was now trying to lock in the headlock, cutting off Sam's air supply and bringing an end to his mission.

As Sam fought for breath and consciousness, he ignored the blurred vision and focused on what he was fighting for.

Singh.

If he faded, she would be killed.

Wallace would hand Sam to the police and while they locked him away in the deepest hole they could find, Singh would never be found.

She would be just another problem that Wallace would have erased from existence.

With one final push, Sam managed to propel himself backwards, taking both himself and his attacker to the floor. As they crashed to the shard covered concrete, the impact drove the air from the attacker who groaned as he released his hold. Sam used the momentum to roll backwards over the attacker and pushed himself back to his feet.

Stood over the man, Sam stamped down as hard as he could, his boot crushing the windpipe of the man. His neck snapped like a biscuit, and Sam could tell by the vacant stare in the man's eyes that he was dead.

They were all dead.

Sam reached down and reclaimed his handgun and then slowly walked towards Wallace's car, massaging his throat. The backdoor of the car finally opened and Wallace, his skin slashed from the shattered glass and his nose bleeding from the crash, stepped out, his hands held high. He looked around, admiring the carnage.

The vehicles were destroyed.

His team lay among the wreckage, all dead.

Blood painted the street, the shattered glass letting it shimmer.

The only thing louder than the ringing in his ears from the collision was the gravity of the situation. After dismissing the battle as being over, Wallace was now looking down the barrel of a gun. One attached to one of the most efficient killers he'd ever met.

The control he'd craved and assumed he had recovered was slipping away once more.

Staring with a vacant look, he surveyed the scene, blown away by the ruthless and pre-meditated attack on his entire team. Good men had just died in the line of duty, paid to protect Wallace. But there was no protecting him from what was coming. The stakes were too high, and the balance of power was about to shift once more.

Before him, walking with a severe sense of purpose, was Sam Pope and Wallace offered his surrender meekly.

'Sam, let's talk about this.'

'Fuck you,' Sam said as he took a step closer, before drilling the handle of his gun as hard as he could into Wallace's temple. The burly man slumped back against the car, his lights out, and Sam stuffed the handgun into the back of his jeans and then reached out, steadying the heavy man before he hit the deck.

The sirens wailed, they were only a few streets away now and Sam heard the roaring engine approach.

He'd hated making the call, but he needed the help. He needed to be able to disappear into the sea of flashing blue lights and sirens. He needed to hide in plain sight and as the lone police car sped towards them, he locked his hands under Wallace's arms and dragged him to the centre of the road.

The police car skidded to a halt, and DI Pearce leapt from the driver's seat, ran around the car, and flung the door open.

Sam dropped Wallace across the backseat, slammed the door shut, and then jumped into the passenger seat.

The engine had already roared to life and Pearce fired up the siren as they sped away down Tower Bridge, leaving the smoking, bullet-ridden vehicles, and the bodies of Wallace's team behind them.

With the mayhem of the attack shaking the city, Pearce and Sam melted into the panic, and made their escape.

They had Wallace.

Sam, knowing the fight was far from over, felt like he was now holding one of the cards.

CHAPTER TWENTY-FIVE

The assault of Tower Bridge was big news.

The story dominated every news station, each one trying to outdo the other with their dramatisation of the events. To be fair, they didn't need to try too hard, as the story itself was spectacular.

A high-ranking government official, on his way to an undisclosed location saw his entire motorcade wiped out in a wave of bullets, before being kidnapped.

Kidnapped reportedly, by Sam Pope.

As the news outlets brought on an endless train of experts, all offering a deep analysis of Sam's state of mind or leading discussions about the impact such an attack would have on the government, Pearce reached over and turned it off. He cursed himself for going along with the plan, and for finally doing what he hoped he never would.

Completely breaking the law.

Ever since he'd begun investigating Sam, he could feel his loyalty to the justice system waning. After helping Sam escape custody over a year ago, he let the vigilante run free from the High Rise, believing the country needed someone like him fighting for them. He still believed it.

Just.

But there was always a limit, as far as Pearce was concerned. While his career of hunting corrupt policemen had made him far from popular within his own organisation, he'd never broken the law himself.

Helping Sam Pope, the most wanted man in the UK, wipe out an entire security team and then kidnap a leading government official was too far. He had become what he'd spent his career fighting and even though he understood the need for the attack, there was no way he could go back.

Pearce was a man of principle and when they became compromised, he knew it would be time to call it a day. What struck him the most was how easy it was to decide it was over, how ready he was to walk away.

As he guided the police car through the increasing traffic of the London morning rush hour, he flicked a quick glance to Sam who sat beside him. As always, Sam looked deep in thought, his eyes absorbing the packed streets as they whizzed by.

Sam had called Pearce on his way to collect his weapons, telling him what had happened, and that Singh's life was at stake. The news hit Pearce like a freight train. He cared for Singh deeply, and although his actions had caused her to push him away, the thought of her being caught in the crossfire of Sam's war filled him with rage.

He held back on reading Sam the riot act. Judging by the tone of Sam's voice, he understood the gravity of the situation and the horror of pulling an innocent woman into his world. Pearce had warned Singh to step back, to stop knocking on the door and asking for the devil.

Eventually, he will answer.

Pearce had driven to the station and signed out the panda car as soon as he could and then he waited near the war zone, knowing that Sam would deliver the exact wave

224

of violence he'd promised. That's what scared Pearce the most.

Behind the complex, broken man was a double-edged sword. One side was possibly the most righteous man he'd ever met, a man who never wavered from right in a world filled with wrong. But on the other side, he was an efficient killer and a knowing criminal, flouting the law and putting people in the ground.

Sam told Pearce he needed three minutes to eliminate Wallace's security detail.

He did it in just under two.

As Pearce had raced towards the massacre, he watched as Wallace emerged from the car, arms raised, and defeat accepted.

Sam delivered the clubbing blow and they quickly made their getaway. In a city swarming with police cars, hiding in plain sight was the easiest way to disappear, as it would take dispatch at least an hour to unpick the tape and see which car turned up at the scene.

They had already switched cars, with Pearce dumping the police car in the same garage that Sam had parked Etheridge's Range Rover. Pearce had helped Sam shift the mighty Wallace from one vehicle to the other, binding his hands behind his back with masking tape.

With rush hour washing through the city like a tidal wave, they ventured into the traffic, with Pearce driving quietly back over the Thames to South London. After the attack, the city had ground to a crawl, with the traffic backed up from the detours put in place.

Trainlines were suspended for a second day in a row and Pearce smiled at the thought of Sam's impact on the Transport for London.

Sam had stayed quiet. He knew Pearce was fuming, the fear of Singh's potential death had created a palpable tension between the two and Pearce had no intention of breaking the silence.

A journey which had begun a year ago, when the city they were crawling through had been rocked by a terrorist attack. An attack that Sam had exposed as a vile cover-up, a despicable link between the Met Police and organised crime. It had created a bond between the two of them, a mutual trust that both men were committed to doing the right thing.

But the cost, now, was potentially too great.

And half an hour later, as Pearce carefully navigated his way through the streets of Dulwich, still hadn't spoken a word to Sam.

They turned onto the street, one which had bonded them together the previous year and Pearce pulled the car to a stop, sliding it in behind a van on the side of the street.

They were parked outside the 'High Rise', the large, four floored building that Sam had laid siege to a year before, a violent ascent that saw him wipe out Frank Jackson's army of goons, before riddling the gangster himself full of bullets.

Pearce had been present for that moment, when Jackson threatened the safety of an innocent woman.

Sam had not hesitated.

He unloaded the clip, ripping the man's chest and stomach to pieces.

Pearce had let Sam leave that night, having delivered the treacherous Inspector Howell to the authorities and exposing the hideous truth.

But now, the building that was once the most feared structure in the city, lay abandoned and derelict. A property developer had purchased the lease of the building not long after Sam had ripped through it like a hurricane. Scaffolding had been erected around the entire structure; the remaining windows removed. A few sheets were pinned to the frames, the thick plastic keeping the rain out, but that was about it.

The bottom had fallen out of the development company, investors pulling out and the building, once a hub of lewd and dangerous appeal, was an empty shell.

A husk of what it was.

Pearce and Sam both looked up at it, and Sam reached for the door handle. He stopped himself, guilt ridden, and he turned to Pearce.

'Thank you, Pearce.'

'Don't.' Pearce gritted his teeth. 'This went too far, Sam.'

'I know.'

'Then why did it? I told you, keep Singh out of it. She was sniffing around the wrong people and now she's being used as leverage. Leverage against you.' Pearce shook his head. 'Jesus Christ, I should arrest you right now, you know that?'

Sam sat quietly, his shoulders slightly hunched. In the backseat, Wallace still lay unconscious.

'I didn't mean for it to get this far,' Sam said quietly. 'But what the man has done to me, what he has done to the world. He needs to be stopped.'

'Then stop him,' Pearce said coldly, looking over his shoulder. 'Bring back Amara, deal with him, and then stop. Because this will only ever end one way.'

Sam nodded and then let the silence sit between them for a moment. He pushed open the door, the bitter chill of a brisk spring morning filtered around him. As he stepped out the car, he rested his hand on the top of the door and then poked his head back in.

'What about you?' Sam asked.

'What about me?'

'Are you done now? With me? With Singh?'

Pearce let out a deep sigh. The thought of it pulled at his heart strings. A heart that was no longer in it.

'I'm done with it all, Sam. The job. The headaches. Everything. After this, I can't go back. I can't be the type of officer I've spent my career hunting down.' He pulled his lips tight, grimacing. 'I hope this is the last time I ever see you.'

Sam nodded respectfully, despite the hurt in the words. He liked Pearce, respected him and to see what he'd done to the man hurt. He offered Pearce a final smile.

'Likewise.'

Sam slammed the door shut, then pulled open the one to the back seat. Pearce heard the sickening crack as Sam broke Wallace's finger, a sure-fire way to bring him back to life. Wallace roared with agony, and Sam slapped him cruelly across the face. Reaching behind him, he pulled the Beretta 92 from his jeans and pointed it directly at Wallace.

'Get out of the car and get in the goddam building.'

With his hands bound, Wallace shuffled out of the car, sneering at Pearce. The man had been a thorn in his side since Sam had resurfaced and he'd pushed for Ashton to remove him. They had shunted him to the darkest corner of the station, given him errands to run but the man was a relentless bastard.

Now, here he was, helping Sam bring him down and he made a promise that if he made it out the other side of this, he wouldn't be so subtle next time.

He would have Pearce killed.

Sam shoved Wallace across the street and through the refurbished front door. Beyond the new frame, the lobby was exactly as Sam had left it.

Decimated by a hand grenade.

Sam had taken the entire building by force, dropping the element of surprise of the criminals guarding it in the form of a grenade which had blown out the entire floor. A

228

few more were put down with pinpoint bullets, before Sam had taken the building floor by floor. As he pushed Wallace up the stairwell, both of them saw the bullet holes from Sam's visit a year prior.

Sam recounted the fight with the horribly scarred man, who he'd sent hurtling to his death in the centre of the stair well.

As they reached the top floor, Sam recounted the fight he'd had with Mark Connor, the brutal beating the man had given him before Sam had ended his life.

The entire fourth floor had been gutted, the sleazy rooms now empty shells, the doors removed in a lame beginning of a refurb job.

The door to the penthouse had been removed, and Sam recalled pushing a hapless criminal through as a decoy, watching as Jackson filled his own henchman with bullets and giving away his position.

It seemed like a lifetime ago.

Since then, Sam had removed all the start-up high rises around London, the smaller ventures hoping to profit from Jackson's death.

He had taken out the head of the Acid Gang, a notorious street gang who maimed innocent people.

The Kovalenko sex trafficking empire had crumbled, both in the UK and Ukraine.

Sam had fought through Berlin station and brought war to the streets of Rome.

Pearce was right.

It needed to end.

It would end.

Sam pushed Wallace into what was once the penthouse, the plastic sheets, stapled to the stone, rustled in the wind. Outside them, the rickety scaffolding shook and rattled, and Sam didn't envy anyone who was out on those at such a height.

It was twenty to ten in the morning, and Sam felt a sudden wave of tiredness crash against him and he blinked a few times, trying to stay alert. Wallace noticed and smirked.

'Why don't you take a nap?'

'Why don't you keep your mouth shut?' Sam kicked Wallace's knee out, causing him to grunt and crumple to his knees. 'Sit down.'

Wallace scowled at him before adjusting himself onto his bottom, sitting on the cold, tiled step. Jackson's oak desk was still in the room, the large desk either too heavy or too valuable to move. Sam made his way to it, looking over the expert craftsmanship, noticing the spatters of Jackson's blood that stained it. Sam turned back to Wallace, and plunked himself onto the desk, looking down on his captive.

For a man who had craved power, he looked beaten. Defeat was not a concept that Wallace was accustomed to, and the idea of being overpowered clearly enraged him. With venom behind his glare, he stared at Sam.

'What are you doing, Sam? Huh? What's the plan?'

'Contact your guy. Farukh. Tell him to release Singh, and then I'll let you go.' Sam shrugged. 'Simple.'

Wallace chuckled, his cruel laugh echoing in the empty building.

'It's really not that easy. See, those files you have. He wants them gone even more than I do. So, my life, in his eyes, isn't enough.'

'Well, that sucks for you.'

'Give it up, Sam.' Wallace snarled. 'We both know how this goes. So here it is. You give us the stick, you let me go, and Singh lives. That much we can do. But if you think you're going to get out of this, then you really are delusional.'

'You are not in the position to be making threats.'

'These aren't threats, Sam.' Wallace countered. 'It's just how it is. This is bigger than you. It's bigger than your little journey and it's what you fail to realise. It's what Marsden failed to realise and it's…'

Sam's fist collided with Wallace's jaw at such a pace it broke his knuckle. A spray of blood and two teeth splattered onto the floor, quickly followed by Wallace himself. Sam shook his hand, the broken bone causing severe discomfort.

'That was for Marsden,' Sam said calmly and then stretched his back. The adrenaline of the morning had seen him through but now, with the brisk, spring chill and a slower pace, the impact from his fall yesterday was locking around his spine like a mechanical vice. Wallace swung his massive bulk to the side, sitting himself up. He drew a large mouthful of blood and spat it forward, not caring if it hit Sam or not. Holding the gun casually in his left hand, Sam squatted down next to Wallace and reached into the inside of his blazer. Wallace moved ever so slightly, and Sam pushed the gun into his throat, making his threat very clearly.

Wallace relented, and Sam could feel the clamminess of the man as he slid his hand into the blazer pocket and removed the mobile phone.

'Passcode,' Sam demanded. Wallace obliged and Sam unlocked the phone, surprised to see a photo of three kids as the screen saver on Wallace's phone. He knew they weren't his own, the man had dedicated his life to the country.

He had no family.

Possibly a sister? Sam only mused for a moment or two before sliding open the contacts on the screen, flicking through the numbers. There was no Farukh, and Sam scowled as he turned to Wallace.

'What's he saved as?'

Wallace chuckled. 'He isn't saved as anything.'

'Then how do we contact him?' Sam demanded.

'He sent the message from a phone. I don't have the number, but you can pull it from the message.'

Sam was surprised by Wallace's helpful attitude, but he knew the game here. The assault on Tower Bridge and subsequent kidnapping had thrown a spanner in the works and Wallace knew he had to adjust his plan. While they didn't hold all the cards, they still had a strong hand.

Sam knew it.

More worryingly, Wallace knew it too.

The fastest way out of this situation was to cooperate and Wallace sat, his legs stretched out in front of him, his arms pinned to his back. His face, slashed from being peppered by shards of glass, bore the irritated look of a man who had been told there was an hour's wait at the doctors.

Sam, ensuring his finger was still resting on the trigger of his gun, just in case, pulled up the message and then clicked on the number.

He pressed call.

As the phone began to ring, he pulled one of the plastic sheets to the side, looking out over the stunning city of London as it glowed underneath the spring sun, the city still reeling from his assault an hour ago.

CHAPTER TWENTY-SIX

As Singh slowly blinked her eyes open, she could feel the thudding ache of her skull. The impact of her collision with the wall had rattled her brain and as she tried to blink away the darkness, she felt a twinge of pain with every blink.

Everything was still dark.

Was she blind?

Had the impact been so severe that it had severed her retina?

Refusing to let herself panic, Singh took a deep, calming breath and allowed herself to recollect. She was blindfolded, that much was certain and judging by the material pressed against her mouth, she had a sack over her head.

It wasn't a preferable situation, but at least her mind had caught up.

Helal.

She remembered the horrible sight of the journalist, dangling from the ceiling, the cable ripping into his throat as it choked the life from him.

She'd rushed to his aid, then everything went black, as

a sack was pulled over her head and then everything went silent.

How long had she been out for?

Was Helal still alive?

As she moved to push herself up, Singh found her arms bound at the wrist, clasped together at the base of her spine. She lay on her front, pressed against the hard wood floor.

Was she still at Helal's?

She began to roll, trying to flip onto her back so she could sit up. Then, she could try to locate an edge or a sharp corner to free herself. A bored voice cut the tension but raised her fear levels.

'Do not bother to try escape.' The man sighed. 'I am watching you.'

Singh felt her breath catch in her throat. After a few moments of nervous thought, she decided to speak.

'Who are you?'

'I am a man who needs to clean up mess. Mess that you have found and made worse.' The man took a deep breath in and Singh could smell the cigarette smoke. 'If Sam Pope is smart, then you will live.'

Singh felt her muscles tighten with anxiety. She trusted Sam, he'd saved her life before, but this was a dangerous game. While Sam, to an annoying degree, was bound to doing the right thing, did that mean sacrificing the truth for her life?

Was Project Hailstorm, and the chance to bring Wallace down, a greater goal than saving one person?

'Where are we?' she finally asked, and within two seconds, felt the cloth whipped from her head. The light was blinding, and she squinted, trying to protect her eyes from the immediate change.

Slowly, the burning light became a blur, and after a few moments, little snippets of clarity began to form. It seemed

234

like she was still in Helal's apartment, the furniture all pressed against the wall, apart from the leather armchair which had been pulled back into the centre of the room.

Sat in it, his meaty arms hanging over the side, a cigarette poking from one hand, was the man who had confronted them at the station. Without his jacket on, he looked like a wrestler, his body so top heavy she wondered how he was able to move. His thick, barrel-like chest filled the entire width of the chair and he drew the cigarette to his heavily bearded face, his bicep almost ripping his T-shirt at the seams.

His eyes, dark and piercing, did not leave her and she followed the smoke as it danced towards the ceiling.

To the dead body of Helal.

Singh screamed at the sight of her associate, his shoulders hunched, his eyes open. His skin had started to drain, a horrible grey tinge beginning to filter through him. As she screamed, the attacker lunged forward from the chair, wrapping his meaty hand around her throat, catching her voice and trapping it.

'You make more noise, I will cut out tongue.' His words were laced with intent. 'Understand?'

Singh nodded and he shoved her away, before taking his seat once again. The concept of time had abandoned Singh, her bout of unconsciousness leaving her in a perpetual state of the unknown. All she knew was that she was in a lot of danger and the chances of her surviving were fading. Before she could contemplate her next move, the buzzing of a mobile phone echoed in the room and the man stood and marched towards the noise. Lifting the phone to his ear, he turned back to stare at Singh.

'Wallace.' Even he seemed like he hated the man.

'Wrong answer,' Sam replied.

'Sam,' Farukh said, a hint of menace in his voice. 'I did not expect to hear from you.'

'Yeah, well it's been a bit of a busy morning.'

'You have stick?' Farukh demanded, not even questioning Sam's voice at the end of Wallace's phone.

'I have Wallace.'

'But do you have stick?' Farukh repeated, his self-preservation overriding any loyalty to the man.

'I do,' Sam confirmed. 'Here's the deal. I want proof of life, you hear me. Put Amara on the phone.'

The man sighed with frustration and held the phone up in the air in Amara's direction.

'Say something. He wants to know I not kill you.'

'Sam…!' Amara yelled, but Farukh pulled the phone back.

'The woman is alive. I not hurt her much. But if you do not give me stick, I will kill her and write your name on wall with her blood.'

'Her life for Wallace. My life for the stick,' Sam said calmly. 'You get what you want, we get to walk away from it. For good.'

'I cannot promise you that,' Farukh responded coldly.

'Well that's the deal. You have till this evening to make your mind up. If I don't see you by ten o'clock this evening, Wallace dies, and your precious files make it onto every news station in the world,' Sam threatened. 'Tell Singh we are at the High Rise.'

'I do not know what that means.'

'I know. But she does. So, you better keep her alive.'

The phone cut off and Farukh chuckled. He had heard that Sam Pope was a dangerous man, but he'd not had him pegged as a stupid one. Farukh was a reasonable man, but he was not to be provoked.

Sam was playing a very dangerous game and Farukh lit another cigarette, deciding whether he wanted to join in.

———

'Pissing him off isn't a wise move.'

Wallace had watched intently as Sam had made the call. Clearly, Sam had hoped that rail roading the original plan would have caught Farukh off guard, but Wallace knew it would have little impact. Despite his position of power, Wallace knew his life meant little to Farukh.

The man was only interested in self-preservation.

As Sam pressed his hand to his busted lip, it was clear he was nervous.

It was a colour not often seen on Sam, and Wallace saw the chance to dig his nails in.

'Also, bringing Singh here? That's not a smart move.'

'Shut up,' Sam said quietly.

'I mean, give her a fighting chance at least, but to put her willingly in harm's way.'

'If she is here with me, then she is a damn sight safer than out there with him. Now, I suggest you shut your mouth before I break your goddam jaw.'

Sam's threat carried enough weight to quieten the large General who grimaced at his treatment. He was a man who commanded such dogged respect, such fear when he entered a room that people would leave. But here he was, on his arse in a dilapidated old knocking shop, being treated like shit by a man who didn't fear him.

The entire mission had fallen to pieces.

Part of him blamed Trevor Sims, the incompetent American who ran the Blackridge task force briefed with the mission to bring Marsden in alive. A series of failures ended up costing both Marsden and Sims their lives, one of which, Wallace regretted. He had known Carl Marsden for over thirty years and had nothing but a deep respect for the man who bloomed so many credible soldiers.

Sam Pope became the UK's deadliest weapon under Marsden's tutelage, and till his dying day, Marsden was fiercely protective of him.

It didn't surprise him that Marsden sought to expose the truth when he finally stumbled upon the files. Like Sam, Marsden was steadfast in his distinction between right and wrong and was clearly willing to die for what he believed was right.

There was no doubt in Wallace's mind that Sam would follow suit, but Singh's life was different.

This was between them.

She was an unfortunate pawn being used in a violent game of chess, and Sam would do anything to keep her alive.

Wallace was aware of Sam's trauma, the loss of his son spurring on his one-man war for justice. It was admirable in a way, a pain like that could be harnessed into making him the ultimate asset at Blackridge. But Sam's quest was more personal, and after not being able to save his son, Wallace was sure that Sam would do anything to make sure he saved Singh.

Anything.

As the day filtered through to the afternoon, Wallace felt himself dozing, his eyes weighing heavy, and he soon sprawled on his side, allowing himself a few hours' sleep.

An hour or so later, he was awoken as a spray of water crashed across his face. Spluttering awake, Sam dropped a sandwich and a bottle of water on his lap, having popped to the nearby Tesco. Wallace, fuming that his chance of escape had passed, was soon calmed by Sam's insistence that he would never leave with the stick.

Wallace relented, agreed, and then asked Sam for the use of his hands. Sam agreed, telling Wallace that any false move would result in a bullet through the knee cap. He had spoken to Etheridge and apparently that hurt like hell.

As the hours ticked on, Wallace watched Sam like a hawk, impressed by the resolute man who was ready to fight until the end.

The sky turned dark and Wallace knew Farukh was drawing out the day. He was hoping that Sam wouldn't be able to source food or sleep, through fear of dropping his guard. It was a cruel move, but Farukh was as brutal as they came.

The Hangman.

Somewhere, in the back of Wallace's mind, the image of Singh and Sam being hung from the roof lingered. He didn't doubt for a second that Farukh was capable of it.

Dangerous, but not reckless.

They needed the stick. Wallace needed proof.

'Did you read all the files on stick?' Wallace asked, looking at Sam who was again, peering out through the plastic, beyond the scaffolding to the street below.

'I read enough.'

'Did you read about Chakari?'

The word struck a chord with Sam, straightening his back as if an ice cube had been passed down his shirt. It had been over a decade since he'd been blown from the mountain face, left to die like his good friend Mac. A local doctor, Farhad, had nursed him back to health, only to give up his own life for the safety of his children.

Sam had never forgiven himself for the orphaning of those boys, knowing that their father's good nature had kept him alive, but got him killed.

Sam had wiped out the terrorist cell responsible for Farhad's death, but it had felt like scant consolation.

The boys were never located.

Mac's body was never found.

'That was a long time ago,' Sam eventually said.

'Yet, we are all haunted by ghosts from our past. Aren't we, Sam?' Wallace continued, his arms resting over his knees. 'You are haunted by the memory of your son. Don't get sensitive about it, it was in the reports that Mrs Devereux filed a year ago. Marsden stopped you from

239

killing yourself and you had to have mandated therapy sessions.'

'You were keeping tabs on me?'

'Absolutely. Sam, you're one of the deadliest soldiers this country has ever produced. All of this, this war against the system, it doesn't have to happen. I know you think I'm the enemy, that I'm the bad guy, but what I am is a necessity.'

'You have killed hundreds of people...' Sam interjected, turning from the makeshift window.

'To save millions,' Wallace snapped. 'In black and white, it looks like I'm a monster, but you don't see the grey areas. The areas where, thanks to my interventions, entire countries are now free of tyrannical reign. Free from oppression. Because of the deaths that I facilitated, there is actual freedom. Men like me will never be celebrated, but we are needed. You, Sam. You could achieve so much more. Alongside me, you could change the world.'

Sam shook his head in disbelief.

'I would rather die than help you mould the world in your image.'

'My image? Sam, some of my work is based on what you created.'

'What the hell does that mean?'

Wallace's face twitched with a smirk, a twinkle appearing in his heavily bruised eye.

'The man who I left you with in Italy. The one who ran you off the road. The one who put two bullets through you.'

'The one who tortured Paul?' Sam stepped forward; his interest peaked.

'A man of that fury. Consumed by that much vengeance. That is not something I can create. Even I cannot generate hatred to that degree.' Wallace flashed his cruel grin. 'That was created by you.'

Before Sam could respond, and wonder further down that rabbit hole, the sound of footsteps echoing from the stairwell filled the room. Sam snapped his head to the doorway and took a step forward. Wallace made a movement to stand, but Sam pressed the gun against the side of his sweaty, blood-stained head, encouraging him to stay seated. As the footsteps grew in volume, Sam determined there were two sets, encouraging him that Singh was still alive.

Moments later, the plastic sheet to the penthouse was pushed aside, and Singh was shoved through. Her face was heavily bruised, with a crude plaster pressed to her eyebrow. Beyond that, and the fear in her eyes, she looked okay.

She greeted Sam with a weak smile, clearly understanding the gravity of the situation. Sam looked to reassure her with a nod, but his eyes were soon drawn to the mighty figure who emerged behind her.

While Sam's lip was scabbed and caked with dried blood, and his body screamed in agony from their last encounter, Farukh looked fine.

As if fighting Sam was as difficult as swatting a fly.

This time, there was no escape.

Fate had pulled them all to the empty, spacious room atop an old war zone, where Sam had made his first statement to the country.

He was ready to fight.

And now, as all four of the occupants took their time to look at each other, he wondered if he was getting ready to fight for what would be the last time.

CHAPTER TWENTY-SEVEN

The entire day had been one big blur.

Since returning to the office among the panic of Sam's attack, Pearce had tried to get his head down and lose himself in the mundane work he'd been given. It had been over a year since he'd been given a real case. The higher ups didn't like the evidence trail he'd presented to them when it was revealed that Inspector Howell had conspired with Frank Jackson to stage a terror attack at the London Marathon.

While they'd acknowledged Howell's deception and sentenced him to a prison sentence that would see him commit suicide, Pearce found himself ostracised. He was shunted to a pokey office in the corner of the building, too small to fit more than one person in it.

He was sneered at by his colleagues, more so than usual and the higher ups had done little to dissuade the officers that he was in cahoots with Sam Pope.

Pearce wasn't just presented as a snitch.

He was presented as a hypocrite as well.

But he'd been able to deal with it. Through his entire

career, he'd developed the thick skin needed and the street smarts to match.

But he couldn't shake the horrible feeling in the pit of his stomach.

The feeling of guilt.

There was no doubt in his mind that Sam's attack on Tower Bridge, the execution of Wallace's men, and subsequent abduction of the General, was the only choice Sam had. With Singh being abducted, Sam needed the ultimate card to play. But by helping him escape, Pearce had willingly aided and abetted the most wanted man in the UK. Sure, before he'd turned a blind eye, but this was different.

This felt like it had gone too far.

The whole afternoon had been one big wrestling match with his conscience, and after what felt like his eighth cup of coffee of the day, he turned and looked at the clock on his desk.

Somehow, it was nearly ten.

Thinking that time was dragging, Pearce had in fact sat in his office for nearly twelve hours, tossing his thoughts back and forth like a tennis ball.

He had scrawled a quick letter, signed it, and then shimmied out from his broom cupboard. The Scotland Yard office was nearly empty, the only people still in attendance were the cleaners, those on the night shift, and a few senior officers who seemed to spend more time at their desks than anywhere else.

As he strode through the corridor he flashed a glance through the window at the bitterly cold evening, watching as a light drizzle began to gently tap against the glass.

Below, the iconic Scotland Yard logo span.

It had always filled Pearce with a sense of pride, but now, the spinning logo only added to the guilt.

He marched through the Task Force office; the desks all

empty apart from one unlucky officer who had been rota'd to the all-night phone line. The young man didn't even look up from his desk as Pearce approached Ashton's door. He took a deep breath and then rapped his knuckles gently on the door.

'Enter.'

Ashton's voice was curt and authoritative, and Pearce obliged. She looked up from her desk, peering over her glasses as the senior detective entered and she sighed.

Pearce had caused her a number of issues over the past year or so, especially regarding her blossoming relationship with General Wallace.

'Evening, Ma'am.' Pearce nodded respectfully, standing proudly with his shoulders straight and hands behind his back.

'What can I do for you, Pearce? It's late.' The final statement told him he was on a time limit.

'I've come to officially start the process of my retirement, Ma'am.'

Ashton dropped her pen and looked up, her finely tweezed eyebrows raised.

'Oh?' She struggled to hide her delight. 'What has caused this?'

'I've been doing this a long time, Ma'am. I've had a hell of a career and I'll be honest; I've loved every second of it. But recently, I've been thinking that I could be doing a lot more good out there than I am in here.'

'I hope this isn't because you were moved to another office?' Ashton offered flippantly. Pearce politely smiled.

'No, Ma'am. It's to do with the fact that the more we try to fix things, the worse they get. My focus was always on how we operated as an organisation. How people such as yourself, and the Commissioner, ran the police to ensure we are keeping the public safe.' Pearce could see a smile forming on Ashton's face. 'And to be honest, Ma'am, the way we operate, the way you operate, makes me think we are doing more harm than good.'

The colour drained from Ashton's face, replaced with a red-hot rage.

'How dare you? You come in here, telling me that we are doing harm when you're the one who's had known dealings with Sam Pope?' She slammed her hands down on the desk.

'Allegedly.' Pearce pointed out, his calmness riling her up more. 'I assume I don't need to work my notice.'

'Get the fuck out of here, Pearce.' Ashton's face snarled like a rabid bulldog. 'I've been waiting for an opportunity to kick you out the goddam door myself.'

'It's been a pleasure, Ma'am.' Pearce bowed before turning on his heel and heading for the door. As he reached out for the handle, he froze. That horrible feeling at the pit of his stomach rumbled once again. He turned back to Ashton, who had already raised the phone, prepping security to escort him from the premises.

'What?' She barked.

'Despite everything, we still need to do the right thing,' Pearce said, almost to himself than to her.

'What the hell are you talking about?'

Pearce felt the horrible feeling of betrayal. Sam was a good man, but it had gone too far.

Pearce had to do the right thing.

Had to.

'Singh and Sam are at the High Rise.' As he spoke, he saw Ashton's eyes light up. 'Wallace had Singh. Sam took Wallace. You need to get her out.'

'You better not be lying,' Ashton spat, hanging up the phone before redialling.

'Not this time. But I'd send guns,' Pearce said. 'Try to keep them alive, okay?'

Ashton didn't respond, she was already mobilising an

armed squad to head towards the High Rise. Pearce quietly left, hoping that whatever impact his decision would have, that Sam would understand. While Sam may have been looking to fight until his dying breath, Pearce had to do whatever he could to keep them all safe.

It would be his final act as a member of the Metropolitan Police, and ten minutes later, with his desk and locker cleared and as he stepped out into the evening rain, he'd made peace with his decision.

It was the right thing to do.

Pearce packed his belongings into his car, took one final look at the building with which he had served his country with such distinction for three decades, before he dropped into the driver's seat.

His car roared to life and he headed for home.

Retired.

———

Farukh didn't take his eyes off Sam. Not once.

As the standoff continued, the tension in the room rose, just as the temperature dropped. Outside the High Rise, a wind had picked up now, crashing rain against the plastic sheets. Sam looked to Singh.

'Are you okay?'

'I've been better,' she replied, offering him a hopeful smile.

'Drop the gun,' Farukh ordered, his voice calm.

'You drop yours.'

Farukh laughed at the insinuation.

'I do not carry gun. I prefer to kill man by my bare hands. To see life choke from him.' Farukh smiled. 'You will find this out.'

Sam pulled the gun away from Wallace's head and tossed it over the desk. He raised his hands up, signalling he was unarmed, and then he drilled his foot into Wallace's spine, pushing him towards Farukh and sending him sprawling across the floor.

'Now her,' Sam demanded and Farukh raised his eyebrows at Singh, encouraging her to move. She stepped across the room to Sam, and they hugged. Wallace, hauling himself to his feet, dusted down his ruined, expensive suit.

'Very touching,' he spat. 'The stick?'

'Yes,' Farukh echoed. 'The stick'.

'Sam, you can't give them it,' Singh pleaded. 'The world needs to know the truth. About him. About you. Everything.'

'Don't be stupid, you daft cow,' Wallace joked. 'You're lucky to still be alive. Now, Sam, hand...over...the...stick.'

Sam looked at the two men and then back to the pleading eyes of Singh. Her right eye was heavily bruised, but her piercing stare still carried enough emotional weight behind it.

She understood.

Sam wasn't just fighting because he had nothing better to do. He was fighting because no one else would.

Knowing Singh was nearest to the doorway, Sam finally sighed and nodded.

'Okay.' Sam reached into his pocket and tossed the stick towards Wallace. His meaty hand clapped it out of the air and his eyes widened with glee. Instantly, he dropped it to the floor and stomped it, the plastic shattering, the memory device cracking into multiple pieces.

All the files. All the proof.

Gone.

Another crushing defeat under the oppressive boot of Blackridge and Wallace turned and nodded to Farukh.

'Kill them.'

Farukh nodded, seemingly pleased with Wallace's end

of the bargain. As Farukh took a step forward, Sam placed a protective arm across Singh's stomach and stepped in front of her.

'That wasn't the deal.'

'The deal's changed,' Wallace casually replied. 'You are both too dangerous to our mission going forward. I hope you understand that. Now I would say it wasn't anything personal, but it definitely is.'

As Farukh took another step towards them, he reached to the back of his jeans, and released the two grips from the leather pouch. Unbuckling the curved blades, he pulled them out with relish, his eyes glistening at the thought of putting them to use. Sam looked at the two men, regretted tossing his gun but then pulled open his shirt.

'You're right,' Sam said defiantly. 'The deal has changed.'

Strapped across his muscular, bullet scarred chest, was a wire. Taped between the two bullet wounds that Wallace himself had administered, Sam let the two men glare at the device, before Farukh turned to Wallace.

'What is this?'

'I don't know,' Wallace stammered. 'Sam, where is that wire feeding to?'

'It's been feeding all day. To a remote location where Etheridge is ready to post to every single news broadcaster on the internet.'

'What has he said?' Farukh demanded, pointing one of his razor-sharp blades menacingly at Wallace. 'Did you mention me?'

'Oh, he told me everything,' Sam lied. 'How you brutally murdered Abdullah Bin Akbar during Project Hailstorm, how you killed his family and murdered his kids in cold blood.'

Farukh turned to Wallace, incensed. Wallace, panicked, held up his hand.

'He's lying. I didn't say any of that!'

Sam continued, ushering Singh towards the door as Farukh took another step towards Wallace.

'How you have killed for several governments. How Project Hailstorm was your idea and that all the deaths should be laid at your door.'

'This is bullshit, Sam. I didn't say anything.'

'I do not take chance.'

Farukh's words echoed in Wallace's ears, as the man swung his arm with the speed and precision of a heavyweight boxer, plunging the curved blade into the top of his stomach. Slicing right through the skin and muscle, the burning sensation roared through Wallace's body, exploding with a cough of blood which shot onto the floor. Wallace's eyes begged for mercy, and Sam and Singh watched on in horror as Farukh pulled Wallace towards the large, plastic sheet covering the nearest window, the blade slicing the large war monger open, his intestine slowly flopping through the tear in his gut. Farukh twisted his hand, rotating the razor within Wallace's inside, dicing his organs, before pulling it out. Blood and remnants of his insides splattered the plastic and Wallace, with his life flashing before his eyes, was reduced to nothing more than a man.

A man about to reach his end.

Without batting an eyelid, the Hangman swung his other hand, the blade slashing the fat hanging underneath Wallace's chin, his throat opening up like a packet of crisps. Before the blood could cover Farukh, he drove his military boot into Wallace's ruined stomach, propelling him through the sheet and into the night.

As the cold wind surrounded him, the rain pelted him, and he felt his throat rip open further and empty, Wallace watched as the top floor of the High Rise raced away from him, and then his life ended.

The fall had shattered his spine and cracked open the back of his head like a cantaloupe.

Wallace was dead, butchered, and laid out for his country to see.

Sam had already ushered Singh towards the door, as Farukh, with the same amount of nonchalance as someone who had just taking the rubbish out, turned to him.

He calmly wiped the bloodstained blades on his lapels, cleaning them as a matter of courtesy, before his eyes locked on.

He raised the blade at Sam, the intent clear.

'You.'

Sam could hear Singh rushing down the stairs, pleased in the knowledge he'd saved her.

This was his fight.

It may be his last.

But Sam had always fought for something. It was who he was.

With the armed assassin making his first steps towards him, Sam raised his fists, ignored the aching pain that coursed through his war-ravaged body and got ready to fight one last time.

CHAPTER TWENTY-EIGHT

'ETA, ten Minutes.'

That wasn't good enough, thought Ashton, who had never felt her heart race with such excitement. Even as night ascended on a Monday evening the London roads were tough to navigate. It was just under six and a half miles, but through the London traffic, it felt like forever. The estimated arrival of the Armed Response Unit wasn't good enough and although they would get there just before she would, she wanted Sam in cuffs as soon as possible.

'Do whatever you have to, but I repeat, we CAN NOT lose him again.'

Her words were as stern as she was worried. The opportunity to catch Sam would all but guarantee her the Commissioner job. While her superior had done an admirable job, there were murmurings that it was time for a change. The Metropolitan Police had taken a bit of battering over the last year, a large part due to the Marathon bombing, another part due to the corruption that Sam Pope had uncovered.

The press was making a hero of him.

A man fighting for the people.

He was a vigilante and a murderer and once Ashton had him in cuffs, she would paint the story for the world to see. With the press leaning heavily on the Met's failings, the notion of replacing the Commissioner had been mooted.

A new leader. A new beginning.

Ashton was the clear front runner and she was hoping that her recent rendezvous with Wallace would tip the odds in her favour.

Bringing Sam Pope to justice would rubber stamp it.

As her driver sped round a corner, his sirens wailing, she held onto the door handle for support. It had been a long time since she'd ventured out into the field, her days as a street officer were long behind her. When she'd started out in the Met, she'd the same doe eyed view as all the other young upstarts pulling on the uniform.

She wanted to help people.

She wanted to make a difference.

The years of long hours and crushing disappointments soon stamped the optimism out of her, replacing it with a cold, hard realism. She played the game then, working hard for those in power and stepping on the toes of those not strong enough to claim it.

Along the way, she'd made some vital contributions to the cause. Her work on Project Yewtree had seen her name lauded in the papers and would no doubt, be one of her more pushed pieces when the time for her promotion came.

Her coronation to the top of the Met.

That was why it was imperative that she brought Sam in, and hopefully, she thought, catch Singh in collusion with him. It was such a disappointment to see her lose her way. Ashton had such high hopes for her and had championed her for leading the Task Force. Not only did she see potential in Singh but promoting a female officer of ethnicity would look great on her record.

Ashton knew how to play the game.

But she'd become a problem and Wallace had made it abundantly clear that he wanted her removed. Without due course, Ashton had struggled, loosely fabricating the stories of her betrayal of the Met but not enough for it to stick. It had been enough to suspend her pending an investigation, but without Pearce, the best internal investigator, on the case, it had hit many a roadblock.

Catching her with Sam would be two birds with one stone.

Factor in that Pearce, the other perennial pain in the arse had willingly stepped aside, it was turning into a good night's work.

She couldn't wait to look Sam in the eye and tell him that she'd won.

Nor could she wait for the grateful thanks Wallace would heap on her for ending what had been a long campaign.

As the car whizzed through the traffic on Loughborough Road, Ashton pulled up the radio, barked further instructions to the team, and stared out of the rain speckled window, looking at the city she couldn't wait to be put in control of.

———

Farukh took two steps towards Sam and then lunged forward with the curved blade, slicing the air inches from Sam's throat. Sam leant back, dodging the attack, before sliding out of the way of the follow up swipe. Farukh wasn't looking to toy with Sam this time.

This was to death.

And Farukh wasn't holding back.

With a grunt of frustration, he swung again, and Sam ducked, latched onto the arm, and wrenched it backwards, the blade dropping from Farukh's hand. Before Sam could move, Farukh's solid elbow cracked the side of his jaw. Sam stumbled to the side, slightly dazed and Farukh charged, slamming his shoulder into Sam's chest and sending him sprawling over the large oak desk and to the hard floor on the other side.

It was like being hit by a double-decker bus.

The man was as thick as a sand block and Sam gasped for the air that had been driven from his lungs. As he clambered on all fours, the thudding of boots closed in on him.

In the corner was the gun that Sam had tossed, but as he inched towards it, a mighty boot crashed into his rib cage, flipping him over onto his back, and driving what little air was left straight from his lungs.

Farukh dropped down to one knee, his leather clad hands shooting out and locking onto Sam's throat.

Sam gasped for air, slamming his fists into the man's meaty forearms, but he just struck the leather of the jacket.

While he wasn't hanging Sam in the traditional sense, the twinkle in Farukh's eye told Sam he was enjoying it. Choking the life from another man was one of the most powerful things he could do, and Farukh pushed his immense weight down, the air supply cutting off completely.

Sam gasped for air, his face turning a sickening purple as his eyes began to bulge.

This was it.

The entire fight coming to an end by the hands of the most dangerous man he'd ever face.

A horrifying thud echoed in the room, as the metal slammed against the back of Farukh's head with enough force to knock it clean from his shoulders.

Moaning with pain as blood splattered to the ground, Farukh wobbled, releasing his hold on Sam's throat. Singh, who had decided to repay her debt to Sam, had returned, wielding a metal pipe she'd taken from the scaffolding.

The first swing had loosened the big guy up.

Her second swing was just a split second too late.

Farukh had already digested the pain, recalibrated, and he caught the swing under his arm, locking the pole in place and he hoisted himself up, driving his forehead into Singh's face and knocking her clean off her feet. Sam gasped for air, gulping greedily as he tried to fill his lungs, aware that Singh was in danger.

Singh tried to get to her feet, but Farukh swung the back of his hand like a tennis racket, his knuckles crashing across her face and sending her sprawling to her knees.

'You bitch,' he spat, furious at the shocking display of disrespect. Never in his life had he been struck by a woman and to him, there was only one penalty.

Death.

Grabbing Singh by the hair, he pulled her to her knees, then with a hard wrench that made her howl in pain, he yanked her head back, exposing her slim neck.

With his other hand gleefully gripping the curved blade, he brought it to her throat and with his eyes locked on her terrified stare, pressed the blade to her skin.

Singh felt the blade just break the top layer of skin, the stinging sensation only adding to the tears as she accepted her death.

Sam slammed into the Hangman with all his might, lifting him off the ground and away from Singh who gasped loudly, narrowly avoiding death.

Sam, with his arms locked around the Hangman's waist, continued charging forward, the brute slamming a hard fist into his already bruised spine.

Farukh slashed at Sam with the blade, and Sam felt the razor-sharp tool slash his arm and shoulder through his bomber jacket.

He kept running.

After a few more metres, Farukh's heels clipped the concrete frame of the window and the two of them spilled out through the plastic sheet, falling dangerously onto the rickety boards of the scaffolding. Sam released his hold and clutched the edge of the board, stopping himself from sliding across the soaked wood to his impending death below.

He wished he hadn't looked at the steep drop, and he pulled himself back, just in time to welcome a hard knee to his chest from the Hangman. Farukh, with the rain crashing against his leather clad body, was irate and he swung a few vicious punches at Sam, rocking his body as he absorbed each blow.

With his left hand still clutching the blade, Farukh swung, but Sam ducked and leapt up, planting Farukh with a vicious left elbow to the side of the head, before sending him back a few steps with a right uppercut.

Farukh took a second, dabbed at his cut lip and smiled.

'A fighter,' Farukh said approvingly, before launching forward with another few rights, which Sam blocked, only to drill a knee into Sam's stomach. As he hunched forward, Farukh drove Sam's face off the metal pole that ran the length of the scaffolding, his nose crushed on impact. Disorientated, Sam stumbled worryingly near the edge and Farukh swung his left hand again.

The blade slashed down the back of Sam's jacket, slicing through his clothes and drawing a mighty gash down his spine. Sam howled in pain, and Farukh drove a hard boot into his spine, sending him sprawling into the railing. Sam flopped over the metal bar, the agony of the assault getting the better of him. On the streets below, he watched as a series of blue lights pulled up outside the building, the police arriving in numbers to no doubt bring this all to a close. He saw the armed team jumping from the back of the van, mobilising, and getting ready to swarm the building.

It would all be over.

But it would be too late.

Slowly, he turned to face Farukh, throwing a few sloppy right hands that the Hangman batted away easily. Farukh reached out and grabbed Sam by the throat, pushing him further over the railing, pressing his slashed back against the cold metal.

'This is the end.'

Farukh's words were calm yet final and he skilfully spun the blade in his hand, pushed Sam's head back to expose the throat and lifted the blade.

The gunshot echoed through the street like a sonic boom and the bullet blew out Farukh's left shoulder. The blade instantly dropped from his hand, clattering onto the wooden walkway. Growling in pain, he turned to see Singh stood, the rain welcoming her to the fight with a wet hug. Her arms were extended, the gun held expertly between her fingers, the barrel smoking from the shot.

As Farukh turned to charge at her, she pulled the trigger again, but this time, the chamber clicked empty.

But it had been enough. Before Farukh could do anything, Sam dropped to his knee, grabbed the blade, and slammed it into Farukh's calf. Roaring like a mountain lion, Farukh fell forward onto his knee, and before he could say anything further, Sam grabbed his thick beard, wrenched his head back, and drove the blade as hard as he could into the centre of his throat.

Farukh gargled, the blood filling his throat instantly and as he choked and spluttered for life, Sam pushed it in further, the curve driving the blade up through his neck and into his mouth.

Farukh's eyes widened, his life ending quickly and as the rain soaked them both, Sam drilled one final punch into Farukh's throat, slamming the blade clean through and he let go.

The Hangman collapsed into a pool of his own blood, a slight twitch reverberating through his body.

An echo of his life.

Farukh was dead.

Wallace was dead.

It was over.

The fight was over.

As the rain crashed against him, Sam looked at his fist, the knuckles split open from the beating, Farukh's blood joining with own in a sickening scarlet glove.

Sam closed his eyes and dropped to his knees, the pain getting the better of him.

Below, he could hear the commotion of the impending police raid of the building.

Somewhere, he could hear the muffled sounds of Singh begging him to stand up.

Sam opened his eyes, and he saw his son, Jamie, stood in front of him, a hopeful smile on his young, innocent face.

'Not yet, Dad,' his son said. 'Not yet.'

Sam closed his eyes once more, bowed his head, and let the water trickle from his brow.

The fight was over.

It was finally over.

CHAPTER TWENTY-NINE

'Sam!?'

Etheridge held his head in his hands. He had been calling Sam's name for the last five minutes, to little avail. Sam's earpiece had been disconnected earlier in the afternoon, no doubt during a heated discussion with Wallace.

From what Etheridge could see through CCTV of the surrounding buildings, someone had been hurled from the top of the old High Rise.

Was it Sam?

He had no way of knowing, but he had one of his screens trained on a CCTV camera which was pointed straight at the door of the High Rise. The building, destroyed a year prior by Sam, was armoured with scaffolding, the windows empty caverns poorly covered in dusty sheets, What was once the most sought after hot spot in the criminal underworld was nothing more than an empty husk, an eyesore of a previous regime.

Sam had cut the High Rise off at the source, destroyed the smaller sister arms of the business until it was nothing but a memory.

But now, inside the building where Sam had truly found his calling, Etheridge worried whether he would ever see his friend again.

The feeling was compounded when the radio piped up, with an all guns blazing Ashton bringing the full blue fury of the Metropolitan Police straight to the doorstep. Even if Sam was alive, his chances of getting away were dwindling with every passing second.

Etheridge felt sick and he popped two paracetamols in his mouth and threw them back with a mouthful of water. He rubbed his chin, the grainy stubble itching, and he realised it had been a few days since he'd showered. Since he'd focused on anything other than the mission.

In that aspect, they had succeeded.

The recording of Wallace's confession had come though crystal clear and Etheridge had made several copies across servers, sticks, and discs.

Just to be on the safe side.

They had what they'd set out for.

Wallace. Bang to rights.

Whatever the outcome of the following events was, Etheridge knew that he would see the mission through to the end. Just as Marsden had willingly given his life for the files, Sam had risked it all to bring the man down.

To burn Blackridge to the ground.

As the excitement rose over the radio and the net began to tighten, Etheridge stared hopelessly at the screen, hoping beyond that his friend would emerge.

———

'Come on, Sam,' Singh said, her words shaking. 'We have to move.'

Singh peered over the railing to the street below, the

blue lights flashing like a street rave, illuminating the rain drops in their glow. The armed team was discussing tactics, and more uniformed officers were arriving, setting up the necessary cordons, keeping the public at bay. Wallace's body had already been discovered on the other side of the building, and several officers were locking down the scene.

They were completely surrounded.

More worryingly, Sam was hardly moving.

Singh leant down, wrapped her arms around Sam's and tried to lift him, but he was almost dead weight, like everything had shut down.

'For fuck's sake, Sam.' She cursed. 'Get up.'

'It's over,' Sam said quietly. 'It's done.'

With visible discomfort, Sam reached up, taking hold of Singh's arm and pulling himself off the ground. The large slice that ran across his spine had pumped warm blood across his back, his T-shirt stuck to him. The blood loss had made him woozy and combined with the probable concussion from the collision with the scaffolding pole, Sam could barely stand.

The rain was cooling, washing the blood from his face, and he stood for a few moments, letting the water crash against him.

Below, he heard the excited buzz of a police force, ready to finally bring him to justice.

Singh, defiant to the end, yanked at his jacket.

'We need to go.'

'Where?' Sam spoke softly, following her as she stepped back through the old window and into the High Rise. The office was splattered with blood, the thick trail from Wallace led to the other window, a horrifying splatter ran the length of the plastic sheet.

It was done.

Wallace was dead and Sam had got enough of a

confession to burn everything he'd built with Blackridge to the ground. He had discovered the truth about Project Hailstorm, the life altering facts of what he himself had been a part of.

The source of the two scars that adorned his chest.

Sam had been through it all.

He had fought.

He had killed.

And now, as he stumbled into the room and dropped to his knees again, he knew it was over. Singh, panicked, rushed towards him, her bruised face wet from tears as much as the rain.

'Come on, Sam. Fight, goddam it.' She slammed a weak fist against him. 'We have to go.'

'It's okay, Amara,' Sam said, trying to smile as he reached a hand up, gently stroking the wet hair from her face. 'It's over.'

'There must be a way out of here.'

'There's only one.' Sam looked her dead in the eye. 'You have to arrest me.'

Singh stood up, her eyes widening with shock as she shook her head.

'What? No. There has to be something else. A fire escape or something.'

'Amara, please.' Sam's voice was twisted with pain. 'It's the only way.'

'Sam, you will go to jail for the rest of your life. Do you understand that?'

'I know. But unless you put me in cuffs and march me out of that door, then so will you.' Sam offered her a smile, his eyes watering and a tear trickled down his cheek. 'The fight is over, Amara.'

She regarded him carefully, knowing then that the man she'd been tasked with hunting all those months ago had turned out to be the man she loved. While it wasn't the usual romance she'd been force fed in books, or the preconceived notion of love conjured up by her parents.

It was love.

Sam stood for something.

What was right.

He had fought, without mercy, without fear, for the things he had believed in. To save an innocent woman, caught up in a diabolical bomb plot. To rescue teenage girls, whom he'd never met, from a fate worse than death.

To avenge his friend, who died trying to do the right thing.

To avenge his mentor, who had fought for the truth.

Sam may not have abided by the law, but he was a good man, and as she looked at him struggling through the pain, she could feel the selflessness of his offer.

His freedom would be devoured by the police in an instant, but it would save her future.

After everything, all the people he'd killed, all those he had saved, he was still doing the right thing.

The man was a hero, and it broke her heart that the justice system would see him as the complete opposite.

Slowly, Singh lowered herself down, face to face with him and she cupped his wet face with her cold hands.

'The fight is over,' she agreed, trying to smile through her tears. 'You won.'

Sam reached up, gently resting his hand on hers, and they kissed. Devoid of the steamy passion of the one they'd shared in the lift the previous day, this one was soft. Tender.

A kiss goodbye.

After a few moments, locked together, Sam pulled away and woozily smiled.

'Let's go.'

Singh wiped her eyes, nodded her agreement, and then

helped Sam to his feet, supporting his weight over her shoulder as she helped him limp towards the door.

Step by step, they slowly made their way back down the stairwell, Sam's compromised mental state reliving some of the moments as he stormed the building the year before. Singh guided him down the steps and as they shuffled towards the front door, she pulled his hands behind his bloodied back and slapped her cuffs on him.

Sam had been arrested.

Singh had got her man.

Amara Singh didn't fail.

But while her career would no doubt fly after this momentous occasion, it felt like failure. As they stepped out into the basking glow of the blue lights, she watched as an entire armed squadron circled Sam like a pack of sharks, their rifles ready, their demands for him to get on the ground, furious.

Sam obliged, gently dropping to his knees, his head bowed forward, the rain crashing against his beaten, broken body. Assistant Commissioner Ashton stormed from the crowd, walking through the armed guard that had surrounded them both and she looked at Singh with astonishment.

'Well done,' she said, her words laced with envy. 'It seems you have done the impossible.'

'He needs medical attention, Ma'am.' Singh pleaded, but Ashton didn't seem interested. With a sneer across her tired face, she looked down at Sam with an undeserved sense of achievement.

'You are done, Sam,' Ashton snapped spitefully. 'You will go to prison and you will pay for the crimes you have committed. No one, not even you, are beyond the Metropolitan Police.'

Singh rolled her eyes, her head aching from the abuse it had taken over the last few days. There had been a time where she would have admired Ashton's gumption, the power play of lauding over Sam in front of so many officers and the public was not lost on her.

But Singh didn't care about that anymore.

She cared about what was right.

What was wrong.

And how Sam had shown her that there was a grey area in between. She looked down at Sam, who was breathing slowly. Ashton, her teeth bared like an attack dog, smirked at Sam for a few more moments before ushering over two of the armed officers.

'Put him in the van.' They hopped to it, reaching down and hauling Sam to his feet.

'Careful.' Singh barged in, to Ashton's furious surprise. Singh helped pull Sam up and he offered her one last glance before he was hauled off towards the van, the two officers caring little for the state he was in.

To all the watching eyes, he was the prize catch.

The most dangerous man walking the streets of London.

Now, beaten and cuffed, he was just another criminal.

As Singh watched, her chest hurting through heart-break as Sam was shoved into the van, Ashton, her coat wrapped warmly around her, sidled up next to her.

'Forget him,' she offered, almost with care. 'Whatever the man did, he is a criminal. And you, you brought him in. This won't be forgotten.'

Singh turned and looked at Ashton, staring a hole through her superior. The harrowing bruising on her face caused Ashton to divert her gaze uncomfortably and Singh smirked, knowing she'd proven to her that she wasn't afraid.

Singh didn't fear anything anymore.

As the sirens of the van began their long, droning scream into the night sky, the van pulled away, making its way slowly through the gathering crowd, ready to whisk Sam off to his future behind bars. Singh stormed away from the scene, bluntly rejecting the offer of medical assistance and decided she was going to take a long walk home.

She needed to clear her head and needed to heal her heart.

Ashton watched Singh leave, annoyed that her rebellious protégé had just solidified her legacy in the police, just as Ashton was on the cusp of ascensions. Still, despite Singh being the one to make the catch, Ashton would still spin it to Wallace that it was under her tutelage.

She'd guided Singh, promoted her quickly and now that shrewd judgement had paid off.

'Ma'am, we have two bodies.' A senior officer snapped her back to the matter of hand. 'One up on the top floor and one sadly on the street.'

'Where?' she asked, and the officer pointed her towards the side street. 'As you were.'

'Ma'am.'

The officer nodded politely and went back to the mayhem and Ashton marched towards the small cluster of officers gathered around a body, the white sheet about to be placed over it.

Ashton felt her legs turn to jelly.

Staring up at her, with his head a crushed mess of bone and brain, was Wallace. The fall had crumpled his spine into a jagged mess of bone, his skull had been obliterated by the pavement.

Wallace was dead.

'Are you okay, Ma'am?' one of the officers asked, but she ignored him. Slowly, she turned back towards the crime scene, marching past the plethora of officers hard at work, the wide-eyed public trying to catch a snippet for their social media accounts.

She made her way back to her car and dropped into the back seat. Her driver remained silent, allowing her to weep as she hunched over on the backseat and howled at the loss of her beloved General.

Sam would pay for his death, she told herself. He would pay dearly.

CHAPTER THIRTY

The following week was surreal.

The world watched on in amazement as what had been dubbed 'The Weekend of War' by the press had come to a close. With all eyes on the Metropolitan Police, Ashton was adamant on putting herself front and centre, happily talking to the media about the long and dangerous journey to bring down Sam Pope.

The man dominated the press, with several of the outlets championing his release, highlighting the people he'd saved and the criminals he'd cleaned from the streets.

While it was hard during interviews to keep her cool, Ashton promised herself she would stay professional. There was one slip, when one of the journalists questioned the integrity of the late General Wallace, probing as to why Sam Pope had targeted the man and what links he had with the mysterious Blackridge.

Ashton had shut down the interview then and there, retreated to her office, and wept for the recently departed. While she was aware it was unrequited, she'd grown fond of the General, their sexual encounters meant more to her than just the feeding of passionate urges.

But he was gone.

Sam Pope hadn't spoken a word since he'd been arrested, beyond signing a confession to the crimes he'd committed. When offered legal representation, he refused, despite being sternly told to accept the offer.

A full confession would mean he would never leave prison and while Sam said he understood, the only names he refused to confess to killing were General Wallace and a Sergeant Carl Marsden.

His lack of responsibility had infuriated the Assistant Commissioner, and she'd demanded a private meeting with Sam. While he sat quietly, almost at peace, she'd berated him for the murder of Wallace and for stripping the country of a fine man. Sam's only response was to call Wallace a traitor, a decision that drew a hard, open palmed slap from Ashton. Disgusted by the vigilante before her, she promised Sam he would rot in prison until the day he died and that she would call on every favour to ensure every day was hell for him.

It fell on deaf ears and Ashton had felt less in control than ever when she'd returned to the office. Now, four days after the arrest, she realised that the story of Sam Pope would never be over.

The press would be tugging at that string forever, with undoubtedly more skeletons existing in numerous closets. She was scared to look further into Wallace, the notion of no smoke without fire had made her tremble slightly in fear.

What if the man she'd slept with wasn't who he'd said? What if the rumours of barbaric actions and global terrorism were true?

It wasn't worth thinking about and Ashton decided to focus on the other pressing matter.

DI Amara Singh.

A week before she was in the final stages of pushing

the reckless detective through the door, much to the delight of Wallace. Now, as the person who had finally brought Sam Pope to justice, she was to receive an excellence award from the Commissioner and was the talk of the office.

The prodigy come good.

It reflected well on Ashton, of course, and she would ride the wave of praise as far as she could. But her suspicions of collusion remained, and she made a silent vow to keep digging, hoping one day to nail Singh for her crimes and let her rot in a dark hole as well.

The entire country was shaking, the public split on whether they wanted Sam to spend his life in prison or to be celebrated as a hero. It was dangerous territory and the last thing they needed were a bunch of senseless copycats taking to the streets in his place.

No, Ashton would make sure Sam was locked away behind as many doors as possible, with the key melted. She would hammer home the narrative of a crazed ex-soldier, who murdered as many innocent people as he did criminals.

The man who killed one of the UK's most respected war heroes.

Ashton looked down at the newspaper on her desk, saw the name Sam Pope emblazoned all over it and immediately tossed it in her bin.

The name would haunt her forever.

————

Never, in his entire career in journalism, had Nigel Aitken ever felt so devastated.

The entire point of a free press was for the country to have access to the truth. People dismissed journalism as an intrusive profession, filled with cameramen with no boundaries and villainous reporters ready to stoop to horrendous levels just to get a scoop.

While in the tabloids that may have held some weight, for the majority, it couldn't have been further from the truth.

Journalists were brave people, willing to knock on the doors where others were too scared and ask the questions no one else could. It landed them in hot water, sometimes even put them in danger, but every journalist worth their salt thrived for it.

The thrill of the story.

But the past week had been different.

Lost among the furore of Sam's capture and the subsequent trail of destruction behind him, Helal Miah had died. An award-winning journalist, willing to go to extreme lengths for the truth, had been brutally murdered by a trained assassin.

Beaten. Tortured.

Then hanged.

It was horrifying and Nigel had shut down the publication for the week, the website showing a joyous photo of Helal's infectious smile.

A loving tribute placed next to it.

Helal had been investigating the links between Wallace, Sam Pope, and Blackridge, his wild articles stoking many flames and had seen Nigel's phone blow up. Several government officials wanted it shut down, telling Nigel that public distrust in the UK armed forces was not something they could afford.

The Met Police had sent a charming detective to talk him down.

But Helal was headstrong, and while his death was tragic, it clearly showed Nigel that he was on to something.

Brutal murders don't happen by accident.

Nigel had wondered how he could honour his friend's

memory, looking through the final article he'd sent. It was a fascinating expose on the state of global terrorism, linking many strands towards the UK government and running the late General Ervin Wallace into the ground.

It was detailed, comprehensive, but it lacked the sufficient evidence that would make it watertight.

Nigel noticed the email in his inbox, the title catching his eye.

All the proof you will ever need.

As the editor of a popular publication, Nigel was accustomed to the odd prank email and opened it, expecting a cruel joke about Helal or a pornographic image.

Instead, what he received made his jaw drop in shock.

An email, sent by Paul Etheridge, detailing how he'd helped Sam Pope bring down the Kovalenko empire and how he'd helped him in his fight against Wallace. The email went to into great detail pertaining to Wallace, Blackridge, and the earth-shattering truth behind Project Hailstorm.

Attached to the email was an audio file and as Nigel played it, the colour drained from his face.

His hand shook.

It was a verbal confession from Wallace, admitting to the heinous crimes.

Nigel opened Helal's article and respectfully began his amendments, his mission to honour his fallen friend being sparked into life with proof that would shock the country to its very core.

———

'You sure about this?' Singh asked with a smile, the bruising down her face had calmed to a dull, purple mark. The cut above her eyebrow nothing more than a scab.

'More sure than I have been for a while,' Pearce said, handing Singh a bottle of beer. She took it gratefully, and Pearce lowered himself down onto the steps of the youth centre. The sun was setting on another lovely spring afternoon, the orange glow of the sun reverberating off the windows. As Pearce slowly sat, he finally felt like a man entering retirement.

'I hear that,' Singh said, clinking her bottle with Pearce's. 'It's been a funny six months.'

'Funny year for me.' Pearce chuckled, swigging his beer. 'But it's time to move on. For all of us.'

Singh nodded, a sadness to her movement. Pearce noticed it and wrapped an arm around her, drawing her in. The restoration of their friendship had been the one saving grace of everything that had happened. In their shared grief for what awaited Sam, Singh had reached out.

She'd forgiven him for her perceived betrayal and thanked him for helping Sam.

In a way, he'd saved her life.

'So…' Singh spoke, changing the subject. 'You're in charge full-time then?'

'Yup. You're looking at the new Bethnal Green Community Centre Manager.'

Singh whistled.

'Get you.' She chuckled and then rested her head on his shoulder. 'I'm pleased for you, Pearce.'

He sipped his beer.

'Please, call me Adrian.'

Singh looked up at him, tilted her head as if deep in thought and then shook it.

'Nah, I don't like that. Pearce it is.'

They both laughed and then sat silently, allowing the calming transition into the evening to relax them both. It had been a hell of journey, one which had seen both of their lives threatened and changed them both forever. As she finished her beer, Singh squeezed his shoulder and then stood.

'I better be going,' she said meekly.

'Do you want a lift?'

'No, the fresh air will do me good.' Pearce stood and she offered him a smile. 'Take care, Pearce.'

'Don't be a stranger okay?'

She nodded, her eyes watering and she buried herself into his chest. He held her for a few moments, gently rubbing her back. Sam's journey had ripple effects, some that could never be altered.

Pearce was no longer in the Met.

Singh had nearly been killed.

While his fight may have finished, there were many nursing wounds.

Wounds that would leave scars.

Singh finally stepped away and disappeared around the corner, losing herself to the busy city. As Pearce watched her leave, Sean Wiseman stepped out from the centre, looking in the same direction.

'She okay?' Wiseman asked, his burgeoning career as a social worker making him care for everyone.

'She will be.'

'What about Sam?' Wiseman popped the cap off his own beer and took a sip.

'I couldn't tell you. All I know is he's a good man. And beyond that, my friend.'

Wiseman silently raised his beer in toast to Sam, agreeing with Pearce's observation. Pearce accepted it, then turned back towards the youth centre, ready to begin the next chapter of his life.

———

The cell was small and the officer on duty made it a mission to slam his baton against the metal door at regular intervals. Sam had found it funny at first, especially as they knew about his military background.

He had slept in war torn bunkers.

The odd metallic bang wasn't going to startle him.

After his arrest he'd been rushed to A&E, the blood loss from his battle with the Hangman had been almost fateful. Chained to the hospital bed, Sam had undergone surgery to repair the damage to his back and had since received over eighty stitches to piece it back together.

The painkillers had been strong but limited and now, with only the regular dose of paracetamol, the solid bed wasn't providing much comfort.

Sat with his back pressed against the wall, the only other significant feature of the holding cell was the metal toilet basin.

Soon, Sam would be sentenced to a life behind bars, with no chance of parole. It was a daunting prospect, but one that he'd calmly accepted.

The fight was over.

He had brought down the biggest terrorist organisation, one that was funded by the very government he'd worked for.

Sam had found out the truth about what happened to him.

How he'd been lied to.

Left for dead.

All of it. Over.

Sam hadn't asked for any access to the news. He was sure he was plastered across it, with dozens of psychiatrists coming out of the woodwork to offer their expert analysis on his psyche, all desperate for their fifteen minutes.

Sam knew he was damaged.

Losing his son had sent him down a dark path, one

which held no chance of redemption. But somewhere along the way, Sam saw a world worse than he could comprehend.

He became a necessary weapon, a means for the world to fight back. So, he did.

He fought back.

He exposed the link between the police and the High Rise. The truth behind the London Marathon bombing and the attempted cover-up.

He had burnt the Kovalenko human trafficking empire to the ground, saving Jasmine, and countless other teenage girls from a life of drugs and sex slavery.

Lastly, he'd ended Wallace's government funded reign of terror and destroyed an untouchable organisation.

While he would rot in prison for the rest of his life, a place where he most likely already had a long list of enemies, he didn't regret any of it.

He closed his eyes and tipped his head back against the wall.

He thought of Jamie, and his perfect, innocent face. His floppy blonde hair.

A vision of his son manifested, and for the first time in years, he smiled at him.

'The fight's over, Daddy.'

With his eyes still closed, Sam felt a smile creep across his beaten face.

An alien feeling spread through him, warming him to his very soul.

Peace.

EPILOGUE

The news of Wallace's death had no effect.

While some may have seen it as a sweet release, for Mac, sat in the hostel in southern Austria, he'd felt nothing.

Was that due to loyalty?

He wasn't sure, but he did owe his life to the man. It was Wallace who had found him in that jail, brutally beaten for years by the Taliban. The horrors they'd subjected him to had broken him.

Physically.

Mentally.

Emotionally.

But Wallace had brought him back from the dead, treating him like the war hero he'd started out to be. That life felt like someone else's, as the fresh-faced young lad had long since evaporated, replaced by the horribly burnt, scarred man who looked back at him from the mirror.

The mission, over a decade ago, had been simple. Sam and Mac were to keep the main road clear, with several sightings of a Taliban recruitment cell reported in the area.

As their unit were taking in supplies to the local village,

it was their job to provide plenty of cover from a distance far enough away that they could evacuate safely.

It should have been simple.

But their position was compromised and as panic had taken hold of Mac, he ran.

Sam valiantly tried to shoot the chopper down, but for once, his impeccable aim was off.

Just another thing to lay at his doorstep.

The resulting missile blast had wiped Mac out and sent Sam sprawling.

His friend never returned for him.

As he'd laid on the crusty old grass of the dying wasteland, he'd wished for death. Unfortunately, the Taliban had other plans, keeping him alive to subject him to an ungodly amount of punishment.

Nothing taught the new recruits more than a savage beating, and the lashings he took were brutal. The skin on his back now was a horrific reconstruction, scar tissue upon scar tissue, all of it a reminder of his torture.

He was beaten.

Spat at.

Urinated on.

Raped.

All of it to show them who was the enemy, and how powerful the Taliban were. Every attempt at suicide was met with a lifesaving doctor, none of them taking enough pity on him to blow his brains out.

Wallace had found him, gave him his revenge, and then rehabilitated him.

With his fury, Mac knew he made a hell of a weapon.

Life had lost all meaning, which meant there was no semblance of a conscience within him. Whoever the target, whatever the age, they were met with a cold, efficient bullet to the brain.

Now, with Wallace gone, Mac realised that he'd been

used. Killed countless people for a cause he couldn't care less about. The one thing he'd been promised was his revenge.

Revenge against the man who had left him to his fate.

Sam Pope.

But now, with his superior dead and Sam behind bars, Mac knew that everything he'd fought for was slipping through his horribly charred hands.

The only thing that mattered, that had made any sense, was killing Sam.

He had come so close in Rome, only to have it snatched away from him.

Without Wallace blocking his path, Mac stared at the mirror, vowing that it would take more than a prison to keep Sam safe.

He had spent months preparing and now, knowing exactly where his target was, he was ready to strike.

Mac hurled his fist at the mirror, shattering the glass which sliced his hand.

As the blood fell from his knuckles, he marvelled at the lack of pain. His nerve endings had been shredded long before.

Now all that existed was a husk.

A shell of a man, fuelled by vengeance.

Vengeance that he was ready to collect.

GET EXCLUSIVE ROBERT ENRIGHT MATERIAL

Hey there,

I really hope you enjoyed the book and hopefully, you will want to continue following Sam Pope's war on crime. If so, then why not sign up to my reader group? I send out regular updates, polls and special offers as well as some cool free stuff. Sound good?

Well, if you do sign up to the reader group I'll send you FREE copies of THE RIGHT REASON and RAIN-FALL, two thrilling Sam Pope prequel novellas. (RRP: 1.99)

You can get your FREE books by signing up at www.robertenright.co.uk

SAM POPE NOVELS

For more information about the Sam Pope series, please visit:

www.robertenright.co.uk

ABOUT THE AUTHOR

Robert lives in Buckinghamshire with his family, writing books and dreaming of getting a dog.

For more information:
www.robertenright.co.uk
robert@robertenright.co.uk

You can also connect with Robert on Social Media:

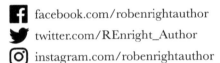

facebook.com/robenrightauthor

twitter.com/REnright_Author

instagram.com/robenrightauthor